SUMMER OF FIRE

SUMMER OF FIRE

Karen Bass

To Mrs. Roy,
best wishes

Coteau Books

Edited by Laura Peetoom
Cover images from Veer
Cover and book design by Tania Craan
Printed and bound in Canada by Friesen's
This book is printed on 100% recycled paper

Library and Archives Canada Cataloguing in Publication

Bass, Karen, 1962-
    Summer of fire / Karen Bass.

ISBN 978-1-55050-415-6

    I. Title.

PS8603.A795S94 2009   jC813'.6   C2009-903369-0

10 9 8 7 6 5 4 3 2 1

2517 Victoria Avenue
Regina, Saskatchewan
Canada   S4P 0T2

Available in Canada from:
Publishers Group Canada
9050 Shaughnessy Street
Vancouver, BC, Canada   V6P 6E5

The publisher gratefully acknowledges the financial support of its publishing program by: the Saskatchewan Arts Board, the Canada Council for the Arts, the Government of Canada through the Book Publishing Industry Development Program (bpidp), the Association for the Export of Canadian Books and the City of Regina Arts Commission.

To Nathan, Jason and Kristen -
three unique and wonderful gifts in my life.

Chapter One

Groggy. Queasy. That's how Del felt as she struggled to wake up and make sense of an announcement in German. One word – Hamburg – pumped alarm through her. This was her stop; if she missed it, who knew where she'd end up?

She jumped up and tugged her suitcase off the shelf above the train window. It bumped her shoulder on the way down and she staggered against the leather seat across the aisle. She grabbed her backpack as her erratic heartbeat rapped out her desire to be at home. To be anywhere but here.

The train stopped. The passenger in front of Del pressed a button on the side and the doors opened. Del hoisted her suitcase and lurched onto the platform. After the silence of First Class, the noise bombarded her.

She stood on the platform – that's where her sister, Cassandra, had said she'd be – and gaped. She'd travelled with her parents so was used to big airports but she'd never seen a train station this colossal. Arched steel beams and glass. Tracks and more tracks, each pair with a platform running between them, a set of stairs and escalators at one end with another set a football field away. At both ends, the stairs led up to stores. People everywhere.

Del's train pulled away. She searched for Cassandra or Mathias but no familiar faces greeted her. She started looking at signs. A big one above the train maps read *Hauptbahnhof*. The word sounded familiar. Del groaned as her sister's directions came to mind: *Don't get off at Hauptbahnhof. We'll meet you at the next station.*

She told herself not to panic. So she'd gotten off the train one stop too soon; she was in the right city. A city she'd never visited.

A city where people didn't speak English. She only spoke English. Maybe panic was a good option.

A double-decker train stopped on the other side of the platform. People gushed out of blue-and-yellow cars like running water. As they surged past Del wondered if she should follow them. At least she'd be moving. The thought made her muscles freeze. A cramp seized her right calf. She pushed her red suitcase over, sat on the hard shell and massaged her leg. All she wanted to do was cry, but not in the middle of the busiest train station she'd ever seen.

Black shoes stopped beside her. A balding man in a navy uniform with a red "DB" on the pocket said, "*Brauchen Sie Hilfe?*"

Had she done something wrong? Del felt her brow wrinkle. "English?"

He motioned toward someone behind Del, then gave her a slight smile. "*Mein englisch ist* not so good. I ask if you want help."

"Oh. That'd be great."

A woman in a matching uniform joined them. He spoke to her in German and she crouched by Del. "Are you hurt? Do you need help?" Her sandy hair was in a tight bun so she looked like a grouchy librarian, but her voice was kind.

Del was so relieved to hear clearly spoken English that words tumbled out. "I got a leg cramp, but my real problem is that I got off the train too early and my sister's waiting at the next station, only I'm here and I don't know how to get there. I don't even know where there is."

The woman straightened, so Del also stood. The woman addressed her partner in German. After he responded she asked, "Were you not to get off in Hamburg?"

"No. I mean, yes. I'm supposed to be in Hamburg, just not here." Del pointed at the *Hauptbahnhof* sign.

"*Ach so.* You were to disembark at Dammtor Station?"

"That sounds right."

"And your sister waits there?" Del gave a small nod. The woman asked, "Has she a mobile phone?"

"Mobile? You mean a cell phone? Yes! I have the number." Del set her suitcase upright, rested her backpack on it and fished out her wallet. She handed a piece of paper from the billfold to the woman. "Can you help me call her?"

The woman spoke to the man again, then led Del toward the centre of the platform. "My partner will continue our rounds. I will help you, then rejoin him."

"Are you police?"

"*Polizei?* No. We are security for *Die Bahn*." She tapped the "DB" insignia. "The train company."

The woman pointed Del to a sickly pink phone, showed her the right change and helped dial. Del's leg jittered. Her shoulders slumped when the voice mail recording came on. Cassandra was on the phone. Del hung up and rubbed her stinging eyes. She dialed again, held her breath. "It's ringing."

"I will leave you. If you need more help go to our office by the main entrance." The woman pointed across the station, then strode away before Del could thank her.

"Fedder," a sharp voice said.

Del hesitated. It sounded sort of like Cassandra. Before she could speak, angry German words battered her ear.

"Cassandra?"

The German cut off midstream.

"Cassandra, is that you?" Del hated how timid she sounded.

"Of course it's me. Where the hell are you, Delora James?"

"I... got off the train too soon."

"Tell me you're at least in Hamburg."

"Yes. In this absolutely huge –"

"You're at Hauptbahnhof? Mathias said that's what happened, but I assured him I'd told you not to get off there. I tried calling Die Bahn to confirm you'd gotten on the train."

Cassandra's brusque tone irked Del. "You thought I'd take off? Thanks a lot."

"Don't be ridiculous. What happened?"

"I was sleeping. We pulled into the station and all I heard was the announcer saying something about Hamburg. I guess I wasn't quite awake and got off without thinking."

A sigh. "Well, stay put. Mathias was so certain you debarked there he's on his way. I'll wait for you two here. Where are you?"

"Where the train unloads."

"On the platform? Don't move. I'll call Mathias and tell him where to find you. Stay where you are."

"You've said that three times."

"Mathias should be there soon. I don't want any more mess-ups, Delora."

"I've told you that I don't like that name. I don't call you Cassie."

"Don't argue. Look, if I've been rude... I just get tense when things go wrong. Stay by the phones so Mathias can find you. I'll call him now."

The line went dead.

Del dropped the receiver into its cradle. Talking to Cassandra was like talking to their mother. It left Del feeling wrung out, and it didn't help that she was so tired she felt sick. She laid her suitcase down again and sat, backpack hugged to her chest. She fought to keep her eyes open.

Mathias was a few metres away when Del spotted him. She'd only met him three times when he and Cassandra had come home to visit; her impression had been of a quiet, serious man.

Now he looked grim-faced. Del stood and exhaled, expecting to be bawled out.

Her brother-in-law halted within arm's length, looked Del up and down, then gave her a smile that crinkled out from his pale blue eyes. "*Wilkommen*, Del. Welcome."

Del returned the smile. "I thought you'd be mad at me."

He picked up her suitcase. "Yours was an easy mistake. Come, we must get to Dammtor before Cassandra calls out a search team."

Chapter Two

Gaze fixed on Mathias's back, Del practically sleepwalked upstairs, through the train station, outside, then down to another platform. Minutes later they were riding a red train between two lakes, a small one on the left and much larger one on the right. They were barely past the lakes when Mathias said, "Here we are."

Unlike Hauptbahnhof, with its dozen or more platforms, Dammtor Station only had two platforms and four tracks. The high, multi-paned windows were church-like, and painted with dull lustre by the mid-afternoon sun. Mathias rubbed the stubble on his jaw and motioned for her to lead the way down a flight of stairs. She almost stumbled on the last step. He cupped her elbow and gave her a questioning glance. She pulled away. "Where's Cassandra?"

"By the main entrance. This way." Mathias wheeled Del's suitcase left then swung right down a corridor lined with stores. Vague impressions of more old-fashioned glass and dark wood panelling sank into Del's awareness.

The sight of Cassandra stopped Del. She'd grown her blond hair out and the ponytail was similar to their mother's hairstyle. She crossed her arms like Mom; stood rigid like Mom; lifted her chin and looked down her nose like Mom. Del's legs itched with the urge to head the other way. She swore under her breath.

Mathias left the suitcase with Cassandra and returned to Del's side. He whispered, "Come. She won't bite. She was just worried."

That showed how little he knew. Before Del could speak, Cassandra said, "Couldn't you follow simple directions? I was expecting a call at four and it's quarter after. It's a twenty-minute walk home. We need to go."

Walk? Del's knees almost buckled. Cassandra had taken two steps toward the exit when Mathias said, "No." She spun around. He added, "Look at your sister, Cassandra. She's exhausted. She was nine hours on an airplane followed by over five hours on a train." He turned to Del. "Have you eaten?"

Del thought. "No."

"Then we will introduce you to a Hamburg specialty. *Backfischbrötchen*. Fish on a bun."

"A fish burger? Those things taste like cardboard."

"*Nein*. You cannot dismiss a Hamburg fish sandwich without tasting it." Mathias steered Del forward. She saw the McDonalds at the end of the hallway and grimaced – he was going to feed her North American fast food? He turned into a store beside the entrance. It looked like a sub joint, with a glass counter, plastic chairs and tables. Mathias began to order for her.

"Hey," Del said. "How do you know what I want?"

He pointed at the German menu. "What would you like?"

Del glared at the unreadable signboard and sat at the nearest table. Cassandra joined her and drummed her fingers on the table. "How are Mom and Dad?"

Del lifted her shoulders. "Same as always, I guess. Busy."

"So... Nothing's new, then?"

Del hesitated. Something in Cassandra's tone implied knowledge. Del stowed the backpack between her feet. "You've spoken to Mom and Dad more than me lately, while you were planning my prison sentence. You tell me: anything new?"

"A summer in Hamburg is hardly a prison sentence. I... thought you'd like the chance to get away." Cassandra's chin lifted but her eyes seemed shadowed by hurt. That surprised Del.

Mathias sat to Del's right and placed a wrapped bun and a bottle of something orange in front of her. He set another bun in front of himself but didn't touch it. "Go ahead, eat."

Del unwrapped the paper. The slightly lemon tang wafting up certainly smelled better than any fish burger she'd had. One bite – crisp coating and tender white fish – and she was sold. She swallowed. "This is really good."

Mathias smiled. "Of course. The fish is fresh. That's the difference."

"Can't she eat as we walk? I want to get home," Cassandra said.

"Then you should go," Mathias replied. "Del needs to revive before she can walk."

Del was puzzled. "Didn't you drive to the station?"

"This is Europe – parking is difficult. It's far easier to walk or bike and take the train. We don't live far. But today we should have driven. It isn't fair to ask you to walk after such a long travel day. Perhaps we should hire a taxi to get home."

The surprise on Cassandra's face suggested that they rarely used taxis. "If that's the case, I'll wait. That'll be as fast as walking."

Del finished the sandwich and Mathias pushed the second one toward her. She eyed it as she drank some fizzy orange juice, then decided she was still hungry. Mathias and Cassandra spoke quietly in German while Del ate the second sandwich. Energy seeped into her limbs and her brain fog lifted. She felt like she could manage a walk, but decided a taxi was better.

Tension vibrated between Cassandra and Mathias. Whatever they were talking about, Del figured it concerned her. She downed half of the orange drink and said, "I'm ready to go."

Mathias led them across the station to a different exit. The sidewalk radiated heat beside a U-shaped driveway jammed with beige taxis. The smell of exhaust was heavy. Across the road a wall of greenery looked like the border of a park. To her left, beyond a patio, a pedestrian ramp sloped up, forking into two walkways, one curving right to the park and one spanning a busy road farther left. To her right, a tall building jutted at least fifteen storeys above the trees. Beyond that was a tower that reminded Del of the CN Tower in Toronto, but shorter.

Cassandra called impatiently. Del purposely strolled toward the taxi where Mathias waited by the open back door. Del pointed at the tower. "What's that?"

"The television tower. Closer is the Congress Centre's hotel. They're the tallest buildings around. If you're walking they're good markers: head to them and you'll get to Dammtor Station."

"Unless you're at Dammtor Station," Del replied. Mathias gave a cheerful nod.

Cassandra leaned across the back seat and peered out. "Is the tour guide finished?"

Mathias's right eye half closed – the first indication Del had seen that his calm exterior could be ruffled. He replied, "This *is* your sister's first time in Hamburg, *Liebchen*." Cassandra retreated into the interior of the cab with a sigh.

Del turned her back on the taxi. "This station looks really old."

"It was destroyed in the war, then rebuilt to look as it did in the late 1800s."

"Cool." Actually, Del didn't care about old buildings, but she took a moment to study the facade, the row of archways along street level, the tall windows above that let light flood the station's train platforms.

The taxi driver's gravelly voice startled Del. She slid into the back seat.

Cassandra whispered, "Must you be so purposely inconsiderate?"

Del replied, "Must you be such a clone of our mother?" She looked out the window as Mathias got in the front and gave the driver their address.

They drove past a grassy park the size of a city block where a soccer game was in progress. Mathias gave a running commentary. "We're going north. This street is Mittelweg. As you can see, it's the business area for this district, which is Rotherbaum. We live east a few blocks, on Pöseldorfer Weg. It's hard to get lost because if you miss our street, you end up in a park beside the big lake we saw from the train, the Aussenalster."

Del eyed him curiously. She'd never heard him talk this much. Cassandra looked increasingly irritated. Finally she said, "Is this really necessary?"

"Yes," Mathias replied in a matter-of-fact way that Del was beginning to appreciate. "I'm trying to help Del orient herself. She will need to know how to navigate."

The exchange switched to German – Del hated how they could exclude her from the conversation – and she returned her attention out the window. Everything blurred as she thought about her home in Edmonton and her best friend, Serena. When they pulled up to a two-storey house with four-storey townhouses on either side, Del had no clue where they were.

While Mathias paid the taxi driver, Cassandra unlocked a pedestrian gate beside a gated driveway, also locked. Del followed her sister up a sidewalk of red paving stones to an oak door set with two rows of oblong windows. Cassandra said, "We rent the top floor from Professor Konrad, who teaches in the same department as Mathias at the university. We share this entrance. Our staircase is in the front hall. We're quiet when we enter so as not to disturb the professor. Understood?"

Del just wanted to get to her room – if she was going to have her own room. What if she had to sleep on a sofa for two months? She'd go crazy without her own space.

Mathias carried Del's suitcase inside. A metre-wide strip of tiles marked the entry; beyond that was a hallway with a gleaming hardwood floor. Mathias indicated that the right door led to the garage and the left to Professor Konrad's kitchen. The rest of the professor's quarters were down the hall. Beside the kitchen, an open staircase of wood and iron led upstairs.

Home, sour home, thought Del as she followed Cassandra to the second floor. A landing surrounded the open stairwell and accessed five doors. Cassandra pointed at each successive door: living room, bathroom, kitchen, spare room (Del's), master bedroom. The landing was empty except for coat hooks, a boot shelf and umbrella stand between the bedroom doors.

Before Del could retreat to her bedroom, Cassandra opened the living room's frosted glass door and said, "We have to talk."

Del almost groaned. Mathias said, "This can wait until tomorrow."

"No, it can't," Cassandra insisted.

Del dropped her backpack by the steps and trudged into the living room. She sidled between a black loveseat in the middle of the room and a square coffee table, and sat in the corner of a burgundy loveseat pushed up against the wall. Beside her, a door opened to a balcony and felt like a possible escape route. Del studied it and waited for the lecture. With their mother, the kind of tone her sister had just used always preceded a lecture.

Cassandra sat on the other loveseat. Mathias retreated to the other side of the room, to a black leather computer chair beside a desk. Del wished she could tell what he was thinking, but his expression was as smooth as the leather under her fingertips.

Her sister cleared her throat. "I want to be very clear on this, Delora." She held up her hand. "I mean Del. We won't tolerate any shenanigans."

Del drew circles on the leather and arched her eyebrows as

high as they would go. "Shenanigans. Is that some fancy college term?"

Cassandra's chin rose a fraction. "Don't play games with me. What term do you prefer? Crap? We won't put up with any crap."

What had their parents said? Del attempted to sneer. "Care to define that?" She continued to trace circles, bigger and smaller and bigger again.

"Mom and Dad said you were sneaking out to raves, getting involved in who knows what. And, my God, Del, they caught you having sex with a guy in their TV room."

"Not a guy. *The* guy. My boyfriend." She maintained her sneer, but anguish squeezed Del's lungs. She pressed one arm against her churning stomach, held herself still so none of the pain of loving Geoff could leak out. "And did they tell you they scared him off with threats and now he won't answer my texts or calls or anything? They ruined my life. And to top it off they sent me here. None of this is any of your business."

"I'm your sister."

"Who's been gone from home for eight years."

"And you're in my home now. So what you do is my concern."

"Only for the next two months." Del silently added, *If we last that long.* She said, "Why did you let Mom and Dad ship me here? Two stinking months away from my friends will kill me. I don't want to be here. Tell Mom and Dad that I'm their problem, not yours."

"Your self-centeredness is appalling. Do you ever think of anything but yourself?"

"I'm a teenager. Thinking about me is what I do best."

"Don't you dare use that mocking, snarky attitude with me. The last thing Mom and Dad need right now is extra worry. You know full well I agreed to this so they could have the summer to try to save their marriage."

Del's finger stopped circling. Her whole being froze, even the air in her lungs. It took a few tries to make her voice work. "What do you mean?"

The moment stretched as the sisters stared at each other. Cassandra said, "You didn't know?"

Chapter Three

The fish in Del's stomach curdled; she swallowed and leaped to her feet to keep from throwing up. Her parents were on verge of breaking up? She wanted to scream at Cassandra that she was a lying hag, but her sister's stricken expression said she really thought Del had known. And Mathias looked like he wanted to sink through the floor.

It's true.

An invisible vacuum sucked the air from the room. Del's breath huffed. She circled the loveseat that Cassandra was on, eyeing the walls and ceiling. Were they closer than they'd been a moment ago? Near the door she planted one foot, spun, searched this strange place, searched for something safe, something familiar. She fixed on Cassandra's face. "Why didn't anyone tell me? What gave you the right to keep it from me?"

Cassandra's face paled to the colour of bleached bones. "We thought Mom and Dad had told you." She lowered her head, entwined her fingers so hard her knuckles whitened.

"No, they didn't tell me! I hardly ever see them. And when I do they just rag –" Del's gut twisted. She swore and fled, snatching her backpack as she tore down the stairs. Her footfalls echoed with metallic clangs. She heard Cassandra yell, but didn't look back.

She vaulted the locked gate, ran down the street, then another. A block later – two? – she slowed and realized she was lost. She came to a park that stretched for blocks to the right and left. Ahead, beyond grass and trees, sunlight glinted off water. Del crossed the street and stopped, attention on the yellow diamond sparkles.

Insistent dinging made her glance around. A man on a bike whizzed past her, almost cracking her elbow. He shouted in German without stopping. Another biker pedalled by, bell ringing. A black-haired girl in shorts halted on the sidewalk and spoke to her. She cried, "I don't speak German!"

The girl grabbed Del's arm and pulled her toward the edge of the sidewalk. Another biker flashed by spewing angry words. The girl pointed at the other half of the sidewalk and spoke slowly. "That is the bike path. This is the footpath. Sie..., I mean, you must stay on the footpath. *Ja*?"

Though side by side, the two paths were different colours. "Oh. Thanks. That would explain the hit-and-run bikers."

The girl smiled and walked away.

Del muttered. "I should get another tattoo. *English-speaking idiot*, right on my forehead." She cut across the grass. Was it allowed? No one yelled at her so she kept going.

The run had vented her anxiety. The lush green of the park restored her calm. She breathed deeply. The air seemed alive, or at least, fresh. Better than the air at home smelled after a rain, but no clouds were in sight.

She was surprised how many people were out on a weekday afternoon – walking, biking, jogging, sitting on benches or the grass. The only time parks in Edmonton were this busy was during special events. She circled trees that looked different than the ones at home. Different leaves, different shapes. One was weirdly different, its trunk swooping like a "C" that had tipped onto its face with branches drooping toward and onto the ground. *Good makeout spot under there*, she thought, then veered away in case someone had the same idea.

There was no beach. A narrow strip of wild grasses marked the shoreline; a border of reeds and lilies bobbed in the current. Del sat two meters from the verge and tried to count the sailboats dotting the lake but they crisscrossed one another's paths so she didn't know which ones she'd counted and which ones she hadn't. A long tour boat puttered by. The amplified voice of the tour guide reached shore, along with laughter.

That she couldn't understand the guide reminded Del of her predicament. This forced holiday was more than punishment for her misdeeds. Her parents were trying to fix their marriage and they didn't think they could do it with her there.

Del remembered how they'd flung accusing words at each other after they'd caught her with Geoff. Why hadn't she realized there was more to those accusations than that one incident? Or maybe she was their only problem. Not wanting to think about it, she dug out her MP3 player and stretched out on her side with her backpack as a pillow. She cranked the music up and watched sailboats. Most had white sails, a smaller triangle in front and a bigger one behind. The hulls were a rainbow of colours. What would it be like to be on that water, wind in your face? It looked like... freedom.

One song melted into another as she imagined sailing. She drifted to sleep a few times, but voices always woke her up. The water turned a vivid, snow-shadow blue that made the sky look pale. A rowing team raced by on a scull. Above the trees and buildings across the lake, an orange haze built along the horizon and rose as if the earth was leaking its colour into the sky.

A tap on Del's shoulder made her gasp. "Mathias! You scared the crap out of me."

Mathias crouched beside her, his eyes a light grey in circles of darkness. He looked ill, maybe scared. Del sat cross-legged and removed her earbuds. "How did you find me?"

"It wasn't easy. I've been looking for hours."

She'd been here that long?

He sighed. "Cassandra has been wanting to call the police. I convinced her to give me until dark." His cell phone rang. "That will be her again. One minute, please." He held a brief conversation in German, then stuffed the phone in his pocket. "She almost called your parents but hoped to not have to worry them. Thank goodness she didn't."

Del hugged her backpack. "Yeah. Don't want to worry them." She squeezed her eyes closed against the burning sensation.

"What's wrong, Del?"

"Wrong? What isn't wrong? Do you think I mean to worry them? Now they're going to break up because I'm stressing them out so much they can't stand to have me around." She touched the barbell in her eyebrow, recalled the argument the piercing had provoked, and pivoted to face the water. "You and Cass don't want me, either."

"That's not true, Del. We do want you. We've never had any of Cassandra's family stay with us. We all need a few days to adjust, yes? The train mix-up was... unfortunate. You may have noticed that Cassandra gets upset when things don't go according to plan. Sometimes she completely –" He frowned, as if he realized he'd said too much.

He hadn't denied her parents were breaking up; things must be worse than Cassandra had said. "I've got two parents and a sister who are master planners. They plan everything, live by lists and schedules and goals. Maybe I'm adopted. The only thing I seem to be able to do with a plan is screw it up."

"We all have our strengths."

Del laughed. "Don't make me laugh, Mathias. None of this is funny."

"A little laughter never hurts. But your sister might hurt us if we don't get back." He hauled Del to her feet. "Are you ready to – what is the saying? – face the music?"

"I've had lots of experience doing that. Stay cool and follow my lead."

Chapter Four

Del scooped a spoonful of mushy granola from the bottom of her bowl and dolloped it onto the semi-dry stuff on top. It sank. She stirred it into grey-brown slush. "Let me go home."

"After you took off yesterday? Not a chance." Cassandra cupped her hands around a mug of coffee. Tendrils of steam carried the rich smell to Del.

Sitting down to eat breakfast together was something Del could hardly remember doing with her parents. They always left for the office early. On weekends one or both were often coming back from or getting ready to go on business trips. If they were home, Dad headed to the golf course with business associates and Mom had a "lie-in", which meant no interruptions.

Mathias opened a cupboard door that was actually a camou-flaged refrigerator. He took three eggs and lowered them into a pot of boiling water. "Would you like a cup of coffee, Del?"

"No, she doesn't," Cassandra replied. "She's too young to drink coffee."

"Germany has age limits for drinking coffee?" Del lifted a spoonful of slush and let it drip back into the bowl. "Must be strong coffee."

Mathias smiled. Cassandra sipped her coffee. "It will stunt your growth."

"Give me a break. Grandma James always spouts that dumb saying. Besides, I'm finished growing." Del shifted, conscious of her worry that her butt was still expanding. Her jeans had been pretty snug this morning. Why couldn't her backside be skinny like Cassandra's?

Mathias showed her a mug with a red coat of arms on it and raised his shoulders in a questioning way. Del said, "No thanks. Coffee smells good, tastes awful." She returned to the topic foremost in her mind. "Look, Cass. If you let me go home, now that I know what's up with Mom and Dad, I'll be on my best behaviour. No sneaking. No unapproved parties. No guys, even. I just want to have fun with my friends. You do remember what fun is, don't you?"

"If you go home, as soon as you're back in familiar territory, you'll fall back into the same routines, the same behaviours that landed you here to start with."

"Thanks for the vote of confidence."

"It's not just you. That's human nature. Change takes time. If it helps, think of your visit here as helping you break a few bad habits."

Del poured some orange juice, splashing a little onto her placemat. She frowned at the orange puddles. Hanging with friends was a bad habit? Maybe sneaking out of the house hadn't been smart, but it was hardly a habit. And Geoff... feeling loved was a bad habit? She winced inwardly. He'd never once tried to contact her. Some love.

Whistling softly, Mathias took the eggs out of the water with tongs, set them in egg cups and transferred them to the table, along with a weird utensil that was ring with teeth all around on the inside and handles almost like scissors. Del picked it up. "What's this?"

Mathias tilted his head. "*Eierköpfer*. I don't know if there is an English word. You could call it an egg decapitator."

"Cool." Del examined it then fit the ring over the top of an egg. "You snip?" She squeezed the handles together and lifted it. A cap of egg shell and egg fell to the table. "Can I do all three?" She clipped off the tops of the other two eggs. "That is so cool."

She set the decapitator down and ate her egg with a little spoon. It was a little runny in the middle, how she liked boiled eggs, though usually she squished them onto toast. When she was done, she sat back. "Is there anything I can do to change your mind?"

Cassandra looked up from her half-eaten egg. "No. Please stop asking."

"Asking is all I can do, isn't it? You and Mom and Dad planned every detail. You have my return train and plane tickets. Mom barely gave me enough cash to get here and you tell me I'll only get a small weekly allowance. Are you enjoying your new job as a warden? What's next? Strip search? Go through my things? Confiscate my belts and shoe laces?"

"You keep poking, hoping for a reaction. No wonder you stressed out Mom and Dad."

Del pushed back from the table so fast, her chair hit the floor. As she slammed the kitchen door, Cassandra called, "I didn't mean it, Delora. Come back!" Del paused by the top of the stairs, considered her bare feet, then sought refuge in the living room. It was cool, and semi-dark with the blinds half the way down. Del decided she needed some fresh air.

The white metal slats were on the outside of the window and door. Del searched for some way to control them and discovered a touch pad behind the curtain by the door. Too many buttons. She turned her attention to the red door handle and silver lever below it. A few attempts at adjusting the lever and the door swung inwards. Del ducked under the blinds. They rattled as she stepped onto a patio, its black floor textured like sandpaper. The only furniture on the deck were a large square planter with a ceramic cat hanging from its edge and a patio table with two white plastic chairs.

Del braced her hands against the white railing. Old-fashioned townhouses surrounded and dwarfed this house. Last night, on her walk back to the house with Mathias, Del had noticed a few other houses, some smaller than this one, scattered among the stately townhouses that butted up to one another to form long walls. Like the way the cliques at her school would close ranks and exclude others by standing shoulder to shoulder.

The way Cassandra and their parents were doing with her. Shutting her out, making her out to be a freak in need of reform. They drove her crazy. Rules, rules, rules. Their way was always the right way; no other opinions allowed. They wanted Del to wear a mask that made her look and act like them, or more accurately, like Cassandra, the perfect older sister. But maybe not so perfect. What had Mathias said? She gets upset when things don't go according to plan? No kidding. Del's mood improved a fraction.

Whistling floated up from the yard. A square-shouldered person in baggy clothes and a wide straw hat carted a wooden toolbox across the lawn, knelt beside a bed of greenery, took a garden tool that looked like a mini shovel from the box and began to dig around the plants. Del watched for several minutes, then said, "Hello?"

The person startled and scanned the yard, gaze finally lifting to spot Del. It was a woman. She removed her hat and pushed aside salt-and-pepper bangs with the back of her gloved hand.

Del said, "Do you speak English?"

"Yes."

"Good. Are you the gardener?"

The woman stood and stretched her back. "The gardener, cook, housekeeper, accounts keeper, secretary and even the boss. You must be my temporary tenant. Delora, isn't it?"

"I prefer Del. Are you Professor Konrad's wife?"

"I haven't been anyone's wife for several years, and I only like my students to call me Professor. In my home I am not much for formality. You may call me Luise." She put her hat back on. "Would you like to help me in the garden, Del?"

Del hesitated. "Okay." She leaned forward and eyed the two-metre drop.

"You might want to put on shoes. There is a sidewalk that runs around the side of the house if you go out the main door."

Del squeezed behind the planter full of cactuses and swung over the rail. She scuttled down a sturdy lattice partly covered by ivy and jumped the last half metre to land on the grass.

Luise, who had watched with tiny spade dangling, spoke in a tone that seemed laced with amusement. "Or you could come down that way." Luise was half a head taller than Del, and despite wide shoulders and hips, lean. She removed a glove and offered her hand to Del, whose hand was swallowed by the larger, stronger one. "I hope you enjoy your stay in Hamburg."

Del didn't respond to that. "What are you doing?"

"Only some weeding."

Luise showed Del which plants to dig out and they worked in silence. Del enjoyed the feel of the cool dirt, its dampness and sweet-mouldy smell. After ten minutes she said, "This is okay."

"Have you never gardened?" Luise sat back on her heels. She sounded surprised.

"I'd just mess things up. Mom has a company hired to do that. The grass looks more like a carpet than a lawn."

"It is the same with professional gardeners here. The yards look like green sculptures. I like grass that invites children to play."

"You have grandkids that come over?"

Luise chuckled. "Do I look that old?"

Del squinted at the face shadowed by the straw hat. It had a few wrinkles, especially around the eyes and mouth, something Del's mother fought with every skin cream at her disposal. "Sorry. I guess it's hard for me to tell."

"No hard feelings. Many of my students find my forty-one years to be more than they can imagine living." She stood and stretched again. "Soon to be forty-two. Time goes by fast. Someday I hope to have grandchildren to play here, yes. I have a ten-year-old son. He lives with his father in Berlin. Usually he would visit for all of August, but this year he is travelling with his father in the Orient. How could I refuse him such a wonderful opportunity? It will be nice to have another young person around instead."

"I'm nowhere near that young. I'm sixteen."

"A young lady, then. Come inside and we'll have something cold to drink. I trimmed and raked before you joined me. I'm ready for a break."

Del picked up the toolbox and followed Luise. They were almost to the patio which was half sheltered under the balcony when Cassandra burst onto the upper deck. "There you are!" She gripped the railing. "Mathias heard a door after you stormed out of the kitchen so we thought you'd gone to your bedroom. We finally checked and you weren't –" She noticed Del wasn't alone. The edge in her voice disappeared like a light switching off. "Hello, Professor Konrad. How are you? I hope Delora wasn't bothering you."

"She was being quite helpful. We were about to have a drink. Feel free to join us."

Indecision seemed to flicker across Cassandra's face. "I'd better not. Laundry day, you know. Don't be too long, Del. I don't want you imposing on Professor Konrad's time." She retreated into her living room and the door's blind lowered as if by magic.

Luise took the toolbox and muttered, "Over three years she's lived upstairs and I can't get her to use my name." She stored the garden tools in a locked outdoor cupboard and led Del into her kitchen. In contrast to Cassandra's white and chrome one, this room was a warm blend of wood, yellow and blue. Light flooded the room through sheer curtains.

Del followed Luise's lead and washed up at the sink. She sat in the chair nearest the window, careful not to bump the parade of houseplants on the wide ledge. Pressure released in a slow exhale. Del hadn't realized she'd tensed up when Cassandra had appeared.

Luise set a glass of murky gold liquid in front of Del. "Homemade apple juice. One of my colleagues gives me some every year. His elderly mother makes dozens of litres and he gets quite sick of it." It smelled stronger than store-bought juice and tasted more clearly of apples. Del commented it was tart but refreshing, then fell silent, aware of sitting in a strange kitchen with a woman she didn't know.

"So." Luise punctuated the word by setting her glass down. "I can't recall where Cassandra said you live."

"Edmonton."

"Is that close to Toronto?"

Del almost choked on her juice trying to swallow laughter. "No. It takes three hours to fly to Toronto."

"Three hours? How many kilometres is that?"

"I don't know. Two or three thousand, maybe."

"Oh my. I do tend to forget how big Canada is. I must look at a map. Is Edmonton on the west coast?"

"No. Do you know the Rocky Mountains? It's just east of there."

"I have heard of those mountains. How far is 'just east'?"

"It takes us, oh, three hours to drive to Jasper. I guess that would be around three hundred kilometres."

Luise's dark eyebrows arched. "We have very different ideas of distance."

"I guess."

Luise poured them each another half glass. "What will you do this summer in Hamburg?"

"Survive." Del didn't see the point of giving a polite answer – another thing her family saw as a fault. Did she ever do anything right in their eyes?

"That sounds very serious. Though I imagine we all like surviving and usually go to great lengths to do so. Your sister tells me that you've travelled but never to Europe, so why would a trip to a European city be such a hardship all you can hope to do is survive it?"

There were lots of things Del felt like saying. She kept it simple. "I'm not here by choice."

A brief knock on the door and Mathias popped his head into the room. "Hello. May I come in or are you gossiping about me?"

"Come in," Luise responded, then spoke to Del in a stage whisper. "Here stands the most handsome man in the university's humanities faculty – what young people would call hot, yes? – and he is so vain he thinks we have nothing better to do than gossip about him."

Del's jaw went slack. Maybe he was fairly good looking but she'd never thought of Mathias as hot. He must have caught her incredulous look, for he cupped both hands over his heart. "You crush me, sister, with such cruel looks. Surely I'm not so repulsive as all that."

"You aren't repulsive. It's just... how can you be hot when you're... so old?"

Luise burst out laughing. The flinch of his eye hinted Mathias had been stung by the remark. But he smiled. "When you're a bone-creaking thirty-one maybe you'll have a different opinion."

"I don't even know if I want to get that old."

That brought another round of laughter from Luise. She wiped at her eyes. "It's hard to believe, I know, but we old people can lead productive lives. Someday you'll agree."

Del gave a non-committal shrug.

Mathias stuffed his hands in his pockets. "I'm going to the bakery. I don't want to traumatize you by making you walk with someone old and almost repulsive, but would you like to see more of the neighbourhood?"

"I can make an exception this time. Thanks for the juice, Luise, and for letting me help in the garden." Del set her glass in the sink and followed Mathias into the hall. "I have to change my jeans. These are grass-stained." Minutes later she was back in the hall wearing indigo jeans and walking sandals. Mathias nodded his approval.

On the doorstep he pointed. "That's east and the direction of the lake. The bakery is a few blocks west, beside Mittelweg."

He unlocked the gate and when they were through a guy bolted toward them and called, "Öffne das Tor, bitte." Mathias paused, then held the gate open. The guy, slightly older than Del, slowed, flashed her a smile and said "Danke." He jogged into the yard and entered the house without knocking.

A cute German guy had smiled at her. "Who was that?"

"Luise's nephew, Felix. I don't know what he'd be doing here today. I thought he had a summer job that was strictly weekdays." Mathias started down the sidewalk.

Del stared at the door. Felix. He was way closer to being hot than Mathias. Hotter than Geoff had been. Too bad about the name – it was almost as bad as Delora.

Mathias said, "Del? Are you coming? What's wrong?"

"Hm? Nothing's wrong. I just saw something interesting, that's all."

Mathias rolled his eyes in an exaggerated way. Del smirked and hurried to catch up.

Chapter Five

Del stabbed the little gardening spade into the soil and prowled the yard's perimeter. She tweaked a small green apple, stroked the velvet orange petal of a tiger lily, brushed her hand across a cluster of ivy, came full circle and flopped onto the grass beside the flowerbed she'd been weeding. A haze of clouds obscured the sky.

"You are restless," Luise said without looking up from the patch of herbs she was tending. "Like an animal at the zoo."

"Perfect comparison," Del replied.

"Why is that?"

"This is my cage. I can go out the gate so long as Cassandra knows where I'm going, but she won't give me enough money to do anything. She said I have to prove myself. Five days in Hamburg and the highlight of my day is walking to the bakery to buy a pastry."

"You went sightseeing yesterday, did you not?"

"Oh yeah. What a blast. Just me and Cassandra." Del rolled onto her side and propped herself up on her elbow. "When I woke up Mathias was gone to some market that's only open Sundays. He was supposed to come back for a late breakfast and we'd all go downtown. But he phoned and told Cass he'd run into a friend who had some kind of bathroom renovation he needed help with, so Mathias did that instead."

"That sounds like Mathias. He is always eager to help."

"I needed help, too. I can almost stand being around Cass when he's there to soften her, or step between us. Without him the so-called tour was a forced march. No stops longer than three minutes. She wanted to march me to some harbour, but I had blisters by then."

"Ah yes. Cassandra said something about this. You 'glued your backside to a bench and refused to move,' is how I believe she put it."

"It worked. We came back by bus." Del rolled onto her back again. She wanted to ask Luise about her nephew, Felix, without seeming too obvious. He'd been gone by the time she and Mathias had returned from the bakery. He must live around here, but how far? Did he speak English? She kept remembering his quick, shy smile and his green eyes and his brown wavy hair. Luise was easy to talk to, but it would be nice to hang out with someone closer to her age.

No one seemed to care how painful it was for Del to not be able to talk to her friends. Cassandra let her have one hour of internet time each day, but with the time difference between Hamburg and Edmonton, she couldn't reach anyone except via email. When her friends were instant messaging in the evening, it was three o'clock in the morning here. Early evening here was late morning there and everyone was at work. No one had been online on Saturday. It made Del want to scream.

Luise interrupted her thoughts. "What did you think of what you saw?"

Del resumed working the dirt around some flowers. "There are lots of church spires."

"Hundreds of years ago that was an indication of a city's wealth. Hamburg was always a successful trading port." Luise removed her hat and rubbed her forehead with the back of her hand. "Did you go inside any of those churches?"

"Saw two near the big train station, but only from the outside. Saw that huge town hall that looks like it could be church and went in the lobby. We went inside what Cassandra said is the biggest church. Mike-something. That's where my feet gave out."

"St. Michaelis. We call it, simply, Michel. It's lovely, especially the pulpit shaped like a ship's prow. Did you go up the tower?"

"No."

"You didn't mention St. Nicholas. *Nikolaikirche*."

Del turned over a clod of dirt. An earthworm squirmed over her spade, searching for a way back into the earth. *To be with its friends*, Del thought bitterly. She flipped it away. "I'm not into old buildings. They all look the same, especially churches. A castle might be interesting."

"Unfortunately for you, there are none in the immediate area. As part of the Hanseatic League, Hamburg had no king or prince but was run by powerful merchants."

"Just my luck. Even if something interesting like that was around, I'd have to beg the money from Cass. Or worse, she'd insist on taking me."

Luise smiled. "It sounds like you value your independence."

"Who doesn't?"

"True enough." Luise stood. "Let's get some juice. We are mostly finished here and I have a favour I'd like to ask of you."

Del held her curiosity in check while they put the tools away and cleaned up. Her leg started to jitter when she sat at Luise's table. The older woman poured one juice then paused to ask if Del preferred mineral water. Del declined. She didn't like the metallic, almost salty taste.

Luise drank deeply, then carefully set her glass on the table. "You look nervous. I'm not asking you to do something illegal."

Del snickered and heard a tremor in the sound. If only this favour involved Luise's nephew. She sipped some more juice. Her leg continued to bounce.

Luise rocked her glass and watched the ripples. "When I turned forty I felt the need to do something significant, something apart from my teaching that would perhaps outlast me. It took a while to decide what, and in the end I found the project right in my family. My grandmother kept journals all her life, and saved them. Boxes of them. I started going through them, not sure what I was looking for, though I loved having her life unfold in those yellowed pages. One period in her life gripped me. I heard some of the story growing up, but not all. I doubt even my mother knew all the details." She took a sip of juice. "The story tugged at my heart. It felt important. I decided to translate it. I finished in May and have been considering my next step. You could help."

Del's leg stilled. She tried to keep disappointment out of her voice. "Help you how?"

"I need someone to read what I've translated, to make sure the English is correct."

"You want me to, like, edit your work?"

"If you find something that doesn't make sense, it would be helpful. I need to know if the story is interesting enough for me to look for an English publisher." Luise stopped her when Del started to open her mouth. "Before you decide, I'd like you to read a few entries. It happened when my grandmother was your age, which makes you a good person to read it. If you are not interested after that, I'll understand. But if you decide to proceed, I wish to pay you."

Del perked up. "Pay me? For just reading a story?"

"I would need you to also tell me your opinion, to provide feedback, perhaps help me come up with a title."

"I'm not a big reader. Maybe your nephew, Felix, could do it for you." Del took a drink and waited to see if she'd learn anything about him beyond those grass-green eyes.

"But you read?"

Del set the glass down and licked her lips. "Mostly only for school. But one of my friends is big reader. Once in a while she drops a book on my bed and says I have to read it. So I do."

"That's more than Felix reads. He mostly sticks to magazines. No, I think you would be the better choice to read this. It is a girl's story, after all."

"I could try. It's not like I have anything else to do."

Furrows settled on Luise's brow. "You are lonely?"

The pressure of unexpected tears pushed against Del's eyes and she lowered her head. "I miss my friends." She realized suddenly that didn't include Geoff. Maybe if he'd once made an attempt to see her after her parents ran him off...

"Mm. And here you are, stuck in a house full of much older people."

The light tone of Luise's words helped the tears retreat. Del finished her juice. "Yeah. Old people who have no clue how to have fun."

"What? Forced marches aren't fun?"

Del gave Luise an incredulous look and the older woman laughed. "Perhaps you should rest your feet more. There's a lounge chair on my terrace. You could relax and read the first two or three journal entries, then let me know what you think. Even if you stop there, I'll pay you ten euros."

"Deal."

Chapter Six

5 Nov, 1942

Oh, Hilde, if only I had been the one to die at birth. But then this awful thing might have happened to you. How could I wish that? The pain still rips me open. I want to scream and still can't.

I'm going to be sick again –

6 Nov, 1942

No one will listen. No one wants to know the truth. I simply must tell someone and it seems you are the only one who will believe me, Hilde, as you sit in heaven and read over my shoulder. Only you. Please bear with me. If I write it down, maybe the memory will flow from my mind to the paper and I won't relive it in my dreams like I did last night.

It is easy to recall the first part of yesterday evening. Instead of the gymnasium, our BDM unit met in an old guild hall two blocks from the school. It was like an old-fashioned gentleman's club. We walked through a dark-panelled room with leather chairs and a sofa in front of a fireplace to get to the meeting room where we piled our overcoats near the double doors and moved the chairs to the side to make room for some games. I always enjoy the relays, even if I can smell myself afterward.

Instead of having a lecture, we organized into small groups and sat on the floor to roll bandages and prepare care packages to be sent to our soldiers in North Africa.

Bette talked about how romantic fighting in a desert would be. I replied that your skin would fry, that you would sweat horribly in the day and freeze at night. It would be scary to be so far from home. And for what? I finished by saying, "It's Italy's fault any of our soldiers had to go there at all."

Bette gave me an irritated look at the same instant our leader swatted me on the head and said, "Garda Kurz, you belong to the League of German Maidens and no BDM member will criticize our soldiers. No matter why, they are in North Africa and will win a mighty victory."

I muttered an apology and said I agreed with her, of course. Mother chastens me because I'm too quiet. It's true I can never think of the proper thing to say. Instead I seem to blurt stupid things, usually at the worst moments.

When the meeting was over, Frau Reifsneider dismissed the other girls and told me to put the chairs back. She had to run an errand and would return later to lock up. Bette lingered by the coats, chatting with the other girls as they left, until only the two of us remained. She offered to help me since she was waiting for Rolf, anyway.

Ever since he asked her on a date three months ago, everything is Rolf this and Rolf that. Bette is far too busy being Rolf's girl to be my best friend. She is even talking about "when we get married" and "when we have a baby." She used to talk about wanting to be a doctor.

We only had three rows left to set out when Rolf knocked on the open door. Bette squealed, rushed to him and threw herself into his arms. Their kiss was so long it was embarrassing and their bodies looked to have melted into one. I went back to moving chairs.

I didn't look when Bette said, "Rolf can't escort us home so we are going to stroll around the block, Garda. We'll be back soon." Rolf muttered something and Bette giggled. I refused to look. I know the way Bette likes to snuggle under Rolf's arm and the way she always beams up at him as if he were her very own Norse god.

A black jacket landed on the chair I had just set out. I nearly yelled. I spun to see Rolf's best friend, Faber Ott, smiling and loosening the tie of his HJ uniform. Bette is forever trying to get me to date Faber. He is her cousin and introduced her to Rolf. But he watches me like a wolf sizing up a rabbit. (If only I'd realized.)

Faber offered to help until Rolf returned. He hauled chairs away from the wall for me to arrange in lines. After we finished, he suggested we wait in the other room. A single lamp cloaked the corners in darkness. I headed for a wing-backed chair, but Faber laid his arm across my shoulders and guided me to the sofa. It squeaked when he pulled me down beside him.

I wanted to slide away from him, but I was beside the overstuffed arm with nowhere to go. I whispered for him to please move away. He snickered. "Shy, quiet Garda. I don't know why you stay in Bette's shadow. You're as pretty as she is."

I folded my hands in my lap. My tongue was thick and refused to form any words.

"You don't believe me." Faber traced my nose with his index finger, holding my chin when I tried to turn away. He said, "Yours is how I imagine a Valkyrie's nose to look. Much better than that ski slope of Bette's. And a firm mouth." His finger ran over my lips. "Not pouting, but determined. You are quiet, but your lips tell me you have a plan. What is your plan now, Garda?"

I told him I would scream if he did not leave me be. He replied that he couldn't imagine me ever screaming, I'm so quiet. His lips covered mine.

I pushed hard. Faber pitched back, but grabbed me when I tried to jump up. He yanked me toward him and we fell onto the sofa with me on top of him. He said that was better.

Everything happened so fast after that, Hilde. Faber rolled and trapped me on my side against the back of the sofa. My heart beat like bird wings against a window. One-handed, he slipped his loose tie over his head and dropped it on the floor, then did the same to my kerchief.

I asked what he was doing, and he told me to relax, that he just wanted to have some fun until the two lovebirds returned. He undid my top button. I tried to squirm free and told him I didn't want to have his kind of fun. He just laughed.

Then his mouth covered mine again and his hands seemed to be every-where. On my breasts, my thighs, even between my legs as they squeezed and kneaded. I can still feel it. I can still smell his beer breath. I couldn't move, so I lay still and prayed he would stop, prayed Bette and Rolf would return, prayed Frau Reifsneider would walk in. Anything.

He kept whispering that I would enjoy it, that I should relax.

Suddenly he drew back and I thought he was finished. He said, "Still no scream? I knew you wanted this." He fondled my breast. I wrenched my arm free and dug my nails into his wrist. He cursed and wedged my arm back behind my back. He tried to kiss me again; I jerked my head aside. Faber gripped my jaw. I could see by his narrowed eyes he was angry. He said, "Your game of hard-to-get is boring. Let's move on to will-ing. We both know you are."

He yanked open my blouse. Buttons flew in all directions. I panicked. I freed my arms and fought. But he was too strong. He pinned my hands with one of his. A scream finally worked its way free, but too late, Hilde. Too late. He clamped his mouth over mine and he ripped off my under-clothes and –

Oh, Hilde, how can I even write it down? It felt like I was being torn apart inside. When Faber rolled off me, I was shaking and so cold. I'm still cold. Still aching.

I curled onto my side, hugged my knees and wept. As if from a dis-tance, I heard him leave. Then there was no sound except the ticking of a mantle clock.

That is how Bette found me.

evening, 6 Nov, 1942
I had to stop, Hilde. I thought I had cried all my tears last night, but I was wrong. After tonight, I might cry forever.

Mother slapped me and called me a liar. Having my own mother not believe me almost hurts as much as the rape. (There, I said it. Such an ugly little word for something that tears such a large wound in your soul.)

I didn't finish telling you what happened last night, Hilde. I need to, I think.

When Bette found me, she tucked in my blouse as if I were a helpless baby. My mind was all fuzzy, but I remember whispering, "Faber forced me. He r-r-" I couldn't say it, not then.

"That's ridiculous," Bette replied. "My cousin has never had to force any girl to anything. Rolf and I have been outside for at least fifteen minutes, waiting for you two to come out. I never heard you scream."

I gaped at my friend. Shock cleared my mind, but again words failed me.

Bette looped my kerchief around my neck and put my coat on and led me to the door. She told me I might regret that we got carried away, but that is was wretched to suggest that Faber forced me. She stuffed my underwear in my pocket.

I don't understand, Hilde. We've been friends since I first joined the BDM. Best friends. And now Bette doesn't believe me.

I don't remember the walk home, but at my door, when Bette turned to go, my voice suddenly returned. I asked her why she waited outside, why she didn't come in.

I will never forget her words: "Because Faber had told Rolf the two of you wanted time alone. I was a little angry that you hadn't told me about your date, but... Now I suppose you two will be at it like rabbits every time you get together. You'll be no fun at all on a double date."

Bette turned up her collar and left. I watched her go. At it like rabbits. My stomach started to churn. I barely made it to the toilet before I threw up.

When my stomach was empty and I hunched over the toilet bowl gasping in the stink of vomit, I realized no one had come to see what was the matter. Papa, of course, was at his usual Thursday night history faculty meeting, where they played chess and won the war over pipes and *Schnapps*. But where were Mother and Erwin?

In the kitchen Mother had left a note on the table, saying she had taken Erwin to a meeting of the Nazi women's auxiliary. I didn't know whether to cry or be relieved. Instead I put on water to boil, and when it was steaming, lugged the pot to the bathroom and dumped the water into the bathtub, then added some cold water. We were only allowed to turn on the water heater one day per week, but I had never needed a bath so badly.

After collecting my nightgown and housecoat, I bathed in the ten centimeters of tepid water, washed blood off my thighs, then scrubbed and cried and scrubbed and cried. My breasts and thighs ached. But inside, where I couldn't wash, I felt like my bones were oil pipes and they had burst and were pouring sludge into my secret places, into my whole body, into my soul. I would never be clean again.

I went to bed in my housecoat. I lay in the dark, fearing that every squeak was Faber come back to do it again. When Mother came home I pretended to be asleep. When Papa came home I wanted so badly to feel his arms around me, but he didn't even open my door.

When I finally slept, it was to dream of Faber covering my mouth as he attacked me. I woke up feeling like I was suffocating. Every time I fell asleep, the same dream assaulted me until I gave up and waited for daylight.

This morning I pretended to be sick. I couldn't bear the thought of going to school, or of seeing Bette. She didn't believe me.

With Papa gone to teach his morning class at the university, Erwin at school and Mother running errands, the house was so quiet. I had always liked that before, but now the silence crushed me. After I wrote today's first entry and cried, I moved to the living room, turned on the phonograph and fell asleep with Papa's favourite Beethoven symphony playing. I would have rather listened to one of his jazz albums, but such music had been forbidden because it isn't German. Mother didn't know but when she had ordered Papa to throw them away, he had hidden them in the attic instead.

A door banged and woke me up with fear in my throat. Papa came into the living room and unwound a scarf from around his neck. He sat on the edge of the sofa and tucked the scarf around my neck. He laid the back of his hand on my forehead. An ache started behind my eyes.

Papa said, "*Liebchen*, you don't look sick. When you are sick, your cheeks get blotchy and your eyes get as round as white wheels with big black hubcaps. But here you lie, unable to look me in the face."

I asked if he shouldn't be getting ready for his afternoon class, and he told me his assistant was taking it for him so he could check on me.

When he said, "Tell me what's wrong, *Leibchen*," more tears spilled over. Papa gathered me in his arms and I cried against his scratchy tweed jacket. He smelled of wool and pipe tobacco and cloves. He coaxed the awful words from me. Then he said nothing, just held me so tightly it almost hurt.

After a long time he picked me up and carried me up to my bedroom, as if I were still ten years old. Papa is only a few centimeters taller than I am and his face was scarlet by the time he laid me on my bed. He looked angry.

I begged him to not hate me.

All the lines in his face sagged. He swiped at a tear (Papa crying?) and gathered me back into his arms. "I'm not angry with you, Garda. I'm angry with myself. I'm supposed to protect you and I failed. It's you who needs to forgive me."

That made me cry again. Papa believed me!

He left me with instructions to sleep. He would talk to Mother and decide what must be done, how best to confront "young Herr Ott."

What I wanted was have another bath and wash away the feeling of filth creeping across my skin like a swarm of spiders. But I stayed in bed, too weary to move, until the clock in the downstairs hall struck five. My stomach rumbled and I realized I hadn't eaten all day, so I brushed my hair and fashioned a loose braid. The mirror showed deep shadows under my eyes. I pulled on wool socks and headed downstairs.

Papa's study door was closed, which meant he did not want to be disturbed. I touched my forehead to the dark wood, trying to soak up some of the peace I enjoyed in that room. My stomach growled again.

The kitchen was empty. There was no sign that *Kaffee und Kuchen* had been consumed. Papa dearly loved his coffee and cake. Maybe he had taken it in his office. Erwin, of course, would be at his German Youth meeting. He spent almost every waking minute with his DJ unit, eager to join the HJ. To be... like Faber.

I determined not to think about him and made myself a sandwich, cutting skinny pieces of cheese so Mother wouldn't fret about how little we had. The bread tasted a little stale and was dry with no butter to spread on it. Today my stomach didn't care.

The half hour chime rang. The outside door slammed. Papa appeared in the kitchen doorway as if summoned by the sound. He stepped into the room just as Mother sailed in and demanded to know where I was.

She stopped, gloves in hand and glared at me. "There you are. Garda Kurz, you should be ashamed. Do you know how much you have embarrassed me?" She gave Papa a scathing look and said she was angry at him, too, for convincing her I had told the truth. Mother tossed her gloves on the table, pulled her hatpin free and dropped in on the wooden surface. I watched it roll onto the floor. She set her hat on top of her gloves.

Papa asked what she was talking about and she said she had gone to Frau Ott with my "outlandish story." He started to protest but Mother demanded that he let her finish.

She radiated anger the way our stove gives off heat. I wanted to shrink into a mouse and scurry away. She said, "Frau Ott and I deeply respect each other. We've worked on many committees together. So when I told her what had transpired last night, she was most distressed. Faber was home so she called him into the parlour and demanded he explain. I'm certain you know what he said, Garda."

I shook my head and turned my empty glass around and around while Mother explained how polite Faber was. He had admitted we had intercourse but insisted I had been willing and that this wasn't even the first time we had been together.

My breath came in short gulps and I whispered that he was lying.

Mother banged the table with her open palm. I flinched. She said that he wasn't lying, that he was a fine young man, the best in his Hitler Youth unit, the perfect Aryan in looks, breeding and behaviour. She said she could understand why I would be attracted to him and should be ashamed of maligning his good character.

I jumped to my feet. "I'm not! He forced –"

Mother slapped me. She called me a liar and a whore.

I could only stare. Mother has never hit me before. And to call me such horrible things... I looked to Papa for help but he only gripped the back of a chair and stared at his white knuckles. I whispered, "How could you think that, Mother? You know it's not true."

"Do I? If I had insisted on your joining the BDM sooner, perhaps you might have better understood the importance of proper modesty. Thanks to your father's interference, I didn't. You've turned out as disreputable as some of his students. You could have had Faber Ott as a husband, but now you'll be lucky if he ever looks at you again. Stupid girl."

I gaped at Mother and silently begged Papa to say something. The only sound was the hiss of burning coal in the stove. Mother picked up her hat and gloves, and marched out of the room, but not before she repeated, "Stupid girl."

Papa followed like a whipped puppy. He didn't even look at me.

Hilde, how am I to bear it?

Chapter Seven

Warm water streamed over Del's body. Keeping her hair out of the shower's spray, she turned and turned again, as if the water could wash away her queasiness. The white-tiled walls and chrome fixtures of the bathroom closed in – clinical, cold, like a hospital – and Del suddenly needed to be surrounded by life. She dried off and slipped into a clean tank top and shorts. Sandals in hand, she found Cassandra at the desk in the living room and told her she was going to the park by the lake.

Ten minutes later she settled near the lake's edge, close enough to hear the water lapping the bank, and curled her fingers into the grass so her knuckles pressed against the cool earth. That distinctive fresh smell she already associated with Hamburg filled her nostrils.

She inhaled to erase the remembered smell of antiseptic and chemicals and human sweat that fills emergency rooms, to forget the way insides knot up during the wait, even when it's for the friend of a friend. She had huddled by Serena who had tried to comfort her sobbing friend. Between physical exams and interviews, it had taken all night. No hope of returning to the party, not that Del had wanted to after she'd heard the girl's choked story about necking with a guy but wanting to stop. Only he hadn't let her. Date rape, the doctors called it.

When Del had made it home at nine o'clock that morning, her parents had been waiting at the kitchen table. She'd told them why she was late, expecting it to erase their worry. Instead, they'd freaked out. That week, they'd pelted Del with lectures about how it "could have been you." She had tried to do the right thing, support a friend, and still they'd stomped on her.

The girl had never pressed charges and until today, Del had put it out of her mind. But a voice from 1942 had reminded her that the incident wasn't likely forgotten by the girl who had been raped. The images formed by those pained words churned her stomach again.

Had Luise given her the story to remind her there were worse fates than being sent to her sister's for two months? She didn't seem that interfering. No, she probably only wanted to know if the story interested Del. It did. How had Garda healed from the rape when her parents hadn't supported her?

Someone in jeans sat beside Del. She stretched stiff fingers and brushed them over the grass. "Hi Ma –" She lifted her head. Of course it wasn't Mathias. He would still be at university dealing with his summer class students. Still she stared.

"Hello. I'm Felix."

Del's tongue wouldn't work.

"You're Del, yes?" She nodded. Green eyes sparkled. "*Sehr gut.* Tante Luise sent me to find a Canadian girl named Del. I would hate to deliver to her the wrong girl. Maybe if you spoke, I would know that a Canadian girl I've found and not one from, maybe, Ireland. You could be Irish with that red shine on your hair. What colour is that named? And are those freckles? Certainly Irish."

Del ducked her head, mortified she couldn't speak. She was never at a loss for words.

He crooked his elbows around his raised knees and one gripped his left wrist with long fingers that Del eyed surreptitiously. "I'm teasing, yes? You now think I'm an idiot."

"No!" Del jerked upright.

"You can speak." Felix offered a smile that flipped Del's stomach, but in a warm and tingling way. "I saw you leave Tante Luise's house a few days ago with Mathias, yes? I thought you were a student, but Tante Luise corrected me." The smile faded.

"She said you were on her terrace reading, then suddenly you left the house. She fears you were upset by what you read."

"I guess I was, but I'm okay now."

He tapped her upper arm. "Nice tattoo. A phoenix? I like the flames for wings."

"Thanks." His flow of words had allowed the tension to drain away. Her usual forthrightness surfaced. "Why'd she send you?"

"No Irish accent. It seems I did find the right girl." He grinned. "My father sent me to drop off some papers and since my aunt was making *Zwiebelkuchen*, she sent me after you."

"Zvee-what?"

"It is translated onion cake. Very good. More a pie, with onions, eggs, bacon, cream. Usually it is eaten in fall but this is my great-grandmother's, her grandmother's recipe and Tante Luise said she was thinking of her today. You must eat some with us." He pointed at the sun overhead. "*Mittagessen*. Lunch."

Del's stomach gave a tell-tale rumble. Felix's smile returned. "That is a yes? After we eat, we could go to the harbour. Have you seen it?"

"No. But, don't you work?"

He frowned at his open palms. "I am... between jobs."

"Oh. The harbour sounds great." Del heaved an exaggerated sigh. "If my prison warden lets me go."

Felix laughed. "We will get you a pass."

The onion cake was similar to quiche and Del had a second helping. To her surprise, Cassandra agreed to the outing, probably because she'd be with *Professor Konrad's* nephew.

While Felix was in the bathroom, Luise handed Del a 10-euro note. "Will you continue reading?" When Del nodded, Luise said, "I'm pleased. But I fear what you read bothered you."

"It reminded me of a night I spent in emergency with someone who'd been date-raped."

"Oh my. That sounds upsetting indeed."

"The girl wasn't a close friend. Reading Garda's story made me realize how awful it must've been for her, for both girls." Del paused. "What really bugs me is how Garda's parents turned their backs on her. How could they do that?"

"It is incomprehensible to me, as well. I think her father tried."

"Not hard enough." Del shoved her hands in her pockets. "Parents are dense sometimes. Mine only pay attention to me when I get in trouble, and Garda's ignored her when she needed them most."

"Most parents are juggling many other responsibilities. It's hard to say what else makes them act the way they do."

"You're defending them?"

"No. I'm saying that things are sometimes very complicated."

Felix reappeared. They walked to Mittelweg in silence and caught a bus to Dammtor. Felix skirted around the rail station. Del hurried to catch up. "Say we aren't walking. My feet are still sore from my last round of sightseeing."

Felix glanced over his shoulder, sidestepped and pulled Del with him. A woman in a skirt sped past on a bicycle, almost clipping Del's arm. He said, "You were on the bike path."

Del frowned at the reddish stones. "I keep forgetting. I almost got flattened my first day here. And Cass had to remind me a couple times on Sunday to watch where I walk."

"You have no bike paths where you live?"

"They aren't the same as here. They're more in parks and stuff. Not many people use bikes to get to work or the store. So how far is this harbour?"

"We could walk..." Del groaned. Felix smiled and pointed to a sign above a set of stairs. "But I thought we'd try this way."

The blue sign only had a white U on it. "I don't get it."

"Have you no Underground in your city?"

"Under... Oh, you mean a subway? Yes, but not much of one. So if the U is for the Underground, what is the S for? I think I saw that in Dammtor."

"The *S-Bahn*, you mean. The S is for *Stadt*, which means city. City trains." Felix jogged down the stairs. "Hurry or we will miss the *U-Bahn* and have to wait five minutes."

"Five whole minutes. Wow."

Halfway down a second flight of stairs cool air blasted Del's face in a refreshing gust. The stairwell opened to a single platform. Felix indicated a digital sign that said a train was arriving in forty-five seconds and gave her the thumbs up. When they boarded, Felix urged Del to sit beside the door and joined her. She was acutely aware of their shoulders brushing. A warning bell sounded and the doors closed.

"Why didn't we have to buy a ticket?" she asked.

Felix's eyebrows curled into arched esses. "You have no pass?" She shook her head. The eyebrows lowered into a frown. "I should have asked when you were unfamiliar with the U-Bahn sign. I hope we meet no inspectors. They check sometimes to make sure people are not cheating."

"And if they are?"

"No ticket? Big fine."

"Oh. Cassandra never mentioned that."

"Here is our stop. We must change trains. We'll buy you a ticket."

They emerged from the *U-Bahn* on the edge of a square lake. Concrete steps led down to a wide boardwalk and rows of tour boats, one of which was pulling away from its dock. They headed away from the lake and Del recognized the view. A rectangular pond full of ducks and swans lay between them and a large plaza in front of the town hall.

Felix pointed behind them to the square lake. "Binnenalster."

Then at the pond. "Kleine Alster." And beyond the pond to a canal. "Alsterfleet."

"Like I'll remember that. There's a special name for the town hall, too. Cass told me. Rat-something. I remember that because people like politicians as much as they like rats."

Felix laughed. "*Ja.* But in German, a four-legs rat is called *eine Ratte.* But *Rat* means council. *Rathaus* is where the town council meets."

"I like my definition better. Your English is great."

"*Ja.* Tante Luise teaches English literature. She makes sure the whole family is good with English. Come. The other *U-Bahn* is on the far side of the *Rathausmarkt.*"

He pointed so Del realized he meant the big plaza in front of the town hall. It was fancy like the legislature building in Edmonton, even the same colour, but was only a city hall. Though it was Monday, people milled all around the plaza, sat on stone steps, basked in the hazy sun. Tour guides herded their flocks, pointing and talking.

In the middle of the plaza, Felix started walking backwards. His brown curls bobbed as he nodded to the side opposite the town hall. "If you want, there are tourist shops under that glass roof. Good prices."

"I've got all summer to shop." *And barely any money to do it with*, she added silently.

Felix's heel caught a ridge on the stone and he stumbled. Del grabbed his wrist to steady him, then realized they stood toe-to-toe and she was looking at his mouth. She raised her gaze to intense green eyes. His relaxed smile made his eyes seem brighter. "Thanks. You can let go."

Del felt like an idiot. Instead of releasing his wrist, she grinned. "Are you sure?"

He laughed, a loose sound that bounced like an echo. She

released her grip. His laughter was like his aunt's. She liked people who laughed easily.

At the next *U-Bahn* Felix showed Del how to buy tickets from an automated machine on the platform and suggested she get a pass since she would be here all summer. The train arrived in minutes. The ride had barely started when the subway went above ground. The elevated track curved and ran along the harbour, giving an excellent view.

They pulled into a covered station, jogged down some stairs, past three food kiosks, then outside onto a bridge that spanned a roadway to a series of interconnected piers beside the river. The freshness Del had smelled by the lake was stronger here. She thought she tasted a bit of salt and paused by the railing to enjoy the cool tang.

An old building with a square clock tower on the closest corner sat to the right of the bridge. Felix pointed. "Landungsbrücken."

"What is it with the long names? I'll never remember a tongue-twister like that."

"It is two words together. Landing, *Landungs*, and bridges, *Brücken*. Not so hard."

"Says you."

"*Ja.* Now you say it."

"Landings-broken."

Felix laughed. "We will work on it, yes?"

Del liked the way that sounded, like today wouldn't be the last day they spent together. "If you're going to try to teach me German, I should warn you I failed French."

"So did I." He laughed and led the way left on the boardwalk past a line of outdoor tourist and food kiosks. Down-sloping gangplanks connected the boardwalk with piers floating on the water. They walked toward a three-masted sailing ship, its deep green hull contrasting with white decks. Felix pointed a lot as he explained how canals and side tributaries branched out from the Elbe River to form the harbour, which was an immense maze. Del enjoyed the sound of his voice. He had an accent and rarely mixed up words.

They were across from the sailing ship, which was a museum, when Felix waved at a man in a captain's hat playing the accordion. "Ho, Kapitan!" was all Del caught before a string of German. Whatever the man said, Felix laughed, dug a coin out of his pocket and tossed it into a container at the man's feet, who offered a gap-toothed grin in return.

They returned the way they'd come. Del said, "My sister thinks you shouldn't encourage panhandlers."

"The tourists like him, and he harms nothing." Felix cupped Del's elbow and pointed with his free hand. "My friend Max. I called him earlier, told him I'd be here."

Max was barely taller than Del, with a wide face and a goatee encircling an equally wide mouth. He took Del's hand and kissed her fingertips. His blond shaggy hair flopped down to hide his face. Del snatched her hand back and wiped it on her shorts. Max shrugged. "Warm day. You two could a drink use. Tables are full. Find a bench. I will drinks bring. *Ja?*"

Felix agreed. They picked a bench on the pier closest to the Landungsbrücken building. Max appeared moments later with three beers in hand. Del's eyes widened. Felix asked, "You don't like beer?"

"I'm not old enough. And, ah, don't we have to be in a bar or something?"

"Not old enough? I thought Tante Luise said you were sixteen." Del nodded. Felix said, "Then you are old enough for beer or wine. And there's no rule about drinking beer on a street."

"Seriously? People can just walk around with a bottle of beer?"

"*Ja*. This is different where you live?"

"Very different." Del took her bottle. Serena would never believe this.

They spent the afternoon watching ships of all sizes, and one float plane, ply the river. They mostly talked about movies. Del drank slowly, having two beers to the Felix's three and Max's four. Max insisted on paying for everything. It was late afternoon when they said goodbye and headed back. Descending from the platform into Dammtor station, Del grabbed Felix's arm. They stood on the stairs as people flowed around them. "My breath will smell like beer."

"And mine. So?"

"My sister will freak out. The age for drinking where I live is eighteen."

His expression turned serious. "We could buy breath candies."

"I'm not sure that would do the trick. How about a stronger taste? I know. A fish sandwich. Mathias bought some from a store here. *Nord*-something."

"Beside the north entrance. Come."

Del used her money from Luise to buy two sandwiches. They doused the fish with lemon. Del started to giggle when they simultaneously lifted their sandwiches. Felix lowered his; Del copied him. Then they raised them again and both started laughing. The guy at the counter gave them a strange look, which made Del laugh harder. It took a minute for her to be able to eat without choking. She couldn't be tipsy after two beers. Could she?

The short bus ride and walk was mostly silent, with Del too busy smiling and stealing glances at Felix to try thinking of witty things to say. Anyway, witty sometimes came out witless, and that was the last thing she wanted.

They had to ring Luise's doorbell – Del didn't have a key yet.

Mathias opened the door. "Come in. We are all on the terrace getting ready to barbeque sausages. Felix, your aunt called and told your mother you'll eat here. Del, why didn't you use your key?"

"You haven't given it to me yet."

He thumped the heel of his hand against his forehead. "I forgot to get it cut, didn't I? A forgetful *Dummkopf*."

Del's toe caught on the mat. Mathias grabbed her arm and pulled her upright before she could fall. He didn't release her but instead sniffed. "You were drinking beer?"

Rats, Del thought. She looked into concerned eyes. "So what? It's legal here."

"True. But you'd best stay away from your sister. And I'd suggest not doing this again."

"Don't start shoving rules down my throat, Mathias. This afternoon is the first fun I've had since I got here."

Felix said, "Did I do something wrong, letting Del have beer? It was only two."

Letting? Del silently fumed. She glared at Mathias. He sighed, muttered something in German and walked down the hall toward the open French doors in Luise's dining room.

"What did he say?" Del asked.

"He said it was going to be a long summer."

"Maybe not so long as I thought." Del smiled at Felix. He smiled back.

Chapter Eight

Del couldn't believe she and Felix made it through the evening without Cassandra discovering their beer breath. Staying away from her became a game. Even Mathias joined in, distracting Cassandra whenever she veered their way with questions like, "Do we need this?" or "Do you think...?" She never caught on but Luise did. She cornered Felix once so likely knew what it was about.

The next day no one was around. Del roamed the apartment, her thoughts bouncing between her afternoon with Felix and what had happened to Garda. When she finally decided Felix wasn't going to show up to relieve the boredom, she settled down with Garda's journal.

9 Nov 42

You are the lucky one, Hilde. All you ever experienced was love. Papa said you only lived for three hours. He held you the whole time. He rocked you and told you how special you were. Do you remember? And from Papa's arms you went to heaven where you have been wrapped in love ever since. Only love.

I spent Saturday and Sunday hiding in my room. I couldn't even write. I stared at the walls for hours, curled under the quilt, hugging my shame. It was my fault. I see that now. I should never have sat. I should have fled. I should have screamed.

No one knocked on my door, except when Papa brought my meals. Twice he looked like he wanted to say something. He didn't.

I've thought about how Papa always says that the more precise and detailed a document, the more useful to historians. I cannot imagine any historian caring about this journal but I have decided to try to write things down with as much detail as possible, even what people say. Someday maybe I will want to remember, though I cannot imagine that, and for now putting things down on paper does seem to stop them from happening over and over in my mind.

Bette never called or stopped by, but now I know why. She was busy.

This morning (Monday), Mother made me go to school and "face the consequences of my foolish actions." She means my so-called lie. Looks might not kill, but hers stab as deeply as any dagger. Aren't mothers supposed to believe their children?

While I was still in the school's cloakroom, shaking the rain off my coat, Bette walked in from the hallway and watched me with arms folded.

My hope for a healed friendship was dashed when she said, "It was bad enough you told me that terrible lie, Garda Kurz, but to denounce Faber to his mother – my favourite aunt – is unforgivable." She stroked her braid and marched to the class. I followed with dragging feet.

In the hall, girls watched with curiosity. When I entered my classroom, every girl turned away. Yes, Bette had been very busy.

I am now the school pariah. It's as if they suddenly discovered I was Jewish. A Jewish leper who has sided with the enemy. I wanted to scream that I was the victim and Faber the monster. But I am quiet Garda. I tried to ignore the hateful sneers and act as if it didn't matter when no one picked me for their team in sports class, that I liked eating my lunch alone and walking home alone.

Pretending is exhausting. I went straight to my room to write this down, because when I'm writing and you're reading over my shoulder, Hilde, I am not alone. I am too weary to cry. Too numb to feel. It's still light out. I'll close the blackout curtain and try to sleep.

11 Nov 42

I love walking the streets of old Heidelberg, with cobblestone roads and stone buildings that seem almost to lean inward on narrow streets, as if protecting me. Now, even that pleasure has been taken away.

School was another day of cold shoulders and hot glares, so I took a winding route home, past university buildings, through small courtyards, down side streets. Though I carried my umbrella, I didn't need it. The sky was a blue strip hanging between peaceful old buildings that whispered to me of years and centuries past, years and centuries to come. The stone soaked up my sorrow as it had for countless others before me.

A movement behind me caught my eye. Rolf and two friends loitered three buildings away. By the way they watched me I realized they had been following me. My heart thudded in my ears and I knew that Faber was close by. Hunting.

I sprinted toward the end of the alley. Someone in a Hitler Youth uniform stepped from hiding and I ran into him. He grabbed my arms and I began to struggle. When he pulled me into a cellar stairwell and pushed me against the door, I saw it wasn't Faber.

That calmed me a little. I said, "What are you doing, *Dummkopf?*"

He didn't answer, but slobbered on my neck. I pushed at him. He held firm and said he wanted what I had given Faber.

My stomach flopped. I struggled. My umbrella caught his thigh. He grunted and lifted his head. Such a stupid expression. He looked puzzled by my lack of cooperation. I kneed him as hard as I could. He doubled over. I hit his head with my umbrella and ran.

I heard footsteps behind me and knew I could never outrun those Hitler Youth – a rabid wolf pack. I ran left, around the corner, past startled pedestrians, between two parked cars and across the street. A block later I stumbled up the stairs of the seminar building where Papa held his Thursday afternoon lectures. I leaned against the wall outside his classroom and tried to calm the terror raging through my mind and squeezing my chest. Someone asked if I were okay. I ignored him, slipped into the room and sank into a chair in the back row.

The smell of chalk and books soothed me, and my shaking hands stilled. Papa paused, nodded at me, then continued pacing back and forth in front of the chalkboard, emphasizing his points with stabs of the chalk he held. This is where Papa feels most at home. Students asked questions; he answered without hesitation. His voice was like a firm caress. I started to listen. This lecture – about the Napoleonic Wars – was one I had heard before. A fellow in the front row asked about Napoleon's Russian campaign.

I didn't hear Papa's answer because the question made me remember that September Sunday over a year ago, when I had entered Papa's study to find him studying a map of Russia on his desk. He had looked worried. When I asked what was wrong he had shown me how far our German armies had advanced into Russia.

I thought it was good to have gone so far in such a short time. Papa agreed but said that if our soldiers didn't capture Moscow before winter, the war was lost.

I asked how that could be, for we certainly have the greatest army of all time. He pointed out that Napoleon had said the same thing.

I must have looked confused because he pulled a book from his shelf and told me to read about the fate of Napoleon's *Grande Armée* in Russia. I never believed the same fate could await our own armies. None of us did, even when men had started freezing and dying last winter. Surely that one terrible season didn't mean the whole war was lost.

Students filed past me. I was so caught in my own thoughts I hadn't heard Papa dismiss the class. I watched him gather his papers and take down his maps. The rustling reminded me of hedgehogs in the garden at twilight.

Papa looked weary as he climbed the steps, and older, as if he had aged ten years in less than a week. I hadn't noticed how thin his hair was getting. He paused by my chair and held out his hand. I took it and we went across the street to the history faculty offices. It was the first time he had touched me since Friday. The warmth of his hand made me want to cry. I thought I had no tears left. I blinked them away. If I cried any more the Neckar would flood its banks.

Papa stopped to talk to his secretary. I circled the desk and studied the gilt-painted name on the door's glass inset: *Professor Jakob Rosenthal*. Papa reached around me and opened the door. I entered the room, crammed from floor to ceiling with books, and said, "Why isn't your name on the door, Papa? A year ago you told me it was going to be changed soon."

He closed the door, crossed to the window, stared into the street. "The work order to change it has remained unsigned on my desk for six years. Do you remember him, Garda?"

I didn't think so. I asked him if I should. He reminded me that I used to call him Uncle Jakob. Said that way, the name did sound familiar. I thought back to when I was ten years old. An image formed in my mind: a small man with dark hair and laughing brown eyes. But in that picture he was holding a little girl's hand. I asked if he had a daughter.

"Yes. She was a year younger than you, *Liebchen*. Like your fathers, you and Judith were friends. You played dolls together. Don't you remember?"

Judith. The name opened a door in my mind and memories tumbled out. I hadn't thought of Judith for years. Because...

She was Jewish. I covered my mouth and glanced at the door, feeling like the secretary outside listened to my thoughts to report them to the authorities. Garda, the school pariah, had once been friends with a Jew. How could Papa have endangered us like that?

Papa's shoulders drooped as he continued to look into the street. I felt ashamed of my thoughts. I crossed the room, linked my arm with his and took care to speak very quietly. "Isn't it dangerous to keep his name there, Papa?"

He patted my hand. "I must protest his treatment somehow, *Liebchen*. I can claim forgetfulness if someone makes trouble over it."

I seemed to remember that Judith's mother had died when she was young. I wanted to know what happened to her and her father. Papa told me that when the university forced Jakob to quit his position, they moved to Brussels. Over half the books in the office are his because they were allowed to take very little when they left. He had said to Papa, "Karl, keep these for me. I'll come back for them when this madness is ended."

I asked what he meant by "madness."

Papa was silent for a moment. "That might not have been the word he used. Today is the anniversary of the end of the Great War, you know. Armistice Day, the British call it. That always makes me think of the horrors of war. And now..."

When I asked him to continue, Papa clasped both my shoulders. His green eyes looked faded and lifeless. "Now the Nazis control Brussels."

I touched the Nazi pin on his lapel. "Aren't you a Nazi?"

"This pin helps me keep my teaching position, *Liebchen*. Do you understand?" I wasn't sure I did, but I nodded. Papa gave me a sad smile. "Your mother is enthusiastic enough for both of us."

My jaw clenched at the mention of Mother. I stared at the red and black pin and asked what happened in Brussels.

Papa explained that he got word from an acquaintance at the university there that Jakob and Judith were both arrested, along with many other Jews in the city. Papa wrote back, asking for details, but the man responded that he knew nothing else and was afraid to make inquiries.

Papa folded his arms around me. I leaned against him, welcoming his embrace. He whispered, "Fear. We are ruled by fear. Me, most of all. I don't deserve your devotion, my girl." Then he asked why I came to class. I had not stopped by like that for a long time.

Something in his tired voice held me back; I decided not to tell him about those HJ idiots. Instead I told him how Bette and Rolf made sure that everyone believes what Mother said about me. Papa called me *Liebchen*, and wished he could do something to make it better. "You must try to be brave. The sun will shine again someday," he said.

"But I feel so alone, Papa," I said, and he told me he would always be there for me.

I closed my eyes and rubbed my cheek against his jacket. What good does his being here do for me if he never says anything? Why hasn't he said anything, Hilde? Why hasn't he told Mother I was telling the truth? Is he afraid of her?

12 Nov 42

Frau Reifsneider stopped by last night, concerned about my absences from the last two BDM meetings. With me on the sofa, squeezed between my parents, she lectured us on the importance of my attendance, for my own well-being and training, and reminded us how unpatriotic it looked to not attend. If I dropped out, she would have to report it. Mother's face turned so red it made her blond hair look white. Papa studied his hands. Mother hustled her to the door with assurances that there was nothing to worry about. We were the most patriotic of families. Mother's loud voice carried into the parlour as she said that she had even spoken to the Führer himself on two separate occasions. That certainly shut the old cow's mouth.

Every chance she gets, Mother likes to tell people about meeting the Führer. Both times were at fancy teas put on by the Party, once before they came to power, and once after. I asked Papa why the Führer would have gone to tea parties. He said it was to charm the rich women who attended them. When I pointed out that we aren't terribly rich, he explained that our connection to the university gives Mother a great deal of respectability in town. She worked hard to secure a place of prominence in the local Party and was one of the hostesses at the teas.

Mother always claims the Führer is charm itself. The picture of him hanging to the right of the fireplace makes him look more judgmental than charming. I whispered, "Why would he charm rich women?"

"To make sure they loosened their fat husbands' fat wallets. Why else?"

Mother walked in. I covered my mouth to stop from laughing. I didn't want her asking what was funny. I suspect she wouldn't think it funny at all.

And I don't think Frau Reifsneider's visit was funny. Because of it, Mother made me go to the BDM meeting tonight. The only good thing was that it was back in the school, otherwise it was a repeat of how everyone has been treating me at school. For games and relays, Frau Reifsneider had to assign me to a team after no one picked me. During the lecture I sat alone in the third row. The ring of empty chairs around me made me think of being in quarantine.

Like twisting a radio dial, I tuned out the lecture and thought about how lovely it would be when I was finished high school and finished with the BDM.

Frau Reifsneider called my name. I blinked. Her nose was wrinkled – a sure sign she was unhappy. I said, "*Jawohl.*" The other girls snickered.

"Yes certainly what, Garda?" Frau Reifsneider said. "I asked why you weren't paying attention."

Foolishly, I replied that I was thinking about going to university to study archaeology.

Frau Reifsneider flushed an alarming shade of purple. She ordered me to stand by her. Then she circled me and lectured about the role of women in the Fatherland, which did not include attending university. Our most sacred calling was to get married and bear children for the Reich. She halted in front of me so her spittle sprayed my face.

She stopped. My ears rang with the silence. She said I was to bring a two-page essay to the next meeting on her lecture's content. Plus, I had to sweep the auditorium before going home.

Hilde, I've never come so close to fainting. The memory of Faber's attack rushed in, as if it had just happened. My knees wobbled. Frau Reifsneider faced the unit and dismissed the girls. I stared at her white blouse and tried to breathe, to move. All I could do was remember. His hands. His mouth.

I realized at that moment that Faber had planned it. He had told Rolf to keep Bette outside. For all I know, he had arranged for Frau Reifsneider to be called away. And now she had ordered me to stay behind again.

Panic began creeping up on me like an enemy soldier preparing for ambush. Frau Reifsneider barked at me to get busy and pointed to the closet. At least I'd have a weapon if Faber appeared. I ran to the closet and grabbed a wide dust mop. A desire to disobey arose, to just go home. I couldn't.

The floor wasn't dirty. I swept quickly, keeping the panic at bay. Fresh sweat dampened my armpits and slicked my palms. The room was empty. I doubled my efforts. My heart raced.

When a voice said, "Garda," I startled and dropped the broom. The wooden handle cracked on the floor like a gunshot. Papa stood in the doorway holding his hat with both hands.

He said it was dark out and he'd come to walk me home. When I started to tell him that Frau Reifsneider had ordered me to sweep, he said, "I won't tell her if you won't. Let's go home."

I put away the broom. I was so very relieved. As I was putting on my coat I asked why his faculty meeting ended early. He said he didn't feel like playing chess. He offered his arm, led me outside and asked why I was left to sweep up.

I explained what happened and how I had to write a two-page essay on how it's my sacred duty to become a mother for the Reich. I don't think BDM means League of German Girls. I think it means *Bund Deutscher Mimiken* – League of German Mimics. They want us to repeat everything they say, true or not. My brain will be pudding if I keep going to those meetings.

When I said that to Papa, he shushed me and warned me to hold my thoughts in my head where no one can hear them, and to hold my dreams in my heart where no one can touch them.

I started to protest and he touched his gloved finger to my lips. "Silence is our shield. Never forget it."

Our shield from what, Papa? What did silence get me when I didn't scream?

Chapter Nine

Del went for a long walk to shake off the melancholy from reading Garda's diary. She headed south along the big lake's shore, past mansion-like buildings, including one that had guards and American flags. When she reached the pair of bridges separating the big lake, Aussenalster, from its smaller sister, Binnenalster, a group of scruffy guys under the first bridge whistled and made loud comments.

For the first time she was glad to be unable to understand the language. She quickly retreated.

Back in the flat, Del leaned over the sink and splashed water on her face. She was patting her face dry when the phone in the living room rang. Seconds later Cassandra knocked on the bathroom door. "Mom and Dad are on the phone."

Del's body clenched. She spun around, intent on escape. "Can't! I'm in the shower!"

"I don't hear –"

Del cranked the corner shower's dial. Water hissed and splashed onto the floor. She closed the glass door and started stripping, tossing her clothes into the bathtub under the window.

Another bang on the door. "Don't be so childish. Get out here."

Del grabbed the shampoo bottle off the counter and retreated under the tepid spray. She took her time lathering up and scrubbing. She shampooed twice. When she bumped the sensitive dial, making the water turn icy, she got out and dressed. Very slowly.

Thirty minutes had passed since the phone call. Her parents would never talk that long. With the time difference, they'd both be on their way to work. Del smirked at the cloudy image in the mirror and carefully followed Cassandra's instructions for cleaning the shower.

Forty-five minutes after the call, Del entered the empty kitchen. She poured some fizzy orange juice with a name she couldn't pronounce, and reluctantly wandered into the living room wearing her best "don't care" expression, knowing Cassandra was going to tear into her. The living room was also empty, but the blind was up on the door and it was ajar.

Cassandra sat at the round patio table with her hand gripping a beer. Another bottle, open and beaded with moisture, was on the table in front of the empty chair. Del couldn't take her eyes off it. Cassandra knew about yesterday? Had she told their parents? Familiar tension clamped onto Del's limbs. Fight or flight. Del had heard the term in science. Her body preferred flight, except her parents had a knack for trapping her, verbally or physically, so she couldn't fly. Had they told Cassandra how to do that? A drop of sweat trickled down Del's neck.

"How far did you walk?" Cassandra's voice was as tense as a bungee cord stretched to its limit. She sounded like she was forcing herself to make small talk.

Del didn't probe. "To the bridges. It looked like there was a path under them. I was going to take it, but some creepy guys appeared so I turned around."

"Homeless. Sometimes they pitch tents on the grass between the street and the train tracks there. The police usually have more serious things to do than chase them off."

Cassandra still hadn't invited Del to sit. The bottle still sweated in the sun. Del's throat dried up so she sipped her orange drink. She wasn't sure what Cassandra thought but she wasn't about to confess anything from looking at a bottle. She leaned against the west rail. "Was that the American Embassy I walked by?"

"Yes."

"Is there a Canadian one?"

"A consulate. It overlooks the Binnenalster on its east side. Do you think you'll need it?"

"What for? I only have a photocopy of my passport in my wallet so I can't lose the original, can I? Isn't that the reason most people go to embassies? Seems like it in the movies."

"I went there the other day, to register you as a visitor to Hamburg and to give them our address as contact information."

"Thanks for telling me. Why didn't you take me?"

"I had your passport and the legal papers from Mom and Dad so I didn't need you."

Just like Mom and Dad, Del thought.

Cassandra added, "Besides, you were gardening with Professor Konrad and looked like you were enjoying yourself. I didn't want to disturb you."

"For the record, Warden, I like getting out of my cage."

Cassandra's lips thinned until they almost disappeared. Her words were tighter than her white-knuckle grip on the beer bottle. "I'll remember that. But for the record, being able to walk along the lake and go to the bakery any time you want hardly constitutes prison conditions. Why are you being so difficult? I thought you'd enjoy getting away from Mom and Dad for a while."

Del scowled into her juice. Away from their parents was also away from her friends, the people who made life bearable. They both heard footsteps on the stairs. Del leaned to see she'd left the living room door open. Mathias appeared, set his briefcase to the side and closed the door. He was loosening his tie when he stepped onto the deck. "You cannot believe how many students insisted they had to talk to me after class."

"All girls, I bet," Del said.

"Why do you think that?" Mathias dropped into the chair and

took a swallow of beer. It hadn't been for her, then. Cassandra
had been waiting for Mathias. Del felt a weird mixture of relief
and disappointment. "Luise said you're considered the hot man
on campus."

Cassandra tsked. "Don't be so disrespectful. It's Professor
Konrad."

Del glanced sideways but didn't respond. "If you're the hot
prof, it's probably like that old movie, you know, about the guy
who hunts for treasure and is chased by Nazis."

"Indiana Jones?"

"That's the one. I saw it on cable last month. He teaches university and girls are nuts over him. Some of them write "love you"
on their eyelids then close their eyes so he can see the message.
Have any of your students ever done that?"

Mathias snorted. "No."

"I bet they flirt with you, though." Del noticed a frown settle
on Cassandra's brow, as if the thought bothered her. Was she
afraid Mathias flirted back?

He smiled. "Perhaps. But I'm too old to be seen as handsome.
Isn't that what you said?"

"No. I said you're too old for me to see you as anything but old."

"Thanks for the reminder."

"You're okay for someone your age, I guess. Maybe college students like old."

He pointed the mouth of his bottle at her. "And maybe we
should change the subject."

Was he waggling the beer bottle to warn Del he might tell
Cassandra about yesterday? Del gave a strained smile and drank
some juice. Cassandra also took a drink and thumped her bottle
on the table. The noise seemed to surprise her. "I waited like you
asked, Mathias."

"Thank you. One moment." He disappeared inside and

returned with a black folding chair. He set it out and motioned for Del to sit. She placed her empty glass on it and stayed where she was. *Here it comes.* It wasn't fair that it was two against one, like when she clashed with her parents. The odds were never in her favour.

Cassandra got an intense look like she was making a plan. She pushed her beer to the middle of the table. "Mom and Dad wanted to talk to you."

"No, they didn't. They wanted to talk to you and hear you say Del is behaving herself and everything is going fine, so don't worry. That's what you told them, right?"

"Of course that's what I told them."

"They believe you. I could tell them anything and they'd ask you to back it up. So why should I bother?"

"They've called three times and every time you haven't been available or, like today, have made yourself unavailable. They're going to start to think you're upset with them."

"They already know that. I told them as they pushed me through security at the airport."

They argued for a few more minutes about Del talking to her parents the next time they called. Finally, Cassandra said, "You're being unreasonable."

"Right. They scare off my boyfriend, take me away from my friends, send me halfway around the world for the summer. They work it so I can hardly scratch my butt without your permission. They don't tell me that part of the reason they want me gone is because they're having marriage problems. But I'm the one who's being unreasonable. Love your logic."

"They were trying to protect you."

"They're trying to make their lives easier. They had it easy the first time around and they don't want to make an effort with me."

"You think things were easy between me and them?" Cassandra

asked. "I bent over backwards to please them. They always wanted me to get more, do better, reach higher. I had an ulcer at seventeen. Why do you think I went to Ontario for university?"

That surprised Del. Why hadn't she known? But she'd only been nine. She shook off a second's sympathy. Ancient history. "Now they're both focused on their precious careers. Half the time they probably wonder why they bothered with me. I know I do."

Mathias interrupted. "You can't mean that, Del."

She wished he wouldn't look at her like he felt sorry for her. Del half turned away from her sister. She crossed her arms and held Mathias's pale gaze. "You have no idea what it's like living in her shadow. All my life she has been Mom and Dad's measuring stick. All my life I've listened to Cassandra this and Cassandra that. If only you got better marks like Cassandra. If only you applied yourself like Cassandra. If only you were pretty like Cassandra."

"They've never said that!" Cassandra cried.

"Oh? More than once Mom has moaned about my bone structure, wishing I had your high cheekbones. And before my grade nine prom, Dad looked me over and said, 'Nice dress. Too bad you don't have a skinny backside like your sister.'"

Cassandra's cheeks reddened and she busied herself with taking a drink. Mathias said, "I know an old professor's opinion doesn't matter to you, Del, but your... backside... is fine."

It might've meant more if Cassandra had said it. Del pushed away from the rail. "Stop asking me to talk to them. If I want to, I'll let you know. And don't give me that 'think about how they feel' crap. They've never done that for me." The lump of hurt in her throat was making it hard to breathe. A walk would clear it up. She started to leave.

Mathias grabbed her wrist. "Don't run away from this, Del.

We want to help. Tell us how we can make this summer less painful for you."

Tears threatened. Del hated that his sincerity made her emotional. Arguing was easier to handle than a gentle touch and kindness. The urge to slap him and run almost won. She pulled away and hugged her torso. "You mean other than flying some of my friends over?"

His lips twisted in a wry grimace. "Yes. Other than that."

"Unlock the chains."

Cassandra slapped the table. "I am so sick of your prison metaphor!" She looked on the verge of tears, too.

Mathias held up his hand. "A bit melodramatic, yes. But let Del explain."

"I want trust. I want to explore the city on my terms. I want a transit pass so I can go where I want without you hovering over me, pointing out boring history stuff I don't care about. I know Mom and Dad sent you a chunk of cash. I want access to more of it so I can do things. Go to movies. Shop. Take a sailing lesson. Whatever I want to do."

Cassandra said, "But –"

"Please," Mathias responded. "I think we should give her requests fair consideration. She's right that being here is not her choice."

A smile started. It disappeared when Mathias gave her a level stare. "But if we agree to some of your requests, you'll have to prove yourself worthy of the trust we give you." He raised his eyebrows as he took a drink of his beer, his meaning more than clear.

He was willing to trust her, unless she screwed up. That was one better than her parents: they just assumed she was going to screw up.

Del spent the rest of the day helping Luise put together new shelving units for her garage. She went to bed early but couldn't sleep. After an hour her thoughts were still spinning so she went to get a drink of milk and noticed a slice of light under the kitchen door. Mathias's and Cassandra's voices were quiet but audible.

"Please don't do this to yourself, Cassandra. This isn't about success or failure."

"With my parents that's always what it's about."

"They've only asked that we do our best. You're the one putting pressure on yourself."

Cassandra's voice rose a notch. "You don't understand."

"Please explain."

"It's... it's like I'm walking a tightrope. Mom and Dad are at opposite ends jiggling the rope, testing me. And Delora is prodding me with a stick, wanting me to fall."

"It's not like that, *Liebchen*."

Del silently retreated to her bedroom. How typical that Cassandra thought this was all about her. Del didn't want her sister to fall. She just wanted everyone to stop expecting her to be a Cassandra clone and let her be herself.

Chapter Ten

15 Nov 42

For three days Papa's words have eaten a hole in my heart. I do not speak out very much, but now it seems even that is too much. Papa does not want me to talk about what happened, what I want, what I think. What is left? Am I allowed to speak about the weather?

Very well. It rained today, Hilde. A lonely drizzle. With my umbrella, I walked up the hill to the castle anyway. When I use the north ramp, I think I hear the wooden carts from long ago rattling up the cobblestones to bring supplies to the castle. Being alone on the incline made the sounds of the past louder. I swung around the switchback and bumped into a uniformed man. My mind screamed, *Run!* My legs petrified. The fear eased when I saw it was a Wehrmacht soldier, not a Hitler Youth. Not Faber. Will I ever quit expecting to meet him at every turn?

The soldier blocked my way, rifle across his chest. In the shadow of the arch, with his helmet pulled low, I couldn't see his eyes. He asked me my business and I stuttered that I only wanted to go to the lower terrace.

When he said they have an anti-aircraft battery there, I asked if it was forbidden to go. Maybe he saw my sadness. He replied civilians were only discouraged and motioned for me to proceed, then followed me through the archway and up the final incline, as if I required an armed escort. My neck hairs prickled. Was he planning to attack me? Only habit kept my legs moving.

A ring of sandbags surrounded a giant gun that crouched like a mechanical insect in the middle of the terrace. There were so few signs of war in the city and now one sat in one of my favourite places. It suddenly felt colder.

My escort halted ten paces away, so I tried to ignore him and leaned on the balustrade. Even the red roofs had a dull cast on this gloomy day.

Heiliggeistkirche (Church of the Holy Spirit) towered above the surrounding buildings like a sentry, its steeple a medieval spear. It reminded me of the soldier at my back. I turned to go.

The soldier's rain-dampened grey overcoat matched the streaked stone behind him. He nodded and said, "Good day, *Fraulein*."

I seized a thread of courage and asked if he thought Heidelberg would be bombed.For a moment he stood, statue-like, then said, "So far the English are only bombing military and industrial targets. Heidelberg is neither. But who can say what those bulldogs will do? We must be prepared."

I scanned the city and tried to imagine what it might look like if it were bombed. I could not. My home a collapsed shell like the rear part of this castle? Unthinkable. Heavy clouds drew my eye. Surely I would hear if English bombers were up there. I asked if he ever fought where bombs were falling.

He limped toward me and explained he was wounded on the Eastern Front in March.

I hadn't noticed the limp, but he had been behind me on the ramp. Curious, I asked, "What was it like?"

He gazed into the distance and told me to imagine the worst storm I'd ever been in, then multiply it a thousand times. I saw his eyes at that moment. Haunted eyes.

Such a fierce shiver ran through my body, I almost dropped my umbrella. Oh Hilde, you know how much I hate storms.

18 Nov 42

Today I was in a toilet cubicle when two girls entered the washroom. The voices belonged to Bette and her new best friend, Elise. I could hear running water. They started talking about me, so I stayed on the toilet though I was finished.

I heard Bette say, "She tried to accuse Faber of rape, if you can believe it."

Elise replied, "That's ridiculous. My brother said he'd heard it's easy to lift her skirt. And Faber is so wonderful. So handsome. What did he see in Garda?"

They both giggled about boys only being interested in what's under my skirt. Bette offered to arrange a double date before Faber goes to training camp.

Elise squealed and cried how wonderful that would be.

The two of them left. I couldn't move, even after the bell rang. I had never understood why Papa didn't go to the police. Now I do. Only girls who are asking for it anyway get raped, and they deserve it, so it really isn't rape. No policeman is going to believe me after they've talked to Faber and Bette and their friends. They are telling everyone I asked for it.

I have been tried and found guilty.

22 Nov 42

Like most Sundays, we ate a late breakfast together. As Mother set a boiled egg in each cup, the bells of Heiliggeistkirche began to ring. They are deeper than the other church bells, stately but comforting, like a father calling to his children, not in alarm but announcing it's time to play. My parents never heed the call.

This week I stopped by the large church twice for somewhere peaceful to sit. I love the soaring pointed arches and the row of smaller ones perched above them – children on their fathers' shoulders. Whenever I leave Heiliggeistkirche, my neck is sore from looking up. The vaulted ceiling hides God just as He hides you, Hilde.

I wish he would let me see you, just once. Are you happy?

I am not. My life is a lonely vigil. No one will go against Bette's decision to ostracize me. The only time someone outside the family speaks to me is when Mother sends me on errands and the shopkeepers ask what I want.

Rations allow one egg each per week, so we save them for Sunday mornings. Papa tutors a farmer's two sons on Saturday afternoons and is paid in cheese that is so creamy and fresh it turns our dark rye bread into a treat. All week long we look forward to that Sunday breakfast of eggs and cheese. This morning it tasted like mud.

Erwin chattered about Feldmarshal Rommel's victories in Africa. Every day the newspaper describes the glorious heroism of his Afrikakorps. Erwin feels an affinity for the field marshal, because they share the same first name, and longs for the day when he can serve under his hero. Erwin is eleven. Surely he can't hope the war will last six years so he can join the fight.

While Erwin babbled I thought of my visit to the castle and that soldier's haunted eyes. He hadn't looked like he thought war was glorious. But nothing could distract me from the thought crouched in my mind – one I cannot bring myself to tell even you, Hilde.

6 Dec 42

I'm sorry for not writing sooner, Hilde. The last two weeks were a haze. I haven't been sleeping well. Twice I was punished in class for dozing off, much to the delight of Bette and her new best friend.

The house is a prison and a sanctuary. Mother watches me. She gets Erwin to spy on me when he's home, which thankfully isn't often. Papa hides in his office, leaving me to face them alone, so I retreat to my bedroom and stare at the storm clouds only I can see.

This morning, as I washed breakfast dishes, Mother and Papa sat at the table having a second cup of ersatz coffee. Mother was talking about a committee she was on with Frau Ott and how the woman had twice called me "your whorish daughter."

Papa whispered, "That's enough, Ulla." Mother replied in her coldest voice that he knew it was true.

The dish in my hands crashed to the floor. I fled. Mother yelled for me to come back, but I grabbed my coat, slipped on my brown shoes and ran outside. A block later I had to stop to tie my laces because I almost tripped.

I wound up at Heiliggeistkirche. The service had just let out and people were visiting by the main doors, so I hurried past, not stopping until I reached the middle of Alte Brücke.

From the old bridge, the castle, warm yellow in the winter sun, floated on a sea of naked trees above the red roofs. It made me want to cry. Everything beautiful becomes a ruin. I thought my life was near perfect, and now it is ruined.

The Neckar whispered to me. For an hour I leaned on the stone railing and studied the river and its traffic. And listened. When I realized what it was saying, fright made me grip the stone so hard my fingers ached. I leaned over the low wall and peered into the cold brown-blue depths calling to me. How simple it would be to sit on the ledge and drop off.

I was bending far over, seeing nothing but the river, when a hand clutched my shoulder. I gasped and straightened up. A young man holding a sketch pad squinted at me and asked if I were Professor Kurz's daughter because he thought he'd seen us together.

A nod was all I could manage. He pushed up his glasses, talked about the river being fascinating but that I needed to be careful I didn't lean too far and fall. Still my voice betrayed me. And worse, tears gathered. He looked uncomfortable while he explained he was in Papa's history class.

I stared at his sketch pad. Couldn't he tell I wanted to be left alone? Or maybe he could tell and that's why he didn't leave. He held out the pad and said, "Would you like to look? I was on Philosopher's Way, sketching the valley. You are in the last drawing."

How could I resist? I took the pad and flipped to that last picture. He must have stood on the north bank to draw it, for three of the bridge's arches spanned across the drawing. I could almost count the bricks. Behind it, the castle ruins were lightly sketched in. I was a dark silhouette above the middle arch of the bridge. A shadow.

A memory?

A tear slipped down my cheek and dropped onto the drawing, wetting the paper river. He took the sketchpad and tore the page out. He said I was important to the picture, adding scale to the bridge so the viewer could judge its size. I reminded him, he said, that beauty such as seen in the bridge and the castle mean nothing if no people are there to appreciate it.

He laid the drawing in my hands. I couldn't take my eyes off it. He asked if he could walk me home and I shook my head. He took my arm, led me off the bridge and left me in the mouth of the gate tower, the portcullis hanging above me like teeth. As he strolled away, I sagged against the tower's wall, wanting to cry.

I wish I were important to something besides a drawing. To someone.

My family is going to hate me even more than they already do. Mother will think her judgment is proved right. I can't bear to tell her, Hilde. I can barely stand the thought of telling Papa, but I must.

It has been a month since that awful night. My period should have started three weeks ago. This must be a bad dream, but I can't seem to wake up. I can't be pregnant. I can't.

Why didn't that young man leave me to do as the river whispered? Now my courage has flown. My bones are water. My hope is dust.

10 Dec 42

At dinner, the smell of frying sausages made my stomach queasy. I couldn't bring myself to eat one. And when I commented that the cheese tasted moldy, Mother got angry with me – she had just gotten it this morning. I ate a bit of bread and potato and asked to be excused to do homework. In truth, I wasn't hungry.

16 Dec 42

Tonight Papa came into his office and found me in his chair. He crouched beside it, stroked my forehead and asked, "What's wrong, *Liebchen*? You have been so quiet and sad these last few weeks."

Under his warm touch, the wall I had built around my secret crumbled.

It spilled out. Papa's face wrinkled like he was in pain. He lifted me, sat and held me on his lap. He didn't speak, but as I lay with my cheek against his tweed jacket, something wet dripped onto my head. Warm silent tears that scalded my soul. I would rather he had yelled, anything rather than cried. I want to shrivel into nothing for the way I've disappointed him.

17 Dec 42

Mother kept me home from school. She sounded almost kind when she told me to stay in bed. I know Papa told her last night. They rarely talk when they go to bed, but I heard their voices through the wall. I couldn't make out the words.

I was reading when someone knocked at the front door. One of Mother's friends come for tea, I thought. A moment later, footsteps clumped up the stairs. Doktor Wiebe barged into my room, Mother right behind him. I dropped my book and pulled my bedcovers up to my chin.

The doctor sat on the end of the bed, looked at me over the top of his round glasses and said, "So you think you are pregnant. When did you last menstruate?"

My cheeks were so hot I expected them to burst into flames. The doctor cleared his throat and repeated his question, so I stuttered it had been the third or fourth week in October. Mother stood behind Doktor Wiebe, arms crossed as she scowled at me.

Then he asked if my nipples were tender. Can you imagine how embarrassing it is to have someone your father's age ask you that, Hilde? I nodded. When he asked about morning sickness, I said no, though I admitted that sometimes my stomach was upset in the evenings.

It turns out morning sickness is poorly named and you can have it any time of day.

Mother asked if we could do a test. Doktor Wiebe replied that we could, but it's expensive and takes several days to get the results. Then he said we needn't bother since I had two common symptoms and had missed two menstruation cycles. He declared, "It is safe to assume your daughter is pregnant, Frau Kurz."

"Can't you do anything about it?" Mother asked.

The doctor promised to do everything he could to see I have a healthy pregnancy.

"No," said Mother. "I mean, can't you get rid of it?"

The air turned electric, as if a lightning storm had surged into the room. Doktor Wiebe's frown was even heavier than Mother's. They looked ready to fight.

The doctor was surprised Mother would suggest such a thing because the Reich has forbidden abortions. He said he was no backroom abortionist, that he does what he can to preserve life. Then he ordered Mother out so he could do an examination and stared at her until she stomped out.

He listened to my heart, took my pulse and a few other things. I paid little attention. I was stuck on the word, abortionist, and so didn't hear him tell me to remove my underwear until he repeated the order in a brusque tone. My eyes widened and he repeated it yet again. Now his frown was directed at me.

After I had done as ordered and scooted back under the bedcovers, he yanked them from my grasp and rolled them down to the foot of my bed, then made me lie on my back with my knees up and legs spread wide. He put on rubber gloves and told me to relax while he poked his fingers inside me. Relax? Oh Hilde, I was mortified. And it hurt. I covered my mouth to keep from making noise but cried the whole time.

Then he took off his gloves and felt my stomach. He pulled my nightgown back down and asked how often I was engaging in sexual intercourse. His bushy eyebrows raised when I whispered that it had only been once. As he tucked my blankets back around me, he asked if the young man had been told.

I shook my head. I wanted to tell him Faber had forced me, but, as usual, my voice had fled. From head to toe, I burned with embarrassment.

Doktor Wiebe opened the door and beckoned my mother. He announced that I was quite healthy and my pelvis size should allow for a normal delivery. Again Mother wanted the name of someone who could help us get rid of the problem.

The doctor fastened his black bag and said he wouldn't endanger his practice by suggesting someone. He has treated women suffering from botched abortions and the safest thing is to let me deliver the baby.

Then Mother blurted, "How am I supposed to explain this? I am on several important committees."

"So now we come to the truth of it," the doctor said. "You are concerned for your reputation." Mother didn't even blush.

He asked me if the young man was Aryan and Mother snapped that, of course he was. The way she went on so proudly about his having just left Heidelberg to do a shortened labour term before joining the Waffen SS, made it sound like we were a couple. I could have screamed.

Doktor Wiebe grabbed his bag and suggested Faber might be willing me marry me. If not, he went on about Herr Himmler's *Lebensborn* program, especially since Faber is SS. Several resorts have been set up to house young single women willing to bear Aryan children for the Reich. I would have excellent medical care and would be out of sight of Mother's friends. The doctor said it was far better than this other foolishness. He said he would draw up a certificate so I could get the extra rations I'm allowed.

The doctor patted me on the shoulder and told me to drink lots of milk. When he left, Mother followed.

Marry Faber? I will throw myself off the bridge first. The thought of an abortion scares me, Hilde. And I don't want to go to some awful breeding farm. I just want this all to go away.

19 Dec 42

Whenever Papa looks my way, he stares at my stomach. He used to ask me how I was feeling, how classes were going, if anything was wrong.

Now I'm pregnant because I was raped and he doesn't ask me anything at all. He doesn't look me in the eyes. He doesn't touch me.

Hilde, could you slip into his dreams and whisper to him how much I need a hug?

21 Dec 42

Erwin spends even less time at home now. No one has told him I'm pregnant, but he must sense something is wrong. After he had gone off to join his DJ unit for the weekend, Mother said it again. "What will our friends think, Karl?"

Papa said nothing; he didn't look up from his coffee. But his shoulders drooped. I think he is embarrassed, just like Mother. She hasn't spoken to me since the doctor's visit. When she talks to Papa she calls me, "your daughter." Every time she says it, he flinches. How he must hate me.

He can't possibly hate me more than I hate myself.

If only I had run away. Or screamed. If only, if only, if only.

Chapter Eleven

Del was crying on the chaise longue when Luise found her on the patio. She felt like an idiot but couldn't stop. The older woman sat on the edge of the lounger and took the diary pages from Del's loose grip.

"Oh my. I was going to suggest we walk to the bakery. Whatever is wrong, Del?"

"I don't know," Del sobbed.

Luise held one of her hands. "You were reading the diary."

Del sniffed and jerked her head yes.

"What were you reading when you began crying?"

Eyes scrunched closed, Del tried to think. It helped dam the tears. Those last words – *if only* – echoed through her mind, but she'd started crying before that. She remembered when – and gasped back more tears.

Luise's grip tightened. "Please tell me, Del. It might help."

Del was torn between fleeing and throwing herself into Luise's embrace. She curled up and laid her head on Luise's knee. A strong hand settled on her hair. "It was... when Garda was on the bridge and –" Del gulped some air. "She wished she was important to someone."

"That was a hard time in her life. I also had difficulty reading that." Del shivered and Luise fell silent for a moment. "It means more than that to you, doesn't it?"

Del nodded against soft denim. "I tried to tell myself that at least I, I still have my friends, but..."

"But they aren't here."

"No," Del whispered.

"What makes you think you aren't important to your family?"

"My parents love their careers. All they want is for me to behave, grow up and get out. Believe me, I can hardly wait." The earthy scent of Luise's fingers wafted around Del's face. "And Cass... just wants to be able to give Mom and Dad a good report."

"Your sister might have other motives. She seemed genuinely concerned when she first mentioned you were coming over. Something about parties and a boy..."

Del pulled away and hugged her legs against her chest. "She told you about Geoff? And did she tell you that Mom and Dad scared him away? Scared away the only person who loved me?" At least, for her it had been love; why hadn't Geoff fought for it, if he felt the same? She whispered, "But Dad said sex isn't love."

"Is that what you thought?"

"I don't know. Maybe. I know it felt good, like I was special."

"Like you were important to someone." Del silently agreed. Luise brushed her forehead with the back of her hand. "Is that the only reason you were crying?"

Del rested her head on her knees. "She was so alone. Why couldn't they see her pain?"

"Maybe they didn't want to, because then they would've had to do something about it."

"Instead they worried about their own reputations." Is that why Del's parents had freaked out about her and Geoff? Because of their reputations? "Can you get pregnant from just once?"

"Yes."

Del bit the inside of her lip. She was lucky she hadn't ended up pregnant. She could have – there was that once when they were both a bit drunk and had forgotten about protection. Her parents would've gone ballistic, worse than Garda's mother. Then they would've rushed her in for an abortion whether she wanted one or not. Then they would've never spoken about it again. Tick it off the list and move on. Who cares how Del feels? Appearances are everything.

Del shuddered. "Were abortions really forbidden then?"

"In Nazi Germany, yes. I believe, later in the war, it was a crime punishable by death."

Down the street, a dog started barking and was quickly silenced. Del felt wrung out. She stared at the grass but didn't see it. If she didn't move she was going to fall asleep.

"Del?" Luise spoke quietly. "You aren't alone. I'm here. Your friends are fairly easy to reach. Even Mathias and Cassandra would listen if you asked."

Maybe Mathias. But Cassandra? Not likely. Del stood. "You said something about the bakery? I need to go every day if I want half a chance at tasting all their different pastries."

Luise let the subject change without objecting. "What will you choose today?"

"Whatever your favourite is."

"Then it will be *Pflaumenkuchen*."

"*Kuchen* is cake. What are *Pflaumen*?"

Uncertainly rippled Luise's brow. "Oval fruit. Purple. As long as my thumb."

"Plums?"

"Yes! Plums. *Pflaumen*. The word was erased from my mind. How silly."

Del tutted. "Sounds like old age to me."

Luise smiled. "Oh hush. Let's go. Clouds are moving in."

The walk to the mall was silent but comfortable.

They were almost there when Del said, "Luise? Have you ever felt really alone? Like, not loved by anyone?"

"I told you I'm divorced." Luise paused. "It was a surprise to me.

One day my husband walked in and told me he loved someone else. During that time I felt very unloved. But I wasn't. My brother and his family did all they could to support me. For quite some time I was too involved in my own pain to feel their comfort."

"That's harsh."

"It's difficult to go through, yes, but it made me stronger. Unfortunately it also made me very reluctant to trust my heart with anyone else."

"You're breaking some guy's heart, Luise. Unreturned love and all that."

Luise laughed. "If only he would introduce himself so I knew he was pining."

The mall was small, only six or seven stores, and it was open to the weather on either end, but there was a glass roof covering the wide sidewalk between the stores. Luise called it a *Passage*, said more like *pass-aaj* with the stress on the end of the word. Just outside the *Passage*, Del admired the mural on the three-storey building – it always made her smile. The building was newer but the mural was a row of old white buildings with old-fashioned wooden trim and a powder blue sky. Today there were thin clouds, but on clear days the top of the mural blended with the sky, creating a three-dimensional illusion.

In the bakery, with prompting from Luise, Del ordered in German. "*Zwei Pflaumenkuchen, bitte.*" The girl behind the counter answered in German, with a lot of words. Del shot Luise a panicked look and she whispered that the girl asked if they wanted a bag. Del nodded. The girl smiled. Del remembered to say, "*Danke.*" The girl sent them off with a cheerful, "*Tschüss!*" Del had figured out from other visits it meant, "'Bye."

Like the road, the sidewalk was narrow, more so because some cars were parked half up on the curb. Twice Del had to slip behind Luise to walk single file past the cars. After jogging to catch up for the second time, Del said, "There is something I'm curious about." Luise indicated she was listening. "Garda's diary is way different from books today that are written like diaries."

"Different how?"

"I don't know. Stiff? No. More formal. Like it was an essay written for marks. Diaries are usually pretty casual."

Luise was silent for a moment. "If you look at diaries of the time, Garda's way of writing fits. In those days I think people kept diaries as an accounting of their lives. They wrote more for posterity, if you will. A lot of thought likely went into most entries."

"Posterity?"

"Yes. A record for future generations."

"Oh. Right." After Del dodged another car, she said, "Garda mentioned hills and a castle. You said there aren't castles in Hamburg, and there sure aren't any hills. She was in Heidelberg, not Hamburg? That confused me."

"Oh dear. I will include a note at the start so it's clear Garda's story begins in Heidelberg."

"I know the name. Where is it?"

"You flew into Frankfurt?"

Del nodded.

"It's a little southeast of there, on the edge of hills that are part of the Neckarwald, the Neckar Forest."

"Neckar. That's the river she referred to."

"Yes. The forest gets its name from the river. The city is quite beautiful. Unlike most cities in Germany it wasn't attacked during World War Two so has a lovely old-town area. Its university is the oldest in Germany, dating back to the fourteenth century."

The clouds fattened up during the walk; a drizzle started as they reached the house. Del watched Luise bustle around the kitchen and considered how relaxed she was with this woman. Her large frame and short greying hair made her the physical opposite of Del's sister and mother. Maybe that was part of why Del felt comfortable. Safe.

Luise set the two pieces of *Pflaumenkuchen* on a plate. "Sitting on the terrace has been delayed by rain. Why don't we retire to the living room for some tea and cake? Too early for coffee and cake, what we Germans call *Kaffee und Kuchen*, but we'll be able to see the garden."

"Sure."

"You have no other plans?"

"No. I'm waiting for a verdict and don't think I should go far until I get it."

"That sounds ominous. On what are you being judged?"

"On everything, I guess. For one, I'd like a transit pass. And I want to be able to use more of the money my parents sent over. I want to be able to do what I want, when I want."

"They are afraid you're too young?"

"No, they're afraid I'll get into the same kind of trouble I got into at home."

Luise glanced up from pouring hot water into her green ceramic teapot, eyebrows raised in questioning curves. "Is that likely?"

"No. None of my friends are here. I don't like partying with strangers, so who is there to get in trouble with?"

"You went out with Felix the other day and seemed to enjoy it." Luise set the teapot on a tray already loaded with cups and the cake. Del held the door open and followed her out.

"Sure. We talked, joked. It was fun. He's like you, easy to talk to."

A smile softened Luise's face. She passed Del her *Pflaumenkuchen*, then a cup of tea. She settled in an overstuffed chair beside the sofa. "How far past the bridge incident did you get?"

Del startled. "Did I leave the diary outside? It'll be ruined."

"No. I set it on the sideboard."

Del retrieved the manuscript and laid it on the table. Luise had printed it out on half pages of paper and trimmed it so it looked about the size of a regular paperback, though it was bound together with elastics. Del flipped to the last entry she'd read. "I'm on December 21."

The phone rang. Luise gave Del a rueful smile and answered it with a blunt, "Konrad." She listened for several seconds, then said something in German, covered the mouthpiece and said, "I'm sorry, Del. I have to take this call. Perhaps you could read until I am finished."

Del nodded and picked up a sheaf of pages.

Chapter Twelve

23 Dec 42

The air in this house is so thick I can't breathe, but I am forbidden to go out. Mother left a note saying so. Erwin found the note and wants to know why I am restricted to the house. I wouldn't tell him, so he hit me and ran from the room.

I sat by my open window all evening, in the dark so Papa wouldn't get in trouble with the Air Raid Warden. Laughter rose from the street, over our roof and into my room. All over Heidelberg people are going to parties, getting ready for Christmas and doing anything they can to forget, for a few days, that there is a war. Surely it will end soon, they say.

I am alone on a battlefield. When will my war end, Hilde?

24 Dec 42

For Christmas Eve we feasted as if there were no war – roast goose and red cabbage and potato dumplings. I don't know how Mother managed to buy everything needed, but it was heavenly. The family is at the Christmas Eve service, which is the only one they still attend. I wasn't allowed to go. My stomach is quite flat, yet still Mother fears one of her snobbish friends will sniff out my secret.

Heiliggeistkirche will be so beautiful with candles everywhere. I wish I could see it. I almost decided to follow them and sneak into the service. If I sat at the back and slipped out during the last hymn, I could get home without being seen.

Breaking rules is not something I've ever been good at, which makes it more painful that anyone would believe the lies being told about me. And now I feel sick because I tried to break an even bigger rule. Oh Hilde, they should have taken me with them tonight.

After they had left, I paced for fifteen minutes, more than enough time for them to walk to the church. When I was certain they wouldn't return any time soon, I went to the kitchen. It still smelled of goose. My stomach felt squeezed by invisible bands. I knew what I was doing was wrong, even if Mother would be relieved.

I climbed onto the counter and jumped down. Twice. Hand on my stomach, I stood in the kitchen and waited for a sign of some kind to tell me a miscarriage had begun.

When nothing happened, I realized the height was probably too small. I lacked the courage to throw myself down the stairs – it would hurt terribly – so I took one of the kitchen chairs to Papa's office. I set it on his desk and climbed onto it. The distance to the floor couldn't have been more than 160 centimetres, but it looked terribly far. I had to take several breaths before I jumped, but I did it.

I hit the floor with a loud thump. Pain shot up my legs and my ankle almost bent over. I crumpled to the floor. After several minutes, the pain died, except in my ankle. I returned the chair to the kitchen, then limped up to my bedroom.

Now I lie on my bed and wait to see if my attempts were successful. It's been an hour. Surely something should have started by now.

Mother wanted to take me to an abortionist so I know she'd be happy with a miscarriage. I'm certain Papa would be relieved, too. But I feel sick at heart, like I've tried to commit murder. It hurts me so much that Mother won't protect me, and yet am I any better?

While the rest of the family celebrates a baby's birth, I'm trying to make sure one isn't born. If the miscarriage happens and this baby has a soul, please take care of it for me, Hilde.

25 Dec 42
Christmas Day is over and I'm still pregnant.

Last night, after the church service, Papa came upstairs to get me for our *Bescherung*. He didn't ask about my limp. While the family opened presents, I sat near the fireplace grate and enjoyed the warmth of the small fire Mother had permitted. I felt like a stranger watching someone else's family laugh and rattle their gifts as they tried to guess what was inside before opening them. I almost expected to not be given any gifts.

Erwin was thrilled with the model *Kübelwagen* I gave him. He said it looks just like the one Feldmarshal Rommel drives in the desert.

Mother and Papa had been harder to buy for. In the end, I picked out a bottle of scent for Mother and a fountain pen for Papa. Small luxuries are easier to find than many necessities, so I was surprised by the night-gown they gave me. I have no idea where they found it since dress shops are quite empty. Violets decorate the bodice and lace trims the collar and cuffs. It's very roomy, an admission that I will get fat. I felt doubly guilty for what I had tried earlier in the evening, and for what I thought then might yet come to pass.

Erwin gave me another journal, which is wonderful since this one is almost full. I'm certain Papa helped him pick it out.

Today was quiet. We have no family close by, so we did not go visiting as most families do on Christmas Day. This evening, Mother and Papa are at a social hosted by the university's president. I chased Erwin to bed, but I know by the crack of light under his door that he is busy putting his model together. I don't care. At least he's not bothering me.

I hear a door downstairs. They are back early. I'll pretend to be asleep.

Here I am, Hilde, back after only 15 minutes. Papa came into my room to say good night, something he hasn't done for months. He sat on my bed and whispered he knew I was awake. When I opened my eyes, he kissed my forehead and said he knew this hadn't been a happy Christmas for me. "Next year will be better," he said.

"What's going to happen to me, Papa?" I asked "I know Mother is planning something. Is she still trying to arrange an abortion?"

Papa stared at me as if a wild boar's head had sprouted from my neck.

After an awkward silence, he wondered what give me that idea. Mother would never endanger my life in such a way. I couldn't bring myself to answer. It never occurred to me that Mother wouldn't have told Papa what had been said during the doctor's visit.

Papa drew his new fountain pen from his inside jacket pocket. He said he knew I wanted him to have it, but the best gift I could give him is if I use it to keep writing in my journal.

When I started to protest, he touched his finger to my lips and said, "Hide the journal if you must, but always tell the truth in it. Someday this war will be nothing but part of someone's history class. Maybe mine. Then we'll be happy for those brave enough to have told the truth."

I took the pen. Papa kissed my forehead again and left. As I write these words with Papa's new fountain pen, I realize that in giving me the pen, Papa was admitting that he is not brave and he hopes I will be. Why does he think I need to be brave? What does Mother have planned?

27 Dec 42

The Christmas break is stretching into forever. I am getting more fearful over what Mother is planning. If she doesn't arrange an abortion, which seems less likely as the days pass, I'm certain she will send me away.

I want to stay in Heidelberg. I love the old town with its scattered university buildings. One of the lecture halls dates back to when the university was started in the 1300s and I love sitting on its benches, seeing the groove worn in the steps by centuries of students. I love the way our house is snuggled up against the foot of *Königsstuhl* and how the dark green hill seems to watch over the whole city. Maybe it hides us from the English bombers.

Hilde, I will do anything if only Mother will let me stay.

28 Dec 42

I'm ashamed to admit I tried it again, Hilde. To start a miscarriage, I mean. I snuck out of the house early and walked six kilometers to the Braun farm, the family whose boys Papa tutors. One of them mentioned once that if I ever wanted to go horseback riding, I should visit.

The air was nippy, which made me glad to be wearing trousers, and everything was dusted with a fine layer of snow. It won't last long, but it looks lovely.

When I knocked, the boy who had made the offer, Johann, opened the farmhouse door. He was surprised to see me. His mother invited me in for a hot drink and to rest my feet. When I explained why I had come (just to ride, I said), they were puzzled that I would want to in the middle of winter, but Frau Braun was accommodating. She sent Johann to saddle their horse and told me to stop by the house after so she could send some ham home with me, for they had butchered a few weeks ago and had plenty.

She didn't ask if I knew how to ride. I suppose she assumed that a professor's daughter would know. In truth, I've only been led around on ponies, and even that was years ago.

Johann seemed to realize I needed help. He held the reins while I mounted, assured me the horse was gentle, then led it to the end of the lane. He warned me the horse has a rough trot.

The road was guarded on both sides by linden trees and was thankfully deserted. As soon as I was out of sight of any houses, I kicked the horse's flanks until it broke into a trot. I now know what "bone-jarring" means. I had to hold the pommel to keep from bouncing out of the saddle. I kicked more. The horse began to canter and it was all I could do to hang on. I decided this wasn't such a good idea, after all.

Before I could figure out how to rein the horse in without releasing my grip on the saddle, a hare darted across the road. I ended up on my back on a crushed bush, air refusing to enter my lungs. Spots danced in front of my eyes until I could draw breath. My ribs pained me. When the air rushed in, I rolled off the bush and gulped mouthfuls of oxygen until the horse nuzzled my hair. I got up and hugged the horse around the neck while I cried against its warm coat.

I'm horrible, Hilde. This fall was what I had secretly wanted. I said I'd do anything to stay in Heidelberg and I had proved it. I knew that this baby growing inside me would soon be no more. But it is so late that Papa has told me twice to turn off the light, and still nothing has happened.

It seems that I will have no choice but to be brave.

Chapter Thirteen

The window in Luise's living room beckoned. The rain came down steadily, adding to the closed-in feeling pressing Del from all sides. She knew part of it was the sense of impending doom expressed by a girl in 1942. It tore at her that someone would be so desperately alone and afraid that she would risk hurting herself by trying to induce a miscarriage. How could her friends and family have abandoned her so completely? Her emergency room visit came to mind. She knew from Serena that her friend's family had stuck by her, and even now Del felt relieved. She couldn't help but wonder how her family would react if it happened to her.

Del was too familiar with feeling like an outsider in her family. She sometimes thought the old *Sesame Street* jingle could apply to them: "Three of these things belong together. Three of these things are kind of the same. Can you guess which one of these doesn't belong here? Now it's time to play our game." Del didn't look like she was part of her family. Father, mother, sister were all slimness and angles and shades of blond. She was rounder, slightly shorter, and her light brown hair was tinted with red. If not for one of her father's sisters having similar looks and build, she would have thought she was adopted.

Footsteps sounded behind Del but she didn't turn from the window.

"My apologies for taking so long," Luise said. "Family can be..." A sigh. "I am a self-confessed fixer. But not everything is easily fixed. Do you still want to talk about Garda?"

Del shivered. "This isn't the kind of thing I usually like to read. I like funny. I like girls with attitude who always have a good comeback."

"Girls like you."

"Is that what I'm like? I always have an answer, but it usually gets me in more trouble."

"Will you stop reading?"

"No."

Luise bundled the diary back into its elastics, silently saying that they didn't have to talk about it. Their tea was cold but they drank it anyway. It was almost better cold. Del liked the *Pflaumenkuchen*, which was more pastry than cake. Luise asked about things Del enjoyed doing in Edmonton and suggested some places in Hamburg that she might want to see.

Cassandra called out from the bottom of the stairs and Luise invited her to join them. Del tried to stay looking relaxed, though she felt her muscles tensing. She tucked her bare feet under her, wrapped both hands around her teacup and held it in front of her like a shield.

"Hello, Professor Konrad. I hope Delora isn't bothering you too much."

Del frowned into her teacup.

"Not at all," Luise replied. "We've been having a nice chat, comparing shopping opportunities in Edmonton and Hamburg."

"Actually, I'm glad the two of you are together. It makes this business easier." Del peered over her cup at the odd statement. Cassandra looked self-satisfied and poised in a blue pencil skirt and yellow blouse. She raised a manila folder and gripped it with both hands. "I need Del to read and sign this. And I would appreciate it if you would witness it, Professor."

"Witness? That sounds rather official. What am I witnessing?" Luise's tone – idly curious – helped Del stay calm.

"A contract," Cassandra said. "I've worked on it all morning." She held it out to Del, who just stared; so she laid it on top of the diary. "Read it now, Del. And sign it."

Cornered. Del set down the cup, her hand hesitating over the folder before she finally picked it up. How could Cassandra put her on the spot like this? And what was she talking about contracts for? Del flipped open the folder and skimmed the crisp document. Then she read it more slowly. Luise said something about fresh tea and retreated to the kitchen. Cassandra waited, arms crossed. One slender foot tapped silently on the Turkish area rug.

Acceptable Behaviour Contract

This contract/agreement is made on (date)_____.

between **Delora James** and **Cassandra** and **Mathias Fedder**.

Delora agrees to the following in respect to conduct while staying in Hamburg with Cassandra and Mathias:

- I will act respectfully toward all residents in the household and any visitors they might entertain.
- I will not, verbally or otherwise, cause distress to the residents in the household.
- I will clean up after myself and keep my bedroom clean.
- I will help out with any chores when asked to do so without complaint.
- I will not climb down from the balcony.
- I will treat all belongings in the household with respect, neither breaking nor abusing them.
- I will inform Cassandra or Mathias when I wish to go out, where I will be and when I will return.
- I will return at the pre-approved time and if I might be late will call to let them know.
- I will only be late for reasons determined to be unavoidable.
- I will not go into areas of the city deemed inappropriate by Cassandra or Mathias.
- I will not associate with people unknown to Cassandra or Mathias.

- •I will not take part in illegal behaviours.
- •I will not take part in underage drinking or take any illegal substances.
- •I will not behave promiscuously or have sexual relations with anyone.

Cassandra and Mathias agree to the following for the duration of Delora's stay:

- • We will provide Delora with a cell phone (for local calls only).
- • We will provide Delora with a transit pass.
- • We will provide Delora with a bank card and access to funds not exceeding 50 Euro per week.
- • We will provide extra funds for purposes of shopping if such purchases are pre-approved.
- • We will allow Delora to visit Hamburg sites alone if such visits are pre-approved.
- • We will allow Delora an extra hour of Internet time on Saturdays and Sundays.
- • We will take all calls from Edmonton and will not force Delora to speak to anyone she doesn't wish to.

Breach:

If Delora fails to meet the stipulations outlined in this contract, her privileges will be revoked and she will be restricted to the house unless accompanied by Cassandra or Mathias or an approved alternate chaperone.

Declaration:

I confirm that I understand the meaning of this contract/agreement and the consequences of a breach of this contract.

Signed: _____

Witnessed: _____

Dated: _____

Del stood on slightly trembling legs. The Manila folder fell to the floor but the two copies of the contract remained pinched between her fingers. An incoherent scream lodged in her throat. She finally lifted her head to try to gauge what Cassandra was thinking. While she had read the contract over, several times, Luise had returned and Cassandra now held a cup of tea. She looked almost smug, as if surrounded by a halo of righteousness she could sense and revel in. The perfect daughter with her perfect plan.

It took three tries but Del finally got some words out. "You worked all day on this?"

A smile flitted over Cassandra's mouth when she nodded. She obviously thought Del was impressed. Del licked her lips. "It's... amazing."

"I knew you'd like it."

"I didn't say that." Cassandra's smugness was replaced by suspicion. Del said, "You left out one important thing." Tears started to build behind Del's eyes but stayed there, pressing hard and giving her an instant headache.

Cassandra set down her cup and perched her fists on thin hips. "What could I have possibly left out?"

"A shred... the smallest shred of trust." Del ripped the contact in half, let it fall to the coffee table and brushed past Cassandra. She wanted to swear foully, but because Luise was there she gritted her teeth, so hard her jaw ached. She headed down the hall.

"Come back here!" Cassandra cried. "Where are you going?"

"For a long walk. I'll come back when I'm ready, so don't send out any search parties."

"Del," Luise called, her voice unruffled. "Take one of my umbrellas from the stand by the door. You don't want to get sick."

"Maybe I do. The hospital is bound to have better company." She grabbed a blue umbrella on her way out.

Chapter Fourteen

Del sat on a bench on the east side of the lake, almost directly across from the park near Mathias and Cassandra's. Nearby was a statue with three huddled figures holding something spear-like. She had walked north around Aussenalster, keeping to the lakeside as much as possible. Five bridges and two hours later, she had finally outpaced her hurt.

Several times she had stopped to watch sailboats, more numerous now that the rain had stopped. The parkland that hugged the lake framed the water with vibrant green that reminded Del of Felix's eyes. Would Luise's nephew ever show up again? He was the only person she'd spoken to who was even close to her age.

Her feet were sore. She checked her wallet: six euros and a bit of change. Not much if she wanted to buy a transit ticket, something her feet voted for with each throb. She sat for a while longer, absorbing the fresh scent of the lake and wet grass, watching triangles of white skim back and forth with a freedom she envied. The afternoon sun dropped low enough to make her squint. Mathias must have returned from the university by now. Had he known about that contract?

Blue patches started to appear and Del felt silly carrying Luise's long umbrella. It could almost serve as a cane. She gripped it midway down the shaft and left the lakeshore behind in hopes she'd find a subway stop. The street led her into a tree-lined residential area of apartments. She zigzagged through the area, keeping the sun behind or on her right. She figured she'd eventually land in the downtown area near the main train station or the town hall.

Her path led to a major thoroughfare running south. The

street was crowded with cars and busses. How did a person buy bus tickets? Since someone else had always bought her ticket for her, she didn't know so didn't try. Cafe tables took up chunks of the sidewalks and people flowed around the obstructions in a babbling stream. Bicycles whirred by on their paths. Here and there, rainbow-coloured flags fluttered from balconies, adding to the kaleidoscope of colour.

Del waited for a walk light behind two young women with arms curved around each other's backs and hands tucked into each other's pockets. They exchanged a brief kiss. Del looked away when spoken English grabbed her attention. A middle-aged couple to the right commented on the busyness of the district. The light changed and Del kept pace behind the couple who sounded American. They were loud, or Del would never have heard them.

She followed, happy to hear English. They discussed their hotel. The woman declared it was nice, all things considered. The man said their travel agent should have warned them the hotel was in the middle of so many sex shops. And had the woman noticed the prostitutes on the corner last night? Drug deals took place in the alley behind the hotel if that Irish couple they shared a breakfast table with could be believed.

Del was listening so intently that she bumped into the man when they stopped for another red light. He grabbed her arm. "What's this? A pickpocket?" He gave her a shake.

"No!" Del replied. "I'm just trying to get back to my sister's."

He smelled like sausage and beer, and mustard stained his red shirt where it curved over top of his protruding belly. "American?"

Del nodded, not wanting to find out he didn't like Canadians. "I heard you speaking English and hoped you'd know where the nearest train or subway stop was."

"We're headin' to that big station now. Hap-ban-hoff." He pronounced the a's like in apple instead of "aw" sound Mathias gave them.

"You should walk with us," the woman said and pulled Del between them. "This area has what you'd call a lot of character, but it isn't a place for a young woman alone. You wouldn't want to be mistaken for something you're not, though thankfully you aren't dressed like that." She was a little heavy but in a way that made her appear soft and pleasant. Her smile was kind. Del found it impossible to take offence.

At the same time she asked Del what part of America she hailed from, the man asked if her sister lived in Hamburg and why. Del decided his question was safer. "My brother-in-law teaches at the Hamburg University and my sister teaches at a college north of the university. They live on the other side of the lake."

"In an area like this?"

Del knew he referred to the unsavoury things he'd complained about when she'd been eavesdropping. "It seems richer. Bigger houses. Quiet streets." She explained that she'd gone for a walk around the lake and hadn't realized how far it was so had started looking for a train to ride back. When he finished admonishing her about the dangers of wandering alone in a strange city, they turned a corner and there was the main train station.

"I know my way from here," she said to the couple. "Thanks for your help."

She jogged across the street, glad to leave their volume and nosiness behind. Several rough-looking men loitered in the shadows of the station near a small building with a sign that read, *Polizei*. More stood near the entrance. One held out a hand. She dropped a coin in his palm then walked under a triple canopy of steel and glass and entered the bustle of Hauptbahnhof.

The first time she'd been here it had felt alien and cavernous and vaguely threatening. After her long afternoon, it felt like a sanctuary. She rode up an escalator and wound up overlooking the platforms and tracks, watching the endless movement below.

Hauptbahnhof was prime people-watching territory. Every walk of life and type of person seemed to cross paths here. All around Del life was unfolding and happening to others. She wanted to be part of the action; she wasn't good at standing on the sidelines. That's what this summer felt like: being forced to stand on the sidelines. Unless she chose to abide by Cassandra's oppressive list of do's and don't's. The thought made her stomach clench. Then it growled.

Del's watch said 5:30. No wonder she was hungry. If she went back to the house now, they wouldn't eat until closer to seven o'clock. She'd collapse from hunger before then. Conscious of her wallet's meagre contents, Del hunted around and found a food court on the ground floor called *Gourmetstation*. No translation needed for that.

She wedged her way between clusters of people as she scanned the variety of kiosks. Greek food, subs, fish, pizzas, pasta, sausages, pastries, Japanese food. It all looked good. In the end she lined up for a fish sandwich and bottled water because it was cheap and left her enough money to buy a train ticket. She found a corner table just vacated. Reluctance to return made her nibble though her stomach wanted her to gobble. The sandwich still disappeared quickly. She downed her water, deciding it was time to head back.

Beside the entrance she'd come in, Del lined up at a *Die Bahn* information booth to find out where to catch the train to Dammtor Station. The woman answered in heavily accented English and also sold her a ticket so she didn't have to use the automated machine on the platform. Outside moisture seemed to float in the air, caressing even as it chilled her skin. In minutes she was back at Dammtor.

Del stepped onto the platform and was stopped by a pair of men in uniforms who spoke in German. She said, "English?" They haltingly asked to see her ticket, then thanked her and turned to another passenger. She hurried down the stairs and out of the station, crossed the busy road and almost got run over by a bicyclist before she spotted the bus she needed – the same Mittelweg bus she and Felix had ridden two days before. Her U-Bahn ticket was good for the bus, too, so she hopped on.

By the time she got off the bus beside the little *Passage* with the bakery, across from a church with a tall steeple, it was past 6:30 and Del was too tired to care what kind of argument she would face with Cassandra. She wanted to eat and crash in front of a movie. Television was out – the only English channels were all news.

She still hesitated for a long time at the gate, gathering courage. At least Mathias had remembered to get her some keys cut. She unlocked the gate, closed it carefully, listening for the click, then walked into the house as if she'd been gone for ten minutes instead of over four hours.

After she stowed the umbrella in the tube-shaped stand she noticed Mathias sitting halfway up the stairs. He looked as tired as she felt. The sound of the door made Luise appear from her living room at the end of the hallway. She lifted a hand in greeting and withdrew.

Del peered up the stairs past Mathias. "Where's Cassandra?"

"Probably still crying."

She had made her sister cry? Guilt twinged, but not enough to make Del do more than narrow her eyes. Mathias sighed. "I feel responsible for what happened today, Del. I mentioned the idea of a contract to Cassandra. But I meant a verbal contract, one where we sat down and discussed what we all wanted to see happen. I didn't explain myself clearly. I never thought she would write up such a –"

"Hateful, rule-filled piece of shit?" Del asked.

Mathias sighed again. "I was going to say such an uncompromising document."

"Uncompromising. That's educated talk for 'my way or the highway,' right?"

"A curious way to put it, I suppose, but apt. We sat down with Luise since Cassandra had involved her as a witness, and discussed the issue. I think perhaps, just as Cassandra likes to have a plan, you don't like rules. Am I correct?"

"I can live with them if I have to, if they make sense, but I'm not crazy about people telling me how to do things. I mean, school's different. I have to get through that, but outside school? Not so much. Deciding on things *together* would've been nice."

"It's not too late for that."

Del had her doubts. Even if they did talk it would be tainted by Cassandra's obvious lack of trust. Not because they knew each other – they didn't – but because their parents had made a judgment call and Cassandra would never go against it. She didn't respond to Mathias's assertion. "I'm hungry and tired."

He rubbed his stubbled jaw, as if considering whether to let the subject change. "Where did you walk?"

"Around the far end of the lake and down to Hauptbahnhof. I came back by train and bus."

"That would make one hungry. It's a good thing I have pork chops and rice warming in the oven, along with a zucchini and tomato casserole."

"Sounds good. I could eat almost anything right now."

"Some day, if you are feeling very brave, I'll introduce you to a Hamburg delicacy."

"Don't say it's raw fish. No way you'll get me eating that."

"No, no." He winked and started up the stairs. "Eel. Cooked, of course."

Del grimaced. "Let me guess: it tastes like chicken."

"Why would you say that?"

"Doesn't everything taste like chicken?"

"Not my pork chops. Come on. I'll see if Cassandra wants to join us, though I think she said something about a headache coming on so we probably won't see her tonight."

That wasn't bad news from Del's perspective. She slipped off her shoes and trudged up the stairs. "We could watch a movie."

"Yes. But when Cassandra feels up to it, Del, we will all sit down and talk. I do not want to spend my summer being a peacemaker."

That was fine by Del because she didn't want to spend the summer being at war.

Chapter Fifteen

29 Dec 42

I got into trouble over my trip to the farm, even though I brought home a ham and half a dozen eggs. Mother was furious I had left the house since she had forbidden it. Papa was worried I had run away. Erwin is on a winter campout with his DJ unit and won't be back until the thirty-first.

As we were eating some of Frau Braun's ham for breakfast, Mother informed me she had visited Frau Ott yesterday while I was out. Since she rarely talks to me, I was doubly shocked – that Mother realized I still had ears, and that she thought a visit to that woman would interest me.

Mother poured some coffee and said, "I suggested that Faber should marry you."

I dropped my fork and gaped at her with horror churning my stomach and climbing up my throat. Papa wondered what reason she gave Frau Ott for the suggestion. Mother replied that she had told the truth, that I'm pregnant and Faber is the father. Papa wanted to know what Frau Ott said to that.

Mother stared down her nose at me. "She said that we certainly couldn't prove such a thing. It's common knowledge that Garda will lift her skirt for anyone."

Papa slammed his cup down and coffee sloshed over the rim. He looked like he wanted to rebuke Mother. Instead he left the table. I fled, passed him in the hall and dashed into the bathroom. All that lovely ham ended up in the toilet.

By now, everyone of Frau Ott's acquaintance knows I'm pregnant, including Bette. She will make sure everyone our age hears. It won't take long before Faber knows, if his mother hasn't already told him.

It shouldn't matter, but it does. It feels like his fingers are raking over my skin again. Is he laughing to know that he took what he wanted, but also that he left part of himself behind?

Mother is calling up the stairs that lunch is ready. I refuse to answer.

night, 29 Dec 42

I snuck down to Papa's office for *Kaffee und Kuchen*. Apparently Mother had gone out for the afternoon. I took a biscuit from the plate on Papa's desk and settled in the small chair opposite his.

He sat back in his chair and looked ready to nod off. I didn't want him to sleep, so I asked him if he still loved Mother.

That woke Papa up. He took a biscuit and frowned at it, dipped the biscuit in his coffee and ate the soggy corner. He finally swallowed and said, "When two people have lived together for so many years, of course there is a kind of love between them, even if it is not that first kind. Your mother isn't the woman I married any more than I'm the man she married." He added, "Our interests are quite different these days."

His answer didn't satisfy me. In truth, it made me angry. He wouldn't even admit that they didn't love each other any more. I wonder whom Mother does love? Erwin, I suppose. Not me, that's certain. I am an embarrassment. How dare I get raped and ruin her spotless reputation?

I turned the biscuit round and round, crumbling the edges so bits landed on my navy skirt. I fought the desire to hurt Papa – fought and lost. I said, "Why were you friends with a Jew?"

When Papa jerked his head up and pain darkened his green eyes, I felt more ashamed than victorious, but not enough to want to take back my words. The mantle clock ticked. I stuffed the biscuit in my mouth and flicked crumbs off my skirt, one by one, while I waited for Papa's reply. Part of me wanted him to yell, to show he has a limit beyond which he will not be pushed, that there is something he will fight for.

Instead, he sighed and explained how he and Jakob had attended university together and eventually ended up teaching together in the history department. Religion wasn't an issue because neither of them paid attention to it and or took part in any kind of worship. They studied history and paid no attention to politics. Even after Mother joined the Nazi party, Papa and Jakob were shocked when the party came to power and started singling out Jews for special treatment.

Papa confirmed that he had said nothing to the department head when they made Jakob quit. I rubbed it in by saying, "So not getting that sign on your office door changed is the only brave thing you've ever done?"

Papa winced and whispered that he deserved that. It struck me that I was behaving a lot like Mother. I clamped my mouth shut. I couldn't believe it when he suggested I could wound him further if I wanted by denouncing him as children are encouraged to do.

I stood and declared, "Unlike some people, I am loyal to those I love." I marched out of the office without looking at Papa, made myself a sandwich, poured a glass of milk (I drink it every day like the doctor told me), and retreated to my bedroom.

It was an awful thing to say. But the worst part, Hilde, is that I'm not sorry.

30 Dec 42

I have tasted happiness again. After so long, I had almost forgotten the way its flavour bursts inside like a mouthful of wild berries and makes every centimetre of you vibrate with life.

At breakfast, Papa announced that he would spend the day with me doing whatever I desired. Though Mother said nothing, I could see she didn't approve by how she scowled into the pot of oatmeal she was stirring. Papa looked me in the eyes – in the eyes, Hilde. He asked me if I'd like that. My grin spread from ear to ear.

For a few hours it was like nothing had happened. Did my cruel words from yesterday spur Papa to be kind? I don't know and don't care. I had my Papa back.

Arm in arm, we strolled the streets of old Heidelberg, looked in shop windows, chatted about the buildings (history is always a safe topic with Papa) and remembered silly incidents from my childhood. We laughed. How I had missed Papa's quiet laugh.

I confessed I had always wanted to see what the rooms looked like inside the Ritter Hotel. Papa marched me into the lobby. Decorative ever-green sprays made the room smell of pine. Papa left me in a wing-backed chair and whispered to the manager. With a snap of his fingers, the man-ager summoned a bellhop who showed us the most luxurious room in the hotel. He told us it is reserved only for Party members.

The furniture was dark wood – cherry, Papa said – with carved legs and fit for a palace. There were fresh flowers in a crystal vase and wrapped chocolate mints on the pillows. The bellhop gave me one and said he'd get a maid to replace it. I decided to save the chocolate and eat it at mid-night tomorrow.

From there, we walked to the Kornmarkt and admired the evergreen boughs decorating the Rathaus. Because of the blackouts, there are no strings of lights, but it looked festive anyway.

We climbed the west stairs to the main castle entrance. The snow from the other day had melted so the steps weren't slippery. Papa was winded by the time we reached the top. He had to rest a few times. There are over 300 steps. Normally I could do the climb without a problem, but I was feeling a little weak-kneed from it, as well.

By the gate tower, Papa stopped to catch his breath. He leaned on a balustrade and looked over the city. I did the same. He drew me close and we stayed for a long time, not talking, just soaking up the weak sunlight and the view of our beloved city. I can't imagine not being here, Hilde. My bones are made of Heidelberg stone; the Neckar flows in my veins.

Papa said, "The climb was worth it, *Liebchen*, even though I did won-der if you were trying to make your old Papa have a heart attack."

He's not really that old, only forty-two. I told him so. He squinted toward the west and quietly wondered if he was old enough to avoid being drafted after all the young men are killed.

Such a thing is impossible. How could one war kill that many men? I said, "It won't come to that. Are you afraid of being in the war?"

Papa gave me a sad smile and said, "As you know, I am afraid of many things. I like my classroom and the routine of my teaching assignments. Outside of that..." He sighed. "But we don't want to speak of sad things today."

I asked then why he didn't fight in the Great War. He told me how he was only eighteen in 1918, and when the Armistice was signed he was training for battle and was relieved to be spared the honour of dying for his country. When I asked why, he explained that his hands shook every time he held a rifle, and that he knew he was not equal to the task of fighting and killing.

He said, "Some people make history. I have always preferred studying and teaching it." When he changed the subject by asking where I wanted to eat, I didn't hesitate.

"*Der Rote Ochsen*." The Red Ox.

Papa chuckled and accused me of wanting him to get in trouble with Mother.

I denied it. After all, if I'm to be a student of the university some day, then I must know what the inside of the most famous student gathering place looks like.

He pointed out that it was where male students gathered. I begged to go anyway.

"Ach, *Liebchen*, when you look at me with those hazel eyes, I can refuse you nothing."

The awful truth hung between us. He had already refused me the thing I needed most – to have him stand up for me. I didn't want to ruin a fairy tale day with ugly words. Instead I linked my arm with his and said, "Does this old man need help going down the stairs?"

He laughed and everything was perfect again.

Papa had me sign the guestbook when we stepped inside the Red Ox. On the same line he added, 'und Professor Karl Kurz.' The Ox is noisy and warm. The walls are crowded with drinking horns, beer mugs and trophies. Several students shouted greetings to Papa as he sat me at a table against a wall. He pointed out the framed letter that "Daddy" Spengel had received from Chancellor Bismarck many years before. Herr Spengel's daughter runs the inn now.

A waiter in a white apron took our order. He brought our drinks first. A beer for Papa and half a glass of red wine for me. The smells of roast pork, fresh bread, cabbage and beer had my stomach growling before our food arrived.

No wonder the Red Ox is so busy. The plates were heaping. I asked Papa how they could serve such large portions with war rationing. He said he had heard that the Spengels had relatives in the country that kept the inn supplied, like how we get extra food from the Braun farm.

After such a large meal both of us were sleepy, so we decided to go home for a late afternoon nap. I slept through Kaffee und Kuchen. Papa brought me milk and a ham sandwich at seven o'clock. I apologized for saying such cruel things yesterday, but Papa said, "You were only doing what I told you to. You were telling the truth. There is no need to apologize."

I stayed in my room and read for the rest of the evening. That way, nothing could wreck my wonderful day. I can't believe after such a long nap, I'm tired. It isn't even eleven o'clock.

Though it's five days late, today was the best Christmas gift Papa could have given me.

31 Dec 42

If November 5 had never happened, I would be at Bette's tonight. She is hosting a party for the members of our BDM unit. Of course, I was not invited.

Instead, I'm staying home to watch Erwin. He arrived back from his week-long campout this afternoon. He went to bed hours ago. When I checked on him a few minutes ago, he was flat on his back, mouth wide open, snoring as loud as a motorcycle.

Mother and Papa are at a party put on by the local Nazi party. Everything about Mother, from her eyes to the sequins on the hem of her gown, glittered. She even wore Grandmother's fur coat for the occasion. Papa looked dapper in his black tuxedo, but not very happy.

I have my chocolate from the Ritter Hotel ready for when the clock strikes twelve.

It feels silly to wish myself a happy new year, especially since I know it will not, cannot, be one. Instead I will hope to be brave, though I don't want to be, and to be thankful I can always tell the truth to you, if no one else, dearest Hilde.

0200 h, 1 Jan 43
My extra blanket is tucked along the bottom of the door so no one knows my light is on. How can I sleep after what I heard? Eavesdropping is rude, so I suppose it serves me right.

Papa and Mother came home less than thirty minutes past midnight. They must have left their party as soon as 1943 began. Their voices rose from the foyer like pungent smoke and I could tell they were arguing. I pretended to be asleep when they came upstairs. My door creaked open and a slice of light fell across my face, but only for a second.

As soon as their bedroom door closed, Mother and Papa took up the argument. At first their voices were low and tense. But as Mother's voice became more strident, Papa's matched it, which startled me. I strained to listen. I had never heard him raise his voice like that.

Curiosity drove me into the hallway. I crouched beside their door. Though it was wrong I couldn't seem to help myself. Their words became clear. I will try to write down exactly what they said.

Papa's voice was tense. "You can't just send –"

"The arrangements are made," Mother said.

"I won't allow –"

"You will not interfere, Karl.'

"I must. It's not right."

"Listen to me, Herr Professor Kurz. One word from you and the university president will hear that it is your child she is carrying. Then see how long your precious career lasts."

I almost gasped. How could Mother make such a terrible threat?

When Papa started to protest, Mother said, "Everyone would believe it. You walk through the town, arms linked like a pair of lovers. You always touch her, guide her into rooms with your hand at her waist, take her hand. With every look you declare your adoration for her."

"Is loving your daughter now a crime?"

"No, but you act like loving your wife is one."

Papa groaned. "Not this again. Since Erwin's birth you have poured your affection on him. Is it surprising I prefer to spend time with our daughter? You can't send her away, Ulla. She is the only joy I have in this house."

"You can't stop me, Karl. Lift one finger and I will ruin your reputation. The whole town will pity me and Erwin, while you will never teach again, at this or any university. Her behaviour is not going to destroy all I've worked so hard to build. And neither are you."

The bed springs creaked. I could picture Papa sagging onto the bed. I splayed my hand against the door, inwardly begging for him to be brave. Quiet shrouded the house.

I returned to my room before I started crying. The pillow made sure my tears were not heard. When they finally stopped flowing, I felt empty. My hope, sparked by the way Papa's voice had risen, was dead, smothered by his silence.

Mother's horrible threat was a bluff. Papa said it himself: his position gives her respectability. If she made such an accusation her reputation would be just as ruined as his. How could he let her bully him like that? Why, oh *why* can't he see the truth and stand up for it?

I hate the way Mother has made Papa so small, how she has whipped him with words until he is too weak to resist.

Where I will be sent? Does it matter? It will not be Heidelberg. Will you watch over me, Hilde? Or is your spirit tied to this place like my heart is?

2 Jan 43

In his weekly newspaper article, Herr Goebbels, Minister of Propaganda, said, "Wherever we look we see mountains of problems." Papa is amazed that anyone in Berlin admits the war is going badly and thinks things must be very bad indeed. His amazement put Mother in a bad mood. Or perhaps I should say, in a worse mood since she has been glaring at me for two days. Do you think she knows I overheard her argument with Papa?

4 Jan 43

I think I need my own bathroom. Every time I turn around I have to pee. It's terrible. I only think about it and I am running for the toilet.

9 Jan 43

For a week awful silence has reigned in the house. I have not been allowed to leave the house for any reason. School is out of the question, and since I'm leaving, what would be the point? I have said nothing about knowing Mother is sending me away, in case she doesn't know I heard her argument with Papa. He has hidden in his office all week. The strain of it made even my pen too heavy to lift.

This morning, Mother brought Papa's big brown suitcase and told me to pack. My train is leaving early Monday morning. When I asked where she was sending me, a sour look puckered her lips and she said to do as I am told.

How do you squeeze a lifetime into one brown bag? All day I tried to decide what to take and leave. I wanted to take all my journals, but there is no room, so I'm only taking this one and the new one Erwin gave me. I will ask Papa to store the others. Most of my clothes will soon be useless, but I must wear something, so I packed as many as I could anyway. Not the BDM uniforms – they remind me of the attack and no matter where I'm sent I will refuse to attend their meetings. No BDM unit would want a pregnant girl in their midst, anyway.

The only photo I packed is one of Erwin, Papa and me, taken last summer up at the castle in front of the half-crumbled powder tower. I'm sure I told you about that day, Hilde. We had hiked up the stairs and had a picnic in the *Schlossgarten*. Will I ever know another perfect Heidelberg summer day? I have to hope so.

The last thing I put in the suitcase was the drawing of the bridge and castle with my little silhouette, to remind me where I belong. Now I will turn off the light and open the blackout curtain so I can look at the stars.

10 Jan 43

Mother allowed me one hour to walk around and see my favourite places one last time. Though the climb was exhausting, I took the stairs up to the castle to look over the city. It was snowing and the red roofs were dusted with white. I lingered longer than I intended and then decided I would take my time. What could Mother possibly do to me as punishment for disobeying her?

So I wandered through the *Schlossgarten* and stood in the castle's courtyard. I left via the lower terrace where the anti-aircraft gun is situated and blessed my luck – the guard with the limp was on duty. I gave him a biscuit (I had two in my pocket) and shared my theory about the hill hiding us from the English bombers. He smiled and said, "I hope you are right, *Fraulein*." He has a nice smile.

Down the ramp, through the Kornmarkt and to the Alte Brücke. Each snowflake that kissed my cheek seemed to say farewell. I stood on the bridge and listened to the Neckar. Today it only whispered, *Auf Wiedersehen*. The water was grey with shattered chunks of ice in it.

My last stop was Heiliggeistkirche. I sat in the church for a long time, letting the peace still my heart which was starting to race with the anxiety of having to return home.

When I walked in the door, I had been gone for three hours. Mother was furious. She sent me to my room. It was no punishment to not have to see her for the rest of the evening.

Papa brought me an *Abendbrot* of bread and ham and cheese, with milk. I stayed by the dresser while he set the tray down. Instead of leaving, he sat down and placed one hand on the suitcase. He looked miserable, as if he were leaving. I don't know why it made me angry.

"So," I said, "Am I to be sent to a *Lebensborn* resort?"

Papa looked startled. "Of course not, *Liebchen*."

"Doktor Wiebe thought it might be a good idea."

Papa rubbed the suitcase. "If you must know, your mother did look into it, but was refused because she couldn't guarantee that an SS soldier was the father." He paused. "I'm glad of it. You must realize if you had gone there, you would have been expected to get pregnant again, as soon as possible, by an SS candidate of their choosing. I could not allow that."

The thought turned my stomach. I said, "How could you have stopped it, Papa?"

He asked what I meant, so I told him about hearing their argument on New Year's Eve, and about the threat Mother had made. I said, "Even though it's a hollow threat you are afraid to risk your teaching position." Could those bitter words really have come from my mouth? I sounded so much like Mother that I thought I might be sick.

Papa hunched over; his shoulders shook. It took a minute to realize he was crying.

With hand outstretched, I approached him as one might a strange dog. When my fingers touched his head, he drew me near, wrapped his arms around my waist and sobbed against my stomach. I couldn't bring myself to step away so I rubbed his back. He seemed like a lost little boy. Though it drained my anger to listen to that muffled pain, my own eyes stayed dry. Perhaps one only has so many tears in her lifetime and I had reached my limit.

Papa regained control. He took my right hand, slid his university ring onto my finger and turned it so the crest was on the bottom. He closed both hands over my fist and said, "Let the world think you are married. You will be treated with the respect you deserve. Remember, silence is our shield. Never let them know what you are thinking."

I was tempted to tell him what I was thinking, but I didn't. My family appalls me. I don't want to be anything like them, not ruthless and power-hungry like Mother, nor cowardly like Papa. What if everyone in all of Germany is like them? If that's true, I will find no comfort or peace, no matter where I go.

Where does that leave me, Hilde? I no longer know who or what I am, or where I belong.

11 Jan 43
Forgive me if my writing is messy today, Hilde. I am on a train. My fingers are cold and I have a headache from the constant rattling and the stink of smoke.

Heidelberg is far behind and though my eyes have stung all morning, I haven't cried. I now know my destination is Hamburg. I am trying not to think about the English having already bombed that city. I must hope they are done with it.

Papa didn't come to the train station. He and Erwin said good-bye at the house. Erwin thinks I'm going to work for Mother's cousin in the north (which is mostly true) and says I'm lucky to be leaving school. But will I go to university some day if I haven't finished high school?

When Papa kissed me goodbye and said he loved me, I did as he has asked time and again: I kept silent. I could see it hurt him. Perhaps now he realizes what his silence did to me.

At the train station, Mother introduced me to my travelling companion.

I cannot believe she arranged to have me escorted by a Gestapo agent. I am no criminal. But so far, Herr Brunner, who is on his way to Copenhagen, has been polite. He gave me a little privacy by sitting across the aisle from me. He offered me coffee from his carafe, but I refused. Now he is reading papers from his satchel.

As we go north, there is more snow and it makes me wonder about the soldiers in Russia – surely they have warm clothing this winter. Mostly, I think about Professor Jakob Rosenthal and his daughter, Judith. Papa said they were arrested, probably by the Gestapo. And they were probably taken somewhere by train. Where? Were they like me, only told their destination when they arrived at the *Bahnhof*? Were they, like me, only allowed one suitcase?

The more I think about Judith, the more I remember what good friends we were and I'm ashamed I forgot her so easily. She was shy and we giggled a lot. She had dark eyes like her father. She was smart and funny and – in my memory at least – very pretty. I have heard and heard why we are superior to Jews, why they are *Untermenschen*, but the Judith I am remembering fits none of those definitions. It seems she was made an outcast only because of her religion. A religion she didn't even practice.

Like her, I am outcast. Cast out.

Chapter Sixteen

Del felt cowardly spending the morning helping Luise in the garden and then using her living room as a reading sanctuary. She
hadn't once heard Cassandra moving anywhere upstairs. It was
weird; usually Cassandra was an early riser. With the schedules
she drew up, she had to be.

The diary was re-bundled and on the coffee table. It kept
demanding Del's attention. Was she subconsciously wanting to
escape into a different world for a while, even if that world was
horrible? She was straightening the elastics for the second time
when Luise walked in, carrying a tray with two glasses of juice
and a plate of miniature pastries.

Del thanked her and took a glass. "Now I know why you gave
me the diary to read."

"Do you?" Luise looked mildly amused.

"Yes. Garda was banished to Hamburg."

"You have found me out. I thought you could identify with
her on that point even if your details are different." Luise walked
to the sideboard and got an envelope out of the drawer. "It's time
to make another payment."

"For what?"

"I said I would pay you for reading."

Del had forgotten. "I'll read it anyway. You don't have to pay
me."

"A bit of spending money only. It's what we agreed." She laid
the envelope on the tray.

Del left the envelope and drank her juice. She rubbed her
arms and shifted her bare legs which were practically glued to the
leather sofa.

"Are you cold?" Luise asked.

"No. Feeling sticky. I was fine after my shower but now... I'm prickly and sticky both." She wiped at her cheek. It felt oily. Great, now she'd probably break out with a thousand zits.

"The humidity level is up. All that rain, now heat. You need fans to keep the air moving." Luise ate a pastry the diameter of a potato chip. "Is humidity never a problem in Edmonton?"

"No. The air there is dry. Smells dusty all the time. I like the fresh smell the air has here. At least, I liked it until today."

The front door opened. A moment later Mathias walked in and asked Del to go upstairs. She wrinkled her nose as she picked up the diary; Luise tucked the envelope under the elastics and patted Del's shoulder. "You will be fine."

At Mathias's direction, Del settled in the living room. He explained he'd gotten a teaching assistant to take his class. He looked worried when Del confirmed she hadn't seen Cassandra all morning. He went to get her. Del grabbed the remote and started flipping through channels. Images flashed. She rarely paused long enough to hear more than six words. She'd gotten by so far with pointing and holding up her fingers in the bakery, and by stumbling across people who spoke at least a little English, but it still felt weird to see lips moving but to not understand what they were saying. Sometimes she wanted to yell, "Stop speaking gibberish!"

Mathias returned alone. He dug out a small parcel from his briefcase. "I almost forgot. This was in the mail for you yesterday."

Del glanced at the Edmonton return address. Something from her parents. She tore the brown paper and pulled out a German phrasebook. "I was just thinking about this. I'd forgotten it on my dresser." Not forgotten exactly. She'd left it, as a protest against the whole banishment thing, but hadn't realized until she got here that she'd only punished herself. A note from her mom said she thought Del might want this. No, "love you" or "have fun." It wasn't even signed, though the handwriting was recognizable. Given the nasty things she'd said in the airport, she shouldn't be surprised. Still, it still bugged her. Just a little.

Cassandra slid sideways into the room like a pale shadow. Del's jaw sagged. The disheveled blond hair was shocking enough, but Cassandra's face was a wreck. She was always so meticulous about her looks. Red-rimmed, blood-shot eyes seemed to float in shadowed caves above blotchy cheeks and colourless lips. Her pink satin dressing gown was creased, as if she'd slept in it. Mathias took a crocheted beige throw from a cupboard beside the desk, wrapped it around Cassandra's shoulders and guided her to the loveseat across from Del.

Cassandra seemed drugged. Her gaze settled on Del and tears welled up, making the redness glow. Her voice trembled. "I'm tired, Mathias. I want to go back to bed."

Mathias kept his arm around his wife. "You've been in bed for seventeen hours, *Liebchen*. We agreed you'd make an effort."

Del pressed into the corner of the loveseat. She hoped Mathias would give her a signal, reassure her, but he kept all his attention on Cassandra. He whispered to her until she started nodding, then kissed her forehead.

The urge to flee started to build; Del fought against it, suspecting that her flight yesterday had somehow triggered this strangeness. She drew her legs against her chest, gripping damp legs with sweaty palms. A trickle of moisture ran down her neck and disappeared beneath her green tank top's scooped neckline.

Cassandra looked about to speak, then she drooped back under Mathias's arm. "Try, Cassandra," he urged. "Del needs to know how you're feeling. We need to work this out."

After a painfully long moment, Cassandra raised her chin. Her voice trembled. "I... I can't do this, Del. Can't live without some guarantees. S-some assurances. I just, I just, I need..." She hid her face against Mathias's chest.

He kissed the top of her head. "Try to understand, Del. Your sister needs structure. She needs order." A wry smile touched his lips. "In that she is more German than I."

Del didn't know how to respond. This was a side of Cassandra she had never seen or imagined. Her pain seemed to be consuming her. Del kept her voice quiet. "I agreed to working something out together. But that contract was insulting. It read like I was a prisoner in a halfway house. Did you see it?"

"I did. Your sister meant well, even if it came out a little heavy-handed."

A little? She'd come across as a freaking dictator. Her feelings must have shown on her face, for Mathias gave her a look of commiseration. He said, "Most of what Cassandra wrote can be summed up by requesting that you treat us with courtesy."

"Maybe the first ones, but the rest of the rules sure weren't being courteous to me. They assumed I'll get into trouble every time I go out. They assumed I'm completely untrustworthy." Her voice took a mimicking tone. "Thou shalt not drink, do drugs or have sex. What is that? I'm sixteen, not a child. And contrary to everyone's opinion, I'm not stupid."

"But sometimes you are thoughtless. Like when you ran away yesterday."

"I didn't run. I said I was going for a walk and I said I'd be back. It was either go for a walk or choke your wife. I think I made the right choice." Del rubbed her sweaty shins and frowned at her toes. "I admit I was gone too long. I should've phoned."

"Agreed. Which is why I picked up a cell phone this morning."

Cassandra jerked upright. "You're going to let her have her way?

You're going to give her a phone and let her run around? How am I supposed to explain that to Mom and Dad? They'll think I'm a total fai –" Hysteria tinged her words. "It's not fair, Mathias. No rules at all? I'll be a wreck all summer. This is killing me."

Mathias framed her face and stared intently at her. "Calm down, *Liebchen*. Calm. Down. If you and Del agree, there will be one simple rule. We will all treat each other with courtesy. Cleaning up, letting each other know where we're going, at least leaving a note, phoning if we'll be late, treating others' belongings with respect and speaking with respect. All of these things are courtesy, Cassandra. Of course, Del will make every effort. And we will do the same. I bought a message board for the kitchen. We can write the courtesy rule across the top."

They seemed to argue with their eyes for several minutes. Del could see Cassandra struggling, wanting to disagree. Finally she blurted, "But what about the other things?"

Del's whole body tensed.

Mathias shook his head. "I know your parents were concerned about some of Del's behaviours. That was there. She isn't there, she is here. She's right. She's old enough that we have to trust her, Cassandra. This will only work if we all trust each other."

"But –"

Mathias covered her lips with his fingers. "No buts. Please, *Liebchen*. I went through some hard years with my parents. I know how much it hurts to not have your parents trust you. We are not doing that to your sister. She gets a clean slate. Understood?"

Del knew a smile would probably freak Cassandra out so she pursed her lips and lowered her head slightly. It felt good to have someone in her corner.

Cassandra chewed her lip for a moment. "I, I don't know. You're asking too much."

"You'll be fine. Get dressed and you can help me put up the message board. We'll write the rule along the top. Okay?"

Finally, she nodded and left the room with the throw still draped over her shoulders. Mathias released a slow breath. Del said, "Thank you so much. You were brilliant."

He rubbed his chin then leaned forward and rested forearms on his knees. "Don't make me out to be a saint, Del. This is the third time in our marriage that Cassandra has broken down. It seems to happen when her plans shatter and she feels she's failed. Instant depression. It's scary as hell, even if it only lasts a few days. I almost left her the last time it happened. I need you to behave. That's all there is to it."

"I'll try."

"Good. And you know that the smell of alcohol on your breath will likely set her off."

So he'd finally decided to mention those beers she'd had the other day. He might be right, but he didn't realize how much "that's all there is to it" had set Del's nerves on edge. She studied him. He looked really tired. His students probably wondered why he wasn't so handsome today. "I'll follow the rule Cass put in that contract. I won't take part in any underage drinking."

Mathias flopped back and sank down. "*Scheisse.* I wish Felix hadn't told you the legal age for beer and wine is sixteen."

Del smirked. "No underage drinking. That's what Cass said."

"Your parents warned us you like pushing limits. Fine. You think you're getting away with something by drinking a few beers here and there. Just remember: you show up in this house drunk, even once, and I'll be the one locking you in your room."

"After I puke on your shoes?"

"No, after you clean up your own puke." Mathias fetched his briefcase. He set a cellphone and a bank card on the table. "We'll have to go to the train station to get your transit pass because they take your picture. Here's your freedom, Del. It's yours to keep..." He stood. "Or lose."

Chapter Seventeen

13 Jan 43

I am sick of trains. They rock and are horribly noisy. Always in the background is the chug, chug of the engine and the clack, clack of the wheels. It is a moving prison and Herr Brunner has confined me to this car. For my own good, he said. There are soldiers in the other passenger cars and he would not want me to suffer inappropriate advances. He doesn't know I am familiar with such treatment, but his warning keeps me in my place.

North of Frankfurt we left the broad Rhine valley behind and entered hills. In each valley is a town blanketed by snow, looking so cozy I longed to get off the train, to take refuge there. Herr Brunner would never allow it, so I contented myself with looking.

The war does not seem to exist in those hidden valleys. But if I walked those peaceful-looking streets, no doubt I would hear about brothers or husbands gone away to fight, to be wounded or maybe die on some distant battlefield.

I hope the soldier at Heidelberg castle is still there when I return. Maybe I can get him to smile again.

It was dark when we arrived at Hannover where we had to change trains. The one we were on was going east to Berlin. The soldiers will likely go farther east, to the Russian Front. Are they afraid to enter that horrible storm? I would be.

That train pulled out of the station, but the one going to Hamburg was late. Herr Bruner and I stood on a deserted platform. After so long with constant noise, my ears were still filled with the clacking of steel wheels. When Herr Brunner asked if I wished to wait inside where it was warm, I told him I preferred to enjoy the quiet. He left his suitcase with me and went to find more coffee for himself, tea for me, and sandwiches for us both.

Like everywhere, the blackout is in effect at train stations. They are favourite targets of the English bombers. As I stood in the quiet and darkness, I became aware of a faint murmuring on the other side of the train yard. I saw a muted light bob through the blackness.

A few words reached me. "*Wasser, bitte.*" The words sounded strange, as if spoken by a foreigner, but it was clear that water was being requested. I heard the words several more times. Suddenly a voice barked, "Silence!"

The night obeyed. The murmuring stopped. I wondered if I had dreamed the sounds.

Minutes later the chugging of an approaching train became audible. Herr Brunner returned, handed me a sack of food and said that was our train. He has been so polite to me that I got brave and asked him about the noises I had heard. For a moment I thought he wasn't going to answer. He finally said, "Do not worry yourself about such things, *Fraulein*. The stationmaster said there is a transport train on a siding. No doubt that is what you heard."

"But I heard voices," I said.

"Yes. Dutch Jews being transported east."

"To where?"

Herr Brunner's long silence made me think I had asked something that should not be asked. At last he replied, "To resettlement camps in Poland, I expect."

Is that where Professor Jakob and Judith were sent? I wondered why they were not allowed water, but thought it better not to ask. Then our train arrived and I was distracted with boarding and getting settled.

This morning I woke with a kink in my neck and saw flat land in every direction, as if it had been pressed by God with a giant iron. Already I miss the hills of the Neckarwald. The sky stretches forever over this level plain. When I was small I used to think that the hills held up the sky. Without hills it feels like the sky will collapse on top of me.

Herr Brunner has just said we will be arriving in Hamburg soon. I cannot see because of a fog. What kind of welcome will Mother's cousin give me? My stomach is fluttering.

Papa's ring feels heavy. After I unpack I will write and apologize for being cruel when I left. If you get the chance, Hilde, whisper in his heart that I miss him very much.

24 Jan 43

I am exhausted. Since I arrived in Hamburg, my time has not been my own and the few minutes I had I used to write to Papa and to Erwin. Even now I want to crawl into bed and sleep, but I need to tell you something of what has happened, Hilde.

Mother's cousin, Ilsa Pflaume, picked me up at the station and took me to her apartment. She is a tall skinny woman with stooped shoulders and from a distance reminds me of a lamppost. This impression is strengthened by her always wearing black, though her husband is alive. He is a supply officer stationed in Warsaw. Her one son is in the navy; his ship's harbour is in Wilhelmshaven and I gather that she hears from him rarely.

Ilsa is severe and very serious about her work, which is in the transport ministry's office. Like Mother, she seems to be a dedicated Nazi. It's through her connections in the Nazi party that she found a position for me.

I thought I was to work for her, but what need does a woman alone in a two-bedroom apartment have of a housekeeper? No, I am living and working with her "dear comrades," Heine and Lucie Wechsler. They are a short couple, both broad shouldered. They appear to be in their thirties and already Herr Wechsler has a paunch. He works in the office where ration cards are handed out and accounted for. Frau Wechsler spends most of her time with charities, especially the Winter Relief fund. They live in a huge house, finely furnished, so I see why they need a housekeeper.

Ilsa informed me this is the couple she and Mother have agreed will adopt the baby when it's born. Why didn't Mother tell me this was what she was planning? It might be the sensible thing, but it would have been nice to have been asked my opinion.

When Frau Wechsler saw me, the first thing she said was that I didn't look pregnant.

She was unimpressed when I explained that the pregnancy was not even three months along. I don't think she believes I am pregnant. Since then, every day she has awakened me at six o'clock with a long list of chores. Washing, polishing, waxing, dusting, ironing. The list is endless. I have not been outside of the house. I feel like a slave.

Frau Wechsler gets irritated if I take a rest and often I have to sit for five minutes. I am so tired all the time. Even my evening "morning sickness" does not impress her. (Luckily, it seems to be getting less severe.) At nine o'clock each night, I fall into bed, wanting to telephone Papa and beg him to let me go home.

What good would it do? We both know he would do nothing unless Mother allowed it. I will find some way to bear this.

27 Jan 43

There was an air raid in the middle of the day! Frau Wechsler was out so I had to hide alone in the shelter in the cellar for several hours. All I heard were distant thumpings but I was so frightened that when the all clear sounded, I stayed, huddled under a blanket for another hour. Finally I had to get back to work or risk getting in trouble. It was hard to leave my refuge.

Hilde, you would not believe the boxes of canned goods in the cellar. A person could live there for a year and not run out of food. There are also wines, chocolate and fancy foods that haven't been available in stores for ages. The laws say we aren't to stockpile food so there is enough for the armies, but perhaps rules are different for those who hand out ration cards.

28 Jan 43

Ilsa came over today and Frau Wechsler allowed me to go to my bedroom for a rest after I had served the two of them their *Kaffee und Kuchen.* Ilsa is distraught. The bombing raid yesterday hit Wilhelmshaven harder than here in Hamburg. She cannot find out if her son's ship was in the harbour, never mind if it was damaged. She told Frau Wechsler she heard the bombers were American. I thought they were only fighting in Africa and the Pacific.

This house is in a rich area north of the Elbe River, a long way from either the harbour or factories. Because of that, Herr Wechsler says we are safe from the bombs. We still go to the cellar if the alarm sounds.

We've had two nighttime raids since I came. The first time the siren went off, I was so terrified I couldn't move. Herr Wechsler had to drag me from my bed. The second time I raced to the cellar. At least I was with the Wechslers, not alone like yesterday. Alone is much worse, Hilde. When I'm alone it feels like the house is going to fall on me and I can barely breathe.

Please let all the bombers stay away – especially during the daytime.

3 Feb 43

I had an overwhelming desire to eat forest berries and cream today. All I could find was a jar of raspberry jam. I ate almost half of it, then vomited it all back up. I may never eat raspberry jam again.

I've been getting leg cramps. I think I am on my feet too much. At least I am not queasy in the evenings any more.

7 Feb 43

My three letters to Papa have gone unanswered. I wish I could talk to him, but the Wechslers won't let me use the telephone for long distance. Who do I have to call in Hamburg, except possibly Ilsa? She comes over every other day or so, anyway.

Papa could explain things so I understand them. Over a year ago he said we would lose the war if we didn't win Moscow and now the most terrible thing has happened.

Yesterday the country finished three days of official mourning. The whole Sixth Army is gone, Hilde, swallowed by the Soviets at Stalingrad. (I had to look in the atlas in the library to find out where it is.) I asked Herr Wechsler how many men had been in the Sixth Army and he said over 300,000. They estimate that 100,000 of those men surrendered. That means 200,000 are dead. *Mein Gott.*

I once attended a youth rally in the Thingstätte on top of *Heiligenberg* – ten thousand young people were there. It seemed like the whole world had crowded into that amphitheatre. How can it be that more than twenty times that number are dead in one battle in a distant city most Germans had never heard of? What made Stalingrad special, that so many Germans died trying to hold it? I must write to Papa and ask. I'll address it to his office in the history department, then perhaps he'll treat it as a student's inquiry and actually answer it.

On Friday night, a general in Berlin broadcast an official message on the radio saying, "The bitter experience of Stalingrad still weighs heavily on our souls," and, "What we used to inflict on the others has happened to us."

What the Soviets did to the Sixth Army is barbaric. I shudder to think that German troops might have so ruthlessly wiped out other countries' armies. My heart wants to deny it, but war seems to turn people into madmen who only seek to bomb and shoot, kill and maim. And rape. Oh Hilde, it must stop soon, before I go crazy, too.

14 Feb 43

Sundays are the only chance I have to write to you, Hilde, because on every other day Frau Wechsler seems determined to keep me busy from morning to night. The good thing is that it gives me no time to feel sorry for myself.

All week I've wondered about what it must have been like for those soldiers in Stalingrad. Trapped, starving, running out of ammunition and hope, their only choices to die or surrender. For what? The heavens are silent and today I am determined to not think about it.

Yesterday, I was washing dishes from *Mittagessen* when Frau Wechsler came in, made herself a pot of tea and drank it at the table. She usually takes tea to her "Morning Room," which overlooks the backyard and has flowered wallpaper, delicate furniture and many plants. She watched me while I worked.

When I went to wipe the table, she grabbed my wrist and laid her other hand on my stomach. My neck and cheeks flamed. My grey skirt is getting tight, but I didn't realize it was obvious to other people.

I stood still, expecting a cruel remark, but she looked up at me with eyes as blue as Delft china, and whispered, "It's true? You really are pregnant?" There was awe in her voice that for some reason almost made me cry. I nodded.

Suddenly, she smiled. She is pretty when she smiles. Her cheeks turn rosy and her eyes get round. I had never realized a face could actually glow with happiness.

With her hand still on my stomach, she asked if I had felt any movement. I didn't think so. She wants me to report to her when I do.

I went back to work, very conscious of her eyes, but she wasn't looking at me, only at my stomach. Like Papa did when I first told him. But her expression was wistful where Papa's had been sad. Why doesn't Frau Wechsler have children? I had to bite my bottom lip to keep from asking such a rude question.

When I was getting ready for bed, I studied my stomach in the bathroom mirror. It looks only a bit bigger. Frau Wechsler must be watching very closely to see the difference. I lay in bed with my hand on my stomach but felt nothing. What am I supposed to feel?

Herr Wechsler has given me permission to use the library. Neither of the Wechslers seem to read books, though he reads the newspaper every day and listens to the radio for hours on end. Walking in to pick out a book made me miss my visits with Papa in his office so much it felt like I had run too far and gotten a stitch in my side. I almost pulled *Effi Briest* off the shelf, then decided I did not want to read about the downfall of a young woman. Instead I found a wonderful illustrated copy of *Peterchens Mondfahrt* and curled up in the leather wing-backed chair. It had been such a favourite when I was young. I read, slept and woke to read more.

Now here it is, only 8:30 and I'm tired again. I want to stay up a little longer. I will turn off the light and open the blackout curtain like I used to do at home. If I stick my head out, I can see the same slice of sky that I saw from my bedroom window in Heidelberg. This must mean you can see me, Hilde. It gives me courage to think so.

18 Feb 43

Herr Wechsler called me into the salon today, handed me a letter and said it was from my father. Ilsa was visiting and got a prudish look on her face. She wanted to know why he was writing to me from his university office.

Without answering I retreated to the hall. All I cared was that Papa had written back! While I was opening the envelope I heard Ilsa telling the Wechslers, "My cousin is beside herself over that husband of hers. She told me he watches his daughter like a husband does a new bride. I think she was relieved to get the child out of the house."

What an awful thing to say, Hilde. I remembered what Mother said to Papa on New Year's Eve, that she'd tell people the baby was Papa's if she didn't get her way. Why would she keep telling such falsehoods after Papa gave in to her wishes? It made me angry. I tried to pretend I hadn't heard anything and went to the kitchen to read the letter.

Papa started, "My sweet *Liebchen*, I was beginning to fear that you would never write to me. I hope this means you have forgiven your sad old father."

Then he talked about what the defeat at Stalingrad could mean, and I realized that he was answering my most recent letter, the one I sent to his office. I think he must not have gotten the other letters. How can that be? If he got the last one, that means that Frau Wechsler is mailing them. Did Mother hide my letters from Papa? Ilsa's cruel words returned. Surely Mother isn't jealous of me? It makes me so upset I cannot even think about it.

Papa says hello from Erwin, who has complained that the house is too quiet without me. Now I wonder if Erwin got the letter I sent to him. I want to write back to Papa tonight, but the pen is getting too heavy and I am starting to misspell the simplest words.

21 Feb 43

This week I realized that I haven't been running to the toilet as often as I had been. It is such a relief to be able to hear water flowing and not panic.

Frau and Herr Wechsler have been arguing all week in quiet tones. Whenever I walk into the room, they quit. I hope they aren't arguing over whether I may stay. Unless Ilsa takes me in, I have nowhere to go. I don't know anyone else in Hamburg. I don't even know my way to the tram, since I still haven't left the house. It's beautiful but is starting to seem like a prison and would certainly feel like one if I couldn't use the library. I long to get outside and walk. Frau Wechsler doesn't want me to because she is afraid I would slip on ice and hurt myself. I suspect she only worries for the baby. What she would think if she knew I had tried to get rid of it?

Frau Wechsler is giving me easier tasks and I am not as tired in the evenings. The other day she told me to polish the silver – bowls, platters, cutlery and candlesticks. She had it all laid out on the dining room table, ready to be cleaned. When I was done, I asked her where the pieces went. She got a puzzled look on her face, said the bowls go here, and the platters there. She fell silent again for moment, then corrected herself. She changed her mind twice about where the candlesticks went.

What an odd response. Surely a woman knows where her own silver-ware goes. Mother is always very particular about such things.

I have written back to Papa using his university address again. I even told him about the air raids we've had – if only knowing I'm so close to falling bombs would give him the courage to demand I return to Heidelberg. I also wrote to Mother, asking if she accidentally laid my letters aside, and could she please give them to Papa and Erwin? Tomorrow, I will ask Frau Wechsler to mail both letters.

It's a good thing Papa gave me some money before I left so I can pay for postage. Though I have been here over a month, I have yet to receive wages. I should ask Herr Wechsler about that, but he is quite gruff with me, especially when he has been drinking, which is most evenings. I've only seen him drunk once, but even so I don't like his growly voice and his deep scowl.

22 Feb 43
I tore up the letter to Mother. It seems I am as afraid of her as Papa is. Instead, the next time I write to Papa I will ask him about the missing letters.

Chapter Eighteen

The silence unnerved Del. The only noise was fans whirring in the living room and each bedroom. She tiptoed around until Mathias took her to Hauptbahnhof for a transit pass. He helped her get cash from a machine, which was easy since she had the choice of doing the transaction in English. He asked if she wanted to return to the house with him – he was anxious to check on Cassandra – or explore on her own. She decided to wander around downtown.

At the entrance to Spitalerstrasse, a pedestrian street leading from the train station, Del drank from a silver, column-shaped fountain with "Water" written in four languages, then started out. The stone buildings and stone walkways trapped the humidity. The air seemed thick enough to wade through. Del was dripping when she joined the line at an ice cream stand. She picked something orange and fruity and ate it as she continued down the shady side of the street, past a "statue" street performer in top hat and tails, painted completely silver. How could he bear working in this heat? She didn't stop, knowing from her tour with Cassandra that he'd stand perfectly still then choose a moment to move when he could startle someone.

What caught her eye instead was a young woman sitting cross-legged in the shade near an intersection with a panhandling cup in front of her. She was also unmoving, head lowered, brown hands palm up on her knees, lap filled with an advanced pregnancy. Del stared at her stomach while Garda filled her mind. Garda's fear, her anguish at having to face an uncertain future and endure an unwanted pregnancy alone. In this city. Del tried to imagine how she'd feel if she had been sent to Cassandra's because of a pregnancy. She shuddered, thankful she'd been spared that.

Were some of these buildings ones Garda would have seen, if she'd ever left the house? Had she ever walked down Spitalerstrasse feeling hot and restless and achingly alone? The young woman looked up at Del with dark eyes brimming with sadness. Del scooped some two-Euro coins from her pocket, dropped them into the cup and hurried away.

She stopped in the tourist shops Felix had pointed out, under glass and chrome roofs in the Rathausmarkt, to buy postcards for her friends. It was hard not to stare at the large selection of cards featuring naked women and gaudy nighttime streets. She wished there was one with a buff guy on it – she'd send it to Serena. She'd love that. Del settled for traditional views of the harbour and the Rathaus and the Alster lakes – three places she'd actually been.

Back at the house, composing a message for each postcard took hours. Del struggled for just the right words to say she was miserable without sounding like she was whining.

The next day she ventured out to buy stamps, armed with directions from Cassandra for getting to a post office. The postal worker didn't speak English. She pantomimed licking stamps and putting them on the cards, which he understood. He refused her debit card. Del's frustration increased until someone in line trans-lated, explaining that Del needed to get cash from a bank machine, then use cash for her purchases. Mathias had explained this yesterday but she had thought he was exaggerating. There weren't many places you couldn't use your debit card in Canada. The clerk set aside her postcards, already stamped.

The bank was close so she only took a few minutes. She returned to the counter, pointed at the cards and waved her money. The postal worker looked affronted. He pointed to the line-up. "*Warten Sie, bis Sie dran sind.*"

His meaning was clear. Del replied, "I've already been through the line."

He repeated whatever he had said, but with more force. Del retreated to the back of the line under several judgmental stares. Waiting wasn't something she excelled at and by the time it was her turn, she slapped the 20-Euro note on the counter and gave the man a glare. He didn't seem to notice, which was more irritating. In seconds she had her change, but not as much as she'd hoped. Obviously fifty euros per week wasn't going to go as far as she'd thought. Her mother's lecture on budgeting time and resources ran through her mind. How annoying that she might be right.

Del returned to find Luise on her terrace enjoying a cold drink with Felix. It was the first time she'd seen him since the beer-breath barbeque. What terrible timing. Another hot, sticky day so her hair was a frizzy mess. Her skin felt slicked by patches of oil and probably looked worse.

Felix's smile was wide and genuine. His hair was feeling the heat, too, and waves had tightened into curls. But in his case, the result was cute. He said, "The person I wanted to see!"

To cover her surprise, Del poured herself some murky apple juice. They'd been expecting her, if the extra glass was any indication. She took a long drink and sat, her composure restored.

"How was your stamp-buying adventure?" Luise asked.

"An adventure."

Felix pinned her with a magnetic green gaze. "Are you ready for another?"

"Always." Del matched his smile.

"Great! Come with me. I'm going to Stadtpark with some

friends. We'll play some football, maybe just lie around." He shrugged. "Whatever we feel like, yes?"

"It's too hot to be running around like crazy people."

Luise replied, "With its lake and shade trees the park is often less humid."

"That sounds good. I'm turning into an oil slick here."

Felix laughed. "Then let's go."

Stadtpark was massive, with huge green areas, a lake, whole forests of trees and presiding over it all, a brick planetarium that had once been a water tower. Like every park area in Hamburg that Del had seen so far, it was busy. Five of Felix's friends met them in the shade beside a huge field. The lake shimmered off to the left and between the trees Del glimpsed a children's wading pool that reverberated with happy shrieks. They staked out a bit of the field and Del joined the four guys in a two-on-three game of soccer. She was basically a moving pylon; all she did was sweat buckets chasing after them. She collapsed for a while under the shade trees with the two girls, then rejoined the guys when one of them produced a Frisbee, something she could actually play. She even got a few compliments on nice catches.

After, everyone sprawled under the trees and guzzled pop that Max produced from an insulated bag. Del didn't mind when the others kept forgetting to speak English. She was happy to feel, even a little, like she was part of a group again.

Chapter Nineteen

27 Feb 43

A fidgety Ilsa showed up this morning. When I told her that the Wechslers were gone to the country for the day, her sour look turned into a skinny pout. I asked her what was wrong.

She told me that Wilhelmshaven was bombed badly again yesterday and Lucie was always such a comfort. Then she fell silent and I got the impression that she was angry she had said anything to me. Cousin's daughter or not, I'm still just the hired help.

When she turned to leave, I asked if she had heard from home. She cocked her head to one side and said, "Your home?" When I nodded, she added, "Why yes, I talk to Ulla almost every week."

I asked her what they talked about.

She said, "About you, silly child. She telephones to make sure you are behaving."

I bit my lip, realizing I had spoken too boldly. But a thought occurred to me and I had to ask, "Did Mother order that I not be allowed out of the house?"

Ilsa stuck her head forward, like a chicken preparing to peck at a pile of grain. She informed me, quite primly, that Mother had only warned them about my being prone to loose behavior, which was nothing they didn't realize given my state.

That hurt so much I blurted, "Since I'm already pregnant, that shouldn't matter now."

Her head jerked back as if struck. She muttered something about my mother being right, then marched out of the house and slammed the door.

Oh, the stupid things that fly out of my mouth. Next time I will bite my lip until it bleeds.

I felt like lice were crawling all over me. I desperately needed a bath.

So, Hilde, I broke the law and ran hot water on a day we aren't permitted to, because I needed to wash away Ilsa's hateful words. I even used a few drops of Frau Wechsler's scented bath oil. Since I had been given the day off, I soaked for almost an hour, until the water cooled off.

I think it put me in the mood for breaking rules, because I went for a walk in the afternoon, though the Wechslers had told me to stay inside. It was cool and overcast. The air was damp but so refreshing. I'm living in a rich neighbourhood. All the yards are large like the Wechslers' and are guarded by stone and wrought-iron fences. A few blocks east is a lake – in the middle of the city! There was a sailboat on the water.

I walked along the shore, then sat and watched the sailboat until it started to rain. There was an odd greyish film on the trees and grass. I wonder what it was?

On the way back, I took a wrong turn and asked for directions to the right street. When I made it to the Wechslers' house, my coat was soaked and I was shivering. I took another bath. Can you believe it? Two baths in a single day. It was glorious. I put on my nightgown though it was only six o'clock, fixed *Abendbrot* and ate it in bed. This must be what it is like to be rich, doing anything you please when you please.

It's ten o'clock and the Wechslers still haven't returned, but I'm too tired to wait up.

28 Feb 43

This morning I confessed to Frau Wechsler I had gone for a walk. I quickly added that the fresh air made me feel quite healthy. She wasn't upset, so I asked her about the lake. It is called Aussenalster. She explained the Aussenalster is connected by a short canal to the Binnenalster and how canals connect that smaller lake with the Elbe River. Both lakes were made centuries ago from the Alster River. The grey film I saw is from machines that make an artificial fog when we have an air raid. Will anything be green in the spring?

Frau Wechsler left the kitchen and returned a moment later with instructions for me to get my coat. Herr Wechsler was taking us for a drive so I could see for myself. I was so excited that I grabbed her hands and whispered, "Thank you." She smiled.

Moments later we got into the Wechslers' black sedan. The interior smelled of leather. I sat in the back and had to restrain myself from bouncing. My first official outing in Hamburg. It had been foggy the day I arrived and I'd seen very little. Plus, trains always take you past the dull parts of a city, factories and such.

It wasn't a long drive. Herr Wechsler made sure I knew his was an official vehicle and wasn't for pleasure. We went around the north end of the Aussenalster where the river enters the lake. Frau Wechsler recited names of districts we were passing through – Winterhude, Barmbek, Uhlenhorst and others I can't recall.

I saw stone buildings and red roof tiles similar to Heidelberg. How do you explain feeling sad and happy at the same time? My heart ached to stand on the Alte Brücke and gaze up at the castle ruins, but Hamburg offered what comfort it could.

It reminded me that at least I'm still in Germany, and not so far from home – not like those poor soldiers who fought and died in Stalingrad, who are still fighting in faraway places like Russia and Africa. It makes me ashamed I was so childish about leaving Heidelberg.

The square little Binnenalster was covered with camouflage, making it look like a grid with a narrow canal instead of a lake. As we drove south along the Aussenalster the city's age began to show. The Aldstadt, with its narrow streets, made me think of Heidelberg's older areas. All that is missing is the hills.

We drove within two blocks of the Elbe River, giving me a few inviting glimpses of water. The Elbe looks much wider than the Neckar. Herr Wechsler said it is even affected by the tides, as are some of the canals. We didn't get closer because of a roadblock. Which Herr Wechsler said was only right because, as well as ships in the harbour, there are a few *Unterseeboote*. Hamburg is where they are made and sometimes repaired.

Imagine, Hilde. U-boats. I missed much of the drive back to the house because I was daydreaming about what the inside of a U-boat might look like. I would love to see one. If I were a man, I think the silence of U-boats, gliding undetected underwater, would suit me best. Quiet Garda in her quiet boat. In a way, I suppose U-boats are like wombs, keeping their men safe until they are ready to surface, just as this baby will stay safe in my womb for the next five months.

I did not see much bomb damage during the tour except for a building beside the Binnenalster. Herr Wechsler may be right about us being safe.

2 Mar 43

I still go to bed at nine o'clock but lately I'm not falling asleep right away. So I lie in bed and think. This isn't always a good thing, Hilde, because I often end up remembering what brought me here. Last night the night-mare about the attack returned. Sometimes the most innocent things bring the memory back, such as Herr Wechsler throwing his black suit jacket over the back of a chair, or his comment one day about how quiet I am.

It's silly, but I cannot sweep the floors when I'm alone in the house. And sometimes, when I hear Herr Wechsler's heavy footfalls on the stairs, I think, 'Faber.'

I'm thankful that Herr Wechsler mostly ignores me. But last night when I was washing dishes, he touched me on the shoulder. I dropped a cup; its handle snapped off. He frowned so hard his heavy eyebrows met over his nose. He set a plate on the counter and said, "You missed this. Try not to be so clumsy. Dishes are hard to replace." Then he left the kitchen.

My heartbeat continued to stutter like a drum roll. I cut myself fishing the handle out of the dishwater. A cluster of soap bubbles turned pink.

I hate the way fear sometimes controls me.

3 Mar 43

It's almost eleven o'clock but I had to tell you this right away, Hilde.

Just now I was lying in the dark, trying to think of pleasant things. I imagined myself in a U-boat gliding through turquoise waters filled with fishes of all sizes and colours. Do U-boats have windows? The one in my imagination did and I could see the fish. It was so peaceful.

Between breaths, I felt something inside, below my belly button. I held my breath and it happened again. It was so faint, as if a tiny tropical fish had swum from my imagination into my stomach and its feathery tail fin had brushed my senses.

I think I felt the baby move, Hilde. It's real. Until now it was only real in my head and not even then, most days. Now it's real in my body. God help me – it is real.

And now I'm crying again. I thought I was finished with crying.

5 Mar 43

I haven't told Frau Wechsler about the movement yet. I have nothing, Hilde, nothing but one suitcase and a hope that I will repack it some day to return to Heidelberg. I hate this secret, though it feels odd and sometimes wonderful, and I hate what it means, but it is mine until I share it. I know that as soon as I tell her about it she will think of it as her baby moving. It's not hers, not yet. Don't worry, Hilde, I will tell her. On Sunday. I promise.

Today, Frau Wechsler was fluttery. Her hair was even out of place. She zipped from one task to the next like a hummingbird between flowers. She is giving a dinner party tomorrow night and insists everything be perfect.

She summoned me into the dining room and pressed a bundle of ivory linen into my arms. "I found this in the bottom of the linen drawer. Take it to the attic, out of sight," she said. "I'll deal with it later. Right now I have to go to the butcher's and pick out meat."

As she flew from the room, she called for me to finish dusting while she was gone. I was already finished but I didn't tell her because I wanted a break.

The linen felt almost silky as I carried it up the two flights of stairs, the second one narrow and steep, almost a ladder. The huge space and steep eaves allowed me to stand upright. Muddy light filtered through two round windows set high in **opposite** walls. Dust layered everything. It had a haunted feel, but sad and neglected, not scary.

There were a few stacked boxes, a tailor's mannequin, and some piles of ancient-looking books with cracked covers. More boxes were hidden in shadow under the high east window. My footsteps echoed. I hesitated in the beam of light, wondering why a luxurious tablecloth had been relegated to the attic. I thought moths had ruined it.

I should have just set it on the box, but I was curious. Instead, I whipped open the folds to take a look. Clouds of dust swirled around my ankles. The cloth was perfect, not a hole to be seen. I turned to let the light fall on it, gasped and sank to the floor to finger the embroidered design in the center of the linen.

A six-pointed star, pale blue and beautiful. The same symbol that all Jews must wear on armbands.

As I traced the blue lines, understanding dawned. Frau Wechsler doesn't always know where things belong because this hasn't always been her house. She banished this beautiful tablecloth to the attic because it speaks of the previous owners.

Jews, once proud of their heritage, now banished themselves. To resettlements camps in Poland? If so, those camps must be cities by now.

Papa's comment about Professor Jakob not being able to take much with him came to mind. I dragged a box from the corner into the light. Dust was so thick on it that it had to have been undisturbed for years. Inside was a black leather book filled with strange, delicate writing. The six-pointed star embossed on the cover told me this too was Jewish. And at the bottom of the box lay the most beautiful seven-armed silver candlestick, heavily tarnished. The Wechslers couldn't have checked these boxes or these things would have been destroyed. Odd they didn't destroy the tablecloth, but maybe Frau Wechsler was drawn to its fine quality.

As I rubbed some of the tarnish off, I remembered a similar candlestick sitting on a mantle. I could almost hear a childish voice saying, "It was my great-grandmother's." I whispered, "Judith?" Nothing answered. The dust motes danced in the dull sunlight.

Anger settled on my skin like a late autumn frost. I shivered and hurried to pack everything away. I dusted off my clothes, not sure if I was angry with the Wechslers or myself or maybe God. I did not deserve to be turned out of my home, Hilde. I did not. My heart whispers that maybe the Jews who owned this house did not deserve their fate, either. How can I know?

6 Mar 43

Frau Wechsler was happy with her party, even though Herr Wechsler got quite drunk. After serving and cleaning all night, my legs ached and my feet tingled so fiercely it hurt to walk. I slept in this morning and no one woke me.

Tonight the news is horrible. The radio reported that over six hundred enemy airplanes bombed Berlin today. Herr Wechsler said Hamburg would never be attacked like that because although we have shipyards, we don't have any important leaders here. He thinks Berlin was targeted because they are hoping to get lucky and kill the Führer. Of course they didn't.

I cannot sleep tonight for worrying. Before I turned the light on to write this, I sat in the dark for a long time, staring at the night, wishing I could see the stars and thinking about home. Has Erwin heard that his hero, General Rommel, is now in charge of the western defences? Since Herr Wechsler mentioned it over *Abendbrot* I have been wondering what Papa would think.

Those faceless voices on the radio say the government is not afraid. I am starting to think that what a person says means nothing; what a person does shows their true thoughts. Surely putting one of our best generals in France must mean they are very afraid of the British.

And what does it mean, Hilde, that Papa did nothing when I most needed him to do, or say, *something*? Silence isn't only a shield; it is also a weapon. And a form of judgment.

Chapter Twenty

Three days after Del had seen Cassandra as a total wreck, she emerged from her bedroom looking poised; hair, makeup and clothing tidy. Her tone was icily formal. She expressed her pleasure that, by Mathias's reports, Del had been following their rules, speaking as if Del had signed that hideous contract.

Del didn't contradict her. She wanted nothing to cause a repeat of that breakdown.

Shortly after, Felix called up the stairs, asking her to come down. Cassandra, heading for her computer, said, "Isn't it nice that Professor Konrad's nephew is being so kind?" Apparently anything or anyone associated with Luise had instant approval. That suited Del.

He waited at the bottom of the stairs, smiling up at her in a way that made Del's stomach flip. They sat on the bottom step. Felix said, "Tante Luise mentioned that your sister is often too busy to take you around Hamburg. And, of course, my aunt is obsessed with her garden and her book projects for the university and rarely leaves the house."

"So?"

"I want you to like my home. I'll show you around if you like."

Del fought against the smile trying to break free. "That'd be okay. But, don't you have a job now? I thought you said something about it to your friends yesterday."

"Only three mornings a week. Clean up at a rental place on the lake. I went this morning and am already here."

"Most of the kids I know who are going to college have to work in the summer to save money. It's nice you don't have to worry about that."

"Ja. You sound like my father." His voice dropped to a whisper. "He's not happy. I told him I might not want to return to school in the fall. I'll find another job soon. But until then, do you want to see Hamburg?"

She gripped the step to keep from wiggling happily and gave an off-hand shrug. "Sure." A cute eighteen-year-old guy as a tour guide? She couldn't believe her good luck; neither would Serena, when she told her. If only she had brought her mom's digital camera.

Rain in the night had washed away the humidity so jeans and a tank top were comfortable again. They walked around the university area, ending up on a street of cafes and stores, including some second-hand places. They rummaged through racks of clothing, laughing at the combinations they found, and searched used records for bands that Felix's mother was hoping to collect. Del quickly discovered that Felix bestowed his shy but sexy smile on almost everyone, but especially girls. Despite not knowing German, she could tell girls sometimes flirted with him. He either didn't realize or ignored it.

Later in the afternoon, they met two of Felix's friends at a sidewalk table of a small cafe. The guy, Jan, had been at the park the day before, and only added nods and smiles to the conversation. The girl, Monika, dark blond and very tanned, was new to Del. She looked a bit like the girl Geoff had dated before her. They'd hardly been introduced when Monika said, "I've never met anyone from Canada. You are... what I expected." The way her gaze raked Del, pausing on her tattoo, told Del that Canadians didn't rate in Monika's list of interesting people.

Del was proud of the way she held her tongue. She was glad that before long Monika declared that she had to get ready for a date. Jan padded after her like a trained pup. Del watched them leave. "Her date can't be with Jan, can it?"

"No. He's too shy to tell her how much he likes her. But she knows. She is dating Max."

Del almost asked who he was dating but didn't want to know. On their way back to Luise's, she studied the townhouses and wondered which one Garda had stayed in. By her description, she'd been in this area, west of the Aussenalster. Some of the townhouses looked new; some old. But even gawking at fancy trim near the roofs and round windows on upper floors, she was intently aware of Felix. He smelled of lemons and sweat.

Over the next few days they continued to explore, mostly different shopping areas. Felix showed her through the maze of shopping malls downtown, many with *Passage* in the title. To Del's surprise he didn't mind shopping. In the mornings, waiting for him to arrive, Del continued to read bits of Garda's journal, about the tedium of her days, how walking was her only pleasure, of her growing stomach and the fascination she had with her changing body, how her fear of air raids disappeared as, like many others, she laughed at the harmless mosquitoes that buzzed over Hamburg, damaging almost nothing and getting swatted down for trying.

Del made sure she kept Luise informed of where she was in her reading. She didn't want her friend to think she wasn't doing her job.

On the weekend Felix and Del returned to Stadtpark for the day. It was even more crowded than during the week. Del was enjoying herself until Max and Monika showed up. The girl set the tone for the group and always seemed to look at Del down the length of her nose. Each time talk switched to German, usually led by Monika, Felix returned it to English. Del could sense the tension between the two. By the awkward glances, everyone could.

The six guys got out a soccer ball and were joined by a few passersby. Del only watched. Felix was slimmer than the other guys, almost skinny, but he was quicker than most of them and could weave with the grace of a dancer. Someone tripped him and he tumbled into a heap. Del started to rise but caught herself. He rebounded and a moment later sent his opponent sprawling. An argument started, making Del wish she understood. The game broke up and the guys returned to the shade. Felix flopped down between Monika and Del.

Max said, "What was that about, Altmann?"

Felix made a rude noise. "Hassles with Dad. I had to take it out on something. We'd played long enough. I'm thirsty." Del got a cold drink from the picnic lunch that Luise had packed them. Felix gave her a thankful smile. "*Danke.*"

"*Bitte.*" Del smiled back, pleased she'd remembered how to respond.

Monika started laughing. She eyed Del. "You have a liking for our Felix, yes? Yes. It is on your face. How you watch him. Smile to him."

Del scowled at her pop can then took a long drink. Monika wasn't finished. "You can't think our Felix is handsome." She laughed again. "You do? Yes, you do. We must fix that wrong thinking."

Max said, "You used to think him not so ugly. When did you date? Two years past?"

"We were children. Now I have you to compare him. He's a child still." Monika stroked Max's heavily muscled arm. When she ordered Felix to sit up, he acted like a puppet, doing her bidding like she was pulling his strings.

Del wondered at his silence. Did he still like Monika? "This is dumb."

"Not at all," Monika replied. "You must see our Felix's, what is the word? *Der Mangel.*"

Felix, who was the best English speaker of the group, narrowed his eyes. "Defects."

"Yes, of course," Monika said. "His defects. Now listen, little *Ananas*." She had started calling Del that during their first meeting. Felix had told her it meant pineapple. Like Del hadn't heard that one before. Monika flicked Felix's hair. "Child curls." She ran her finger down Felix's nose. "Too straight. His nose … like a boat sail, yes?" She didn't wait for an answer. "And this mouth. When our Felix smiles not, he is like a sad clown." She pinched his chin. "Look. His chin sticks out like the nose." She squeezed one bicep. "So skinny. A child, not a man. No whisker, no muscle."

Felix's silence frustrated Del as much as Monika's arrogance. "And you know what your worst trait is, Monika? Your mouth. It's way too big. Everyone has faults."

"You would know," Monika snapped.

"Yeah, I would. But I know that poking fun at a friend isn't fun at all." She stood. "I can't believe you'd all just sit and listen to this crap." She didn't look at Felix. His silence was almost unbearable. "Have your so-called fun." As she started to walk away, Felix said, "Wait, Del. I'll come with you."

Monika said something in German that made the others laugh. A few voices called something that sounded like, "*Tschüss*, kin-der-hew-da."

Felix had the soft-sided cooler slung over his shoulder when he caught up. Del was secretly relieved he'd come, since she wasn't sure how to get home. She glanced at his hand gripping the navy strap but didn't want to look at his face. "Why'd you let her do that?"

"It's an old joke with Monika. It means nothing."

"No? I bet the joke started when you two stopped dating, right?"

"You might be right." He nudged her. "But you should've let it be. Monika doesn't like it when anyone disagrees with her. It's easier to keep quiet."

Del said nothing more until they were at the edge of the park. She stopped and faced him. "Did you believe her?"

"About my looks? She told the truth."

"Maybe technically."

"The lecture didn't convince you?" A hint of his usual smile pulled at his mouth but he didn't let it take over. "Do you think I'm good looking?"

"That's a phrase stuffy Cassandra would use. The term my friends and I use is hot. Do I think you're hot?" Del started to walk away but Felix grabbed her wrist.

"Do you?" His tone was teasing.

"If I told you, your head would explode. I don't feel like cleaning up a mess." She walked away, knowing that she'd as good as told him the truth. Maybe he wouldn't get it.

He laughed. Not usually prone to embarrassment, Del suddenly felt like running away. Before she could, Felix grabbed her wrist again. "Let's go to the park by the lake. We don't want to let this picnic lunch go to waste."

Chapter Twenty-One

19 April 43

I love walking, Hilde. It is the one time I feel free. The bigger my stomach grows, the less Frau Wechsler makes me work, so the more time I have for walking. The doctor has assured her this will strengthen me and help make delivery easier, so long as I do not overdo it. Since I have not been sleeping well, I get up and walk at dawn. It is quiet, a lovely time to be outside.

Something odd happened during my morning walk. I was south of Dammtor Station on the edge of the park and was sitting on a bench having a rest. I had taken bread and a small jar of water. I nibbled half of the bread while resting and was taking a drink when a column of men came into view. There must have been fifty or more. They were marching, but it was sloppy. When they came closer, I realized how ragged they were. They marched past with eyes lowered. I saw patches on their dirty uniforms. Most read, *Ost*. They were prisoners from the east, probably housed in that compound near Dammtor station. I saw a few patches with "P" on them and thought that must mean Poland.

Herr Wechsler has warned me about prisoners in the city. There are even women prisoners. We are to stay away from them, never talk to them, never look at them. As if they do not exist. But these men were very real, and some looked sick. They also smelled bad. One prisoner looked like an older version of Erwin. I watched him shuffle by when a movement made me turn. My bread was gone! I had left it on my cloth bag on the bench. I tried to see who had snatched it, but could not. It happened so fast I almost wondered if I had eaten all my bread and had forgotten doing so.

I could have called out and the guards at the front and back of the column would have found the thief, but I did not have the heart. How hungry must you be to steal food from a visibly pregnant girl?

I must tell you before I forget. Herr Wechsler told us our army uncovered a mass grave in a place called Katyn. They say it is several years old and the dead are Polish officers who were killed by Soviets. Over 4100 bodies. I wonder if those Polish prisoners I saw today know? Does it make them angry at the Soviet prisoners they work beside? How could the Soviets do such a terrible thing? Maybe they really are as evil as our leaders say.

29 April 43

Easter was depressing. The only good thing is what I discovered southeast of the Rathaus: Nikolaikirche. It's lovely and peaceful. But I felt the pain of being away from Heidelberg so keenly, Hilde, that I don't want to talk about it. There is something I should tell you, though. I have been breaking the law. Can you imagine? And I will keep doing it, though I must think up more clever ways of going about it.

For the last ten days, I have walked at dawn almost every morning. Five times I went to that same bench where the prisoners walked past me, hoping they would again. They did. They must work in some factory or warehouse south of here. Each morning I purposely left bread on my sack and looked away. Every time it was gone when I looked back.

Their gaunt, hungry faces are a torment. I do not care if they are prisoners, no men should be made to work without enough to eat. When I think of all the food hidden in Herr Wechsler's cellar, I want to cry. So I decided that Herr Wechsler will feed some of those poor men. If I ever get caught I will have to pretend that I did not notice, which is why I need to think up clever ways to leave the food along the path they take. Tomorrow I will follow and see where they go.

1 May 43

I am writing this before I get out of bed. I had another strange meeting, only this time not with prisoners. I followed that column yesterday. They went to a warehouse near the river. I could see it down the street so had to look. When I arrived on the banks of the Elbe, I realized how tired I was. I rested on a bench beside the St. Pauli Landungsbrücken.

It was wonderfully refreshing to sit and watch the ships on the river, which is much wider than the Neckar. Quite a few solders passed by, though none of them looked at me, except for one sailor in a black-and-white striped shirt. He sat beside me for a minute or two, then finally asked if I was waiting for someone.

I told him I was resting before heading home. I had not realized how far the river was.

He told me my accent says I'm from the south, not from Hamburg.

I admitted I was from Heidelberg. He noticed Papa's ring and assumed I was the wife of a sailor so I did not correct him. He introduced himself as Werner Hoenig. His post is on a U-Boat. A radioman. Imagine, Hilde. I have met someone who works on a U-Boat! I have so many questions to ask him. I do hope we meet again.

I think we might. He asked to escort me back to the house. He was concerned I would come to the river alone in such times. "Some of the sailors are not respectful to women." He said it like he was an old man, but he is only nineteen or twenty. I let him escort me home. He is easy to talk to and so it seemed a short walk. When we got there, he said his father lives close by, but not in a fancy house like mine. I told him I was a guest, that it was not my real home.

He insisted on introducing himself to Frau Wechsler and explaining why he had walked me home. She was polite and thanked him. When he left she forbade me from returning to the river, saying it was too far and that Landungsbrücken was too close to the shipyards, which is one place the British target when they fly over. I do not know why she is concerned. The bombers are long gone by the time the sun rises. Her thoughts, as always, are with this baby I am growing for her. It is the only reason she cares for my welfare.

evening

Today Frau Wechsler gave me the lightest and easiest jobs. When I was done I asked to walk to the lake. She reminded me not to go farther and said if I had many days like yesterday I would have feet the size of an elephant's and would be confined to bed. That would be the end of my walks. It sounded like a threat, which made me doubly glad to be out of the house.

The pleasant afternoon seduced me. I removed my shoes and stockings to let the grass tickle my toes. I do love the park beside the Aussenalster. The green is sickly from those fog-making machines but it still reminds me of the green hills surrounding Heidelberg (except here it is flat) and the blue water calms me no matter what my mood. I lay on a blanket under a tree and watched branches wave above me. I realized the only hill in the area was this mound beneath my baggy dress that Frau Wechsler bought from a woman with four children and no more need for such clothing. I rested my hand on my stomach and smiled.

You might think it strange I can smile, Hilde, but when I feel movement, I do not think of the awful way this life in me began. I am awed by the miracle of what my body is doing.

This is how I was lying when a familiar voice asked if he could join me. It was the U-Boat sailor. When I started to sit up, Werner insisted I stay down, that I looked very comfortable. I rolled onto my side to face him. He is a little strange looking, slight, with straight dark hair and green eyes with a ring of brown around the pupil. His face is narrow, much like his body. His nose is a little big. He reminds me of a stork, if storks were short.

Werner might look strange, but he is wonderful to talk to. He is in Hamburg because he and his "Number One" and the second engineer are the nucleus of a new crew. They are going over their new U-Boat, making sure everything is working while the rest of the crew is assembled. He is very proud of that, though when I asked he did not want to tell me about life on a U-Boat. "It's noisy and gets stinky," is all he said before changing the subject. I was a bit disappointed to know U-Boats aren't quiet like I thought.

Our conversation buzzed about like bees in a flower garden. In the middle of it, the baby started moving. He could see that something was happening – my face had flushed – and when I told him, he looked interested. He watched my stomach, not in the greedy way Frau Wechsler does, but with a look near to the awe I feel at such times.

Shortly after, he left, saying his father would be expecting him for *Kaffee und Kuchen*, not that they'd had any coffee for a very long time. The Wechslers have plenty of coffee – real coffee, not the ersatz stuff most people drink. I would give some to Werner, but I doubt they would let me. I am not supposed to speak about the food in the basement.

I am tired of silence, Hilde. I so enjoyed talking to Werner that I do not think I want to be quiet Garda any more.

Chapter Twenty-Two

Loud voices lured Del onto the deck. One loud voice, really. It came from the terrace below. She crouched and hugged the wall as she crept forward. Eavesdropping was rude, but what about when you couldn't understand a word being said? She had never heard German being spoken with such vehemence, except in movies. As she peeked between the deck's fence slats she half expected to see someone in a Nazi uniform.

A man in khaki slacks and a blue golf shirt paced back and forth. He was big and broad, a male version of Luise, right down to the salt-and-pepper hair. It had to be her brother. Del inched forward to see if Luise was on the receiving end of this tirade. She couldn't imagine the professor allowing someone to speak to her like that.

It was Felix. He slouched in a deck chair, unresponsive, like when Monika had put him down at the park. The man – Felix's father, Herr Altmann, she assumed – seemed to puff up. His face turned red. Even from a distance, Del saw spittle fly from his mouth. He waved his arms.

When Del thought he might hit Felix, Luise appeared. She stepped in front of Herr Altmann and spoke in a low, steady voice. When he tried to step around her, she blocked his path. He gradually deflated. Minutes later he gave a nod and followed Luise into the house.

Felix hadn't moved through any of it. Del leaned over the railing to make sure the coast was clear, then shimmied down the lattice. She jumped to land in front of Felix. He flinched, jerked up his head – and instantly the Felix she liked was back, smile and all.

"You shouldn't scare people like that," he said. "Where did you come from?"

Del pointed up at the deck. "Was that your dad?" The smile disappeared. Felix nodded. Del brushed a twig off her shorts and dropped into a chair. "Why'd you just sit like that?"

"What am I to do? Fight him? He's twenty centimetres taller and probably thirty kilograms heavier. He'd squash me. And believe me, I can't yell louder. I could leave, I suppose, but he'd start in again when I return."

"Leaving is probably what I'd do. It freaks me out when people yell at me like that." Del ran her hands over the smooth surface of the patio table. "What was he so pissed off about?"

"Same old thing. Get a job. Go to uni. Make something of yourself." He shrugged dismissively. "I will when I've figured out what I want to do." His expression darkened. "Bad enough being the oldest, but I'm the only son. He's always pushing me to do better, as if I have to be more successful than him or he's failed. And when I don't work hard enough, I'm the failure."

"My folks are always putting pressure on me, too. Do this, don't do that. Why can't you be like your sister?"

Felix turned his chair so it faced the table. "I'm glad you're not like your sister. She always seems so... serious. You're fun."

Before Del could respond they were interrupted by a sharp, "Delora!" They both looked up. Cassandra had a death grip on the railing. "I've told you not to climb down from the deck. I swear you're trying to drive me crazy." She spun and disappeared.

Felix arched his brows. "She seems a little tense."

"I tend to do that to people, especially Cass and our parents." She squinted at the deck. What Felix said about his dad reminded her of Cassandra saying how much pressure she'd felt growing up. And there was that late-night talk Del had overheard – Cassandra on a tightrope. She had it all: great job, great husband, nice home. How could she ever feel like a failure?

Luise joined them. "*Guten Morgen*, Del. I did not hear you come down the stairs." She glanced at the lattice in a knowing way. "Your father left, Felix. He was calmer. I don't appreciate how you forced me to get involved today. I have other things to worry about."

"*Entschuldigung*." He whispered to Del, "That means sorry." He continued, "Dad was in the shower so I left a note saying where I was going. We'd argued last night. I didn't know he was going to follow me."

Luise sat with a sigh. "Enough. Del doesn't need to be burdened with our family spats. So, Del, are you enjoying touring with Felix?"

How should she answer? She really enjoyed being with him, though she wished he'd flirt with her instead of treating her like a cousin he happened to get along with.

Luise prompted, "Do you like Hamburg? Yes, no?"

Del swished her hands back and forth over the table. "Yeah, I like it, as much as you can like a place that reminds you of a tabletop."

"What do you mean?"

"It's nice, but really flat. No hills or valleys, nothing to make the streets more, I don't know, picturesque." She quickly added, "I like all the canals and lakes and stuff. That kind of makes up for the..." She tapped the tabletop and gave a wry grin.

Felix laughed. "You've just decided where we're going today."

"I have?"

"Yes. I'm taking you to Blankenese."

"So this Blawnka-nay-za has hills? That doesn't count. A different town having hills doesn't make Hamburg less flat."

"Blankenese is in Hamburg. Don't you have names for different districts in your city? This is Rotherbaum. Up near the park is Winterhude, and east is Barmbek. There is Sankt George, Altstadt, Sankt Pauli and Altona and –"

"I get it. Yes, we have names for different areas of Edmonton."

Del told Cassandra where they were going. Luise supplied another picnic lunch. It took them almost an hour on a bus and two trains before Felix announced they'd arrived. They exited a train station that looked like an Italian villa on the outside. Del teased Felix that it didn't look very hilly to her, but as they walked, the streets folded down into a crease that opened to the Elbe River. They stood on the east ridge overlooking winding treed streets, real villas and red-tiled roofs – a postcard come to life.

"This is cool," Del said. "Are we really still in Hamburg?"

Felix's smile was wry. "I have to confess it used to be its own village."

"Ha!" She elbowed him in triumph.

He grunted and rubbed his ribs. "But it is part of Hamburg now. Come on. We'll go down and eat our lunch on the beach."

It being a Monday and overcast meant there weren't many people around. They explored the streets, finding steep stairways, overlooks and winding paths beside roads barely wide enough for a single vehicle. They relaxed on the narrow beach, protected from the river by a low wall that served as a walkway. They waded in the river, both getting soaked to mid-thigh when the wake of a container ship caught them off guard.

On their way out of the valley, they discovered different stairways and switchbacks. Several times Del stopped on stairs thinking her lungs would explode, only to have Felix grab her hand and pull her along to the next landing, where she would try again to catch her breath. When they reached the top of the east ridge, both winded and laughing, they stopped to rest, leaning on the rail of a lookout spot.

Felix asked, "Is this hilly enough for you?"

"Not bad. You need to come to Edmonton so you can see a real river valley. Sure your river is wider, but ours is in a valley probably three or four times deeper than this puny little dip."

"Puny?" He poked her shoulder, then cupped his hand over it.

Their gazes locked, and all Del could see were the vivid green eyes holding her captive, all she could hear was their breathing. She thought he was going to kiss her. She wanted him to, so much that her lips dried up from the heat scorching them. She licked her top lip. Felix seemed to startle. He frowned across the valley and the feeling was gone. Had it been real? Had she imagined the intensity in his eyes? He wouldn't look at her again so she couldn't tell. She felt so frustrated she wanted to kick his shins. Instead she turned and marched down the street.

Felix called after her. She spun around. Smiling, he pointed in the other direction. "The train station is that way."

All the way back, Del kept thinking what a perfect day it would have been, if only he had kissed her.

Chapter Twenty-Three

14 May 43

Oh Hilde, it has been such an awful day I do not know how to start. But as Papa always urges me, I will begin at the beginning, and it began fine. I went for my dawn walk and cleverly handed off some bread to my marching prisoners at a corner where I pretended to be waiting to cross. As the men marched around the corner, I waited until half the column was past me, then with the guards at either end out of sight, I stepped forward and handed a whole loaf to the nearest prisoner and stepped back. I knew that loaf would be long gone before they got to the factory. The prisoners, even if their heads are up before, walk past me with heads down. I think it is their way of protecting me, of making the guards think they don't notice me. But they do. Does it gives them courage to know someone cares about their fate?

When I returned to the house, I had barely stepped inside when Frau Wechsler accosted me and told me I had a visitor waiting in the salon.

I was puzzled as to who could be here. Papa came to mind. My fingers fumbled as I undid my coat. Surely Papa had found his courage and was taking me home.

It was not Papa. It was Frau Ott, standing in front of the cold fireplace with her stole draped over her shoulder and her hat tilted over one eye. Her face looked scrunched, like she was wearing a corset three sizes too small and couldn't breathe. As soon as I stepped into the room, her attention dropped to my stomach. It felt like she could see through my dress and skin to the baby itself. I laid my hand on my stomach's mound. I wished to protect myself from her scrutiny, to protect the helpless baby.

Frau Ott sat in the chair by the fireplace, with a suddenness that hinted her legs had no strength. I perched on the edge of the settee. I wanted to flee this awful woman's presence. What could she possibly want?

In the silence, Frau Ott pulled out a twisted handkerchief and began to twist it more. She started speaking, stopped. Her eyes closed for a second then she said, "I have come to request that you move back to Heidelberg, to live with me until the baby is born."

I rose, circled the settee and gripped its back to steady myself. Faber's mother wanted me to live with her? How could she think I could even stand to live in the house of the person who had violated me, much less want to? I shook my head. Only manners and fear kept me from leaving. I thought I might throw up.

"Do not reject my offer out of hand!" Frau Ott cried. "How dare you be so ungrateful!"

I could not speak. After weeks of being able to talk I was quiet Garda again. Then I realized Frau Ott was near tears and was as white as the linens in Frau Wechsler's cupboards. I forced myself to speak, though only a whisper. "Why?"

Tears spilled down parchment cheeks. She looked much older than I remembered. She pressed her fist to her breastbone and gasped until the tears stopped and she could speak. Faber was killed on the Eastern front, only two weeks after arriving there. She stumbled over some nonsense about him not having time to become the hero he should have been, then started inhaling sharp, short breaths.

I could only stare. Faber was dead. The beast who had raped me was dead. Forgive me for thinking it, Hilde, but even as Frau Ott struggled to breathe it felt like I was able to inhale freely for the first time since that awful night in November. I was free from the fear he had bound me in, free from the threat of his presence. Frau Ott calmed again. I still couldn't understand her thinking. I should have expressed my sympathy, but instead blurted, "You called me a whore."

Frau Ott seemed to regain her arrogance. She said she was protecting her son from scandal. She had no qualms about me being in a scandal. I started shaking my head again. She stood abruptly and insisted I return with her.

I refused.

"You must," she said. "Faber was my only son. You carry his child."

I could feel words rising in my throat. I could not stop them, nor did I want to. "Now you believe me?"

"I never disbelieved you. His charm was too strong for more than just you to resist."

"He did not charm me. He forced me."

Frau Ott demanded I never say such a thing. Her grandchild would not have such a terrible lie hanging over his head. She said I would only be allowed to remain with them if I abandoned my belligerent attitude.

It took me a moment to understand that she wanted me to return to Heidelberg with her, give birth to Faber's bastard, and then leave so she could raise another Faber. She allowed that I could stay if my attitude improved.

I backed up until I bumped the door and reached behind to grip the door handle with both hands. The movement made my stomach stick out more. It drew her gaze, which made it easier for me to tell her, "I will only say this once, Frau Ott. I will never go anywhere with you and I find your nerve at coming here appalling. You gave up any claim to this baby when you called me a liar. Please leave. I want nothing to do with you."

I walked out of the house and went directly to the lakeside. Then, under a tree, with only the lake as my witness, I cried. I longed to return to Heidelberg. To Papa. But not under those conditions, to be Frau Ott's brood mare. It was too awful, Hilde. Her every word played over and over in my mind.

I do not know how long I cried, only that at some point a familiar figure knelt beside me. I turned to Werner and soaked his shirt with tears. The flood eased. He pulled a handkerchief from his pocket and said, "I was going to offer you this, but I'm not sure you need it now." He pressed it into my hand, cupped his hand over it and asked what was distressing me.

He called me dear. Dear Garda. It almost made me start crying again. I held it back and instead was beset with hiccups.

"I am your friend," Werner said. "I will listen if you wish to tell me."

I told him about Frau Ott's visit and her news of Faber's death. He interrupted me, assuming I had lost my husband, and tried to express his condolences. I could not keep up the pretence. I told him everything. I was killing our friendship, but I had to tell him. For once, the truth had to be spoken and believed. I knew Werner would believe me.

He did. More than that, he claimed he still wanted to be my friend.

I started crying again. When he asked what was wrong, I could barely speak past the tears to tell him that those words were the kindest I had heard since that terrible night. I'd long since stopped believing anyone cared about my fate. I knew then I was falling in love with him. We talked for a long time. He was horrified a family could turn away like mine had, and his dismay gave me strength. It made me love him more.

When he walked me home, he stopped at the gate and confessed he had been looking for me to tell me his news. His face seemed to change from sad and thoughtful to proud and back again. He took both my hands and told me his U-Boat was shipping out tomorrow at dawn. He knew it was too much to ask that I come down to Landungsbrücken to watch them sail past, but he hoped, if I was awake, that I'd wish them good sailing and happy hunting.

I had to swallow a surge of nausea. I shook my head and said, "All I can wish, Werner, is that you return."

Oh Hilde, watching Werner walk away was worse than facing Frau Ott. To find love, to find such a dear friend and lose him, all in the same day, is crushing.

15 May 43

You have to know I was at Landungsbrücken when the sun rose, Hilde. I was so afraid I would not wake in time that I was awake half the night. There was a cluster of women and a few older couples on the dock. I stood a short distance away and scanned the river, wondering if they would come from upriver or one of the side channels.

A woman approached me and asked if I was Werner's friend.

Her question surprised me. I nodded. In the dim light I studied her. She was seven or eight years older, tall and slim in a tailored skirt suit, the kind that was fashionable several years ago, when there was still enough material in supply to make fashion possible. She offered a gloved hand. "I am Tilli Gronwald. Actually Mathilde, but no one calls me that. My husband is Werner's captain. They served together on their previous U-Boat."

"You mean Werner's 'Number One?'" I asked.

"Yes, that was Klaus's rank before his promotion," She said. "My husband is happy to have Werner on his boat and always says he has the best ears in the fleet."

I smiled at her then and agreed he was a good listener.

She explained how Klaus is much like a father to his crew. He had made Werner tell him why he was upset when he returned to the boat yesterday. My story came out. Werner told his captain my baby's father had died and he was worried about leaving me alone.

Tilli offered to be my friend. She said she had not lived in Hamburg for very long either. She said we could wait together for our men, her husband and my friend. When she asked if I would like that, of course I said, "Yes."

She patted my arm and pointed upriver. "Here they come. The officers and some of the men are standing on the deck, bidding Hamburg farewell."

I wondered if Werner was an officer.

She laughed and explained that, yes, a radioman is always an officer, though of a lower rank. She added that he was one of the most important men on a U-Boat because without Werner's ears, Klaus was blind.

I puzzled over that remark but did not ask more. The sun was rising as the U-Boat glided past. Werner stood near the grey tower shaped like a large smokestack. He pointed and started waving, so I know he saw me. I waved back. The baby chose that moment to kick, as if also saying goodbye. I hope he comes back soon, Hilde. We have so much to talk about.

Chapter Twenty-Four

Mathias was twenty minutes late. In the shade of a tall linden tree, Del straddled a smooth-topped stone fence. She alternated between watching the trains on their elevated tracks, coming and going from Dammtor station, and eyeing the entrance to the university administration building that the fence surrounded. Mathias had a letter to drop off there, he'd said. Tomorrow was Cassandra's birthday. They still hadn't bought her anything and he had promised he'd go with her today.

The grey stone building, with a white porch supported by white pillars, red-tiled roof and central glass dome, looked old and dignified, with ivy covering one whole wing. Del wondered if Garda had walked by this building. She often mentioned Dammtor station in her diary.

Over the past two weeks, Del hadn't read as much of the diary as she had at first, maybe because after Werner left on the submarine, Garda slipped into a tedious existence of visiting Tilli, waiting to hear from Werner and fascination with the life growing inside her. Del needed to tell Luise that the May 1943 entries were boring. Not only that, but she'd need a history lesson to understand some of it. Garda kept putting in things like the Ruhr Valley being bombed so much – though Del could understand Garda's relief that her mother hadn't sent her there.

Fed up with waiting, Del swung her leg over and slid to the sidewalk. She'd been to Mathias's office once before; she'd drag him from behind his desk.

Del cut past a red brick hotel that was almost triangular, its blunted point banked with windows. Her pace quickened as she

passed other university buildings, some newer and blockish looking. A bicyclist zipped by. At least she now remembered to stay
on the foot path.

Head down, she turned a corner, walking faster still as she
neared the building that housed Mathias's office. She skirted a
tree at the foot of the stairs to the entrance and halted.

Mathias sat on a ledge beside the doors and a woman stood
near his knee. She was young enough to look great in a mini skirt,
with dark bobbed hair and dangly earrings. Her expression was
pouty and she licked her lips in such an obviously flirting way
that Del wanted to slap her. Mathias had the nerve to be smiling.
When she whispered something, he laughed.

Del clenched her fists. She stomped up the stairs and loudly
said, "Hey, Mathias. We're supposed to go shopping for your wife's
present." The woman jerked back and blushed. Del crossed her
arms. "Your wife. Remember her?"

The woman picked up a book bag and fled into the building.

"A student?" Del asked.

"Yes."

"You screwing her?"

"Del!" Mathias dropped to his feet. "*Schei* – That is... insulting. *Mein Gott.*"

"Are you?"

"No. She was trying to charm me into a better mark. No
harm."

"Yeah, right. Looked to me like you were enjoying it way too
much."

"We weren't even touching. Her attempt was so ... obvious,
that I found it funny."

"Should we ask Cassandra if it's funny?"

Mathias snatched up his briefcase and jogged down the stairs.

"Don't do that, Del. I've been your shield for weeks, reassuring Cassandra and pointing out how good you're doing. Do you know how upset she got when I told her you were having the odd beer? After all that you throw this one little thing in my face?"

Del had to take long strides to keep up. "How do I know it's little? She was coming on to you. How many other students do that? How many times have you given in?"

He stopped and grabbed her arm. "Never. But between how high-strung Cassandra's been since you came and your constant prodding, it's looking better all the time."

Del yanked free. "So you're going to screw around on my sister and blame it on me? That's great. I thought you were one of the good ones and now you start acting like Mom and Dad. What's with that?" She slapped at a tree branch, took two steps and spun around. "Maybe they're right. Maybe I'm a walking disaster." She cut across the road.

Mathias stopped on the curb. "Del! Where are you going?"

"Shopping for my sister's birthday. By myself." She walked backwards down the sidewalk. "Go make love to your wife, Mathias. Maybe it'll ease your conscience. Here's an idea: for her birthday, take her somewhere for the weekend. Away from me. That'll make you both happy." She headed to Dammtor.

For two hours Del roamed Europa Passage, not finding anything to buy. She wound up at the west end of the four-storey mall, in a leather chair in a bookstore overlooking the Binnenalster. The flow of pedestrians and traffic and tour boats weren't enough to distract her from nagging thoughts.

Was she stressing Cassandra's marriage, like she had their parents'? What was it that made her push so much? She didn't mean to. Words poured out sometimes with no more control than a river spilling its banks. She rarely regretted what she said because it was true, but she sometimes regretted the results. As destructive as a flood. She needed to be more like quiet Garda, keeping her thoughts to herself or writing them down instead of saying them.

Her cell phone rang. "James." She had gotten in the habit of answering the way many Germans did, only saying her last name.

"*Guten Tag*, James. I called the house but Cassandra said you were shopping."

"Hey, Altmann. I thought you were helping your dad today." Del wondered if Felix could hear her smile in her words.

"We're done. Some of us are going to a movie. Want to come?"

"Dubbed?" She couldn't stand dubbed movies – the words never matched the mouths and, being in German, she barely understood a single one.

"I talked them into going to one that is in English with German subtitles."

"In that case, you've got a deal."

"*Sehr gut*. Where are you?"

"Europa Passage."

"The cinema is close. I'll meet you at the entrance near the Rathausmarkt and we'll eat." They arranged a time. On her way out of the bookstore Del bought a gift card for Cassandra.

The movie was a typical summer blockbuster, with explosions, big guns and lots of skin. Del didn't pay much attention. She was mostly interested in the way her leg and Felix's were so close she could feel his warmth, and how when she rested her head on the back of the seat close to his shoulder, she could smell his spicy cologne. Whenever she moved, their arms or their legs would brush and a tiny charge of electricity would skitter up her limb. She wished he would put his arm around her, maybe pull her close like Max had with Monika. But he only nudged her once in a while and whispered, "Did you see that?"

Why couldn't he see she wanted to be more than friends? Or worse, maybe he saw but didn't want to act.

After, they walked several blocks to the Jungfernstieg U-Bahn stop, along the Alster canal for a block and past a guy urinating into the water. *Gross*, thought Del, but kept quiet because everyone ignored it. When they reached Dammtor station, the others decided to buy a beer and sit on the patio. Felix offered to escort Del when she said she should get home. As they were leaving, Felix's friends called out, "*Tschüss, Ananas. Tschüss, Kinderhüter.*"

When they were on the other side of the station, Del asked, "What does that mean?"

"I told you it means pineapple. Pay no attention. They give everyone nicknames."

"No, I mean what they call you." Del stuffed her hands in the pockets of her shorts to stop herself from what she really wanted, which was take Felix's hand.

"Maybe I do feel like having a beer. Hang on while I buy one." He slipped into a convenience store beside the main door that sold mostly soft drinks and candies, a few sandwiches and pastries. He emerged with two bottles. He handed her an *Orangensaftschorle*, and took a drink of his beer. When he lowered it, Del grabbed it, took a long drink and handed it back to him with a "thanks for asking" look. She opened her bubbly orange drink.

She asked. "Are you going to tell me your nickname?"

"*Kinder* means children." He scowled as he took another drink.

"They call you, what, childish?"

"Close enough. Come on. Let's get you home."

They talked about the movie and Felix regained his cheerfulness. She didn't care what Monika said, she thought Felix was hot. And nice. And fun. She'd confessed in an email to Serena that she really liked him. She didn't want to scare him away by being too out-front with her feelings, but if he were any more dense he'd be a slab of concrete.

Felix said good night at the gate. Del figured he was returning to hang with his friends. She would like to have stayed out longer but had decided Cassandra needed some consideration, especially after Mathias's behaviour earlier. Maybe he hadn't been doing anything, but he'd been smiling, which meant he might have been thinking about it.

Guys were such jerks sometimes. Except Felix. He'd never been anything but nice.

Mathias and Cassandra were curled up together on the black loveseat watching television. Del lay down on the burgundy loveseat and gave vague replies about the movie. They seemed more interested in each other than in Del's evening. Maybe Mathias had taken her advice.

"Guess what Mathias is giving me for my birthday?" Cassandra said. "He's taking me away for the weekend to Luebeck. Isn't that romantic?"

Del squinted at Mathias. She bit her tongue to keep from asking a sarcastic question about where he'd come up with that idea. "Sounds fun. What's a Luebeck?"

"It's a town northeast of Hamburg with a beautiful medieval *Aldstadt*, I mean old town. We've been there a few times. Our favourite hotel has a suite available. It'll be like our first anniversary." Cassandra kissed Mathias, then said, "The only thing we're worried about is you."

"I'm not a kid. I can handle a weekend by myself."

"We'd feel better about going if you ate your meals with Luise and always let her know where you are. We've asked and she's agreeable."

If she had to have a babysitter, at least she liked Luise. For Cassandra's sake, Del decided not to argue. "Sounds like it's settled. But what about that party the birthday girl is supposed to throw? Isn't that what Luise said the custom is?"

"We were planning that for next week anyway."

"Great." Del stood. "Good night."

Mathias caught up with her by her bedroom door. He whispered, "Are you still angry?"

She also kept her voice low. "You really do think you're hot stuff. I haven't thought about you all day. After all, it doesn't matter where you get your appetite, so long as you eat at home. Isn't that what they say?"

"You didn't seem to think that earlier."

"Earlier I'd just seen a chick in a mini wanting to lock her lips onto yours."

"I would never do that to Cassandra."

"Changed your mind, eh? Good." Del opened her door.

Mathias barred her from entering. "It works both ways, Del."

"What do you mean?"

"It would worry Cassandra and your parents if you got too involved with a guy here."

"Too involved?" Del laughed. When Mathias asked her what was funny, she replied, "You're talking about Felix. I can't even get him to peck me on the cheek. I don't think there's any worry about us getting *too involved*."

Chapter Twenty-Five

14 June 43

The doctor came today. He says I am healthy, even with reduced meat rations. This surprises him, but he does not know about Herr Wechsler's store of goods in the cellar. Rations keep getting reduced and reduced. Many people look worn out, and most of the children are now outside the city so there aren't many happy sounds of playing. People are silent and so tired. The raids aren't the least funny any more. We wake at the slightest sound, ready to flee into shelters. In the morning everyone has dark shadows under their eyes.

It's embarrassing how my stomach sticks out, Hilde. I am my own parade. My stomach leads the way and the baby is the drum corps. How that baby kicks and punches me. The doctor is happy about this, but he is not the one with bruised ribs.

It is hot again today. The sticky air sucks my energy. I wanted to visit Tilli, but Frau Wechsler let me use the telephone to call and tell her I will visit tomorrow instead.

evening

I am so upset. I walked into my room after my bath and found Frau Wechsler reading my older journal, the one that describes that awful night. She was very embarrassed at being caught and said it was an accident, that she was turning back my covers for me and bumped it off the shelf. I cannot bear the thought of her reading my private thoughts. I will mail the journal to Papa tomorrow and ask him to keep it hidden in his university office. As soon as this journal is full (it is getting very close), I will do the same with it. Until then I will find a hiding place in my bedroom for it.

15 June 43

I almost do not want to write today, Hilde.

I often walk to Tilli's. If I could swim it would be a short trip since her apartment is directly across the lake. Today I took the tram north to Winderhude, then another south to Uhlenhorst. Her district has a lot of apartments, but all the trees help it stay cooler, and I think they often have a breeze off the lake that we do not feel. Her apartment is on the second floor and those two flights of stairs tired me out. As soon as Tilli opened the door, I plopped into a chair beside the open window, greedy for a puff of wind. I made a loud "oof" when I landed. I fear a very pregnant woman plopping into anything is a dreadful sight.

Tilli was still wearing her air raid overalls, which surprised me. She was fidgety, pacing and playing with a pencil. She kept putting it to her mouth as if to smoke it. Rationing has forced many people to stop smoking and Tilli once confided that she was one of those.

Finally she sat down and told me she had visitors after she returned from her air raid shift this morning. Everyone has to do these shifts, even Herr and Frau Wechsler. I am exempt because of the pregnancy. She took two breaths then said, "The U-Boat is missing in action."

She might as well have been speaking Russian. I said, "What do you mean, missing?"

She took another big breath and spilled the story. Klaus's boat had been laying mines in a convoy route when he received a distress call from another U-Boat that was trying to harass a convoy. He answered the call, distracted the convoy escorts and allowed the other U-Boat to escape.

All I could think was that Werner would have been the one to hear that distress call. I asked, "But how does that make them missing? Surely they escaped."

Tilli chewed on the end of the pencil for a moment, then told me that the other captain saw Klaus take damage and lost contact with him after that.

I could not bear the thought that Werner had perished. I kept insisting they had escaped. She stood up with a stomp of her foot and snapped the pencil. "Stop it," she cried. "If they had escaped, they would have reported in. If the radio was damaged they would have fixed it and reported. There are only two possibilities. They sank or were taken prisoner."

I had nothing to say after that. If this heat does not suffocate me, I think sadness will.

Chapter Twenty-Six

Freedom. Del had almost forgotten what it felt like. Sure, Mathias and Cassandra had given her a longer leash, but she had to report every move. Now they were gone for the weekend and she was sailing. Riding, actually, since she wasn't doing anything. But she was in a sailboat, skimming across the Aussenalster, Felix at the rudder of their rented skiff. Del had hugged Luise when she had given them some money and told them to get out on the water.

The sails billowed as they zigzagged – Felix called it tacking. The hull sent a slight vibration across Del's skin; wind rifled her hair. She peeled off her T-shirt and lay back in her bikini top and shorts.

"Hey, James!" Felix called. Del propped herself up on her elbows, almost bumping the boom. He pointed. "You should be wearing your life jacket."

His gaze strayed to her mauve bikini top and lingered for a moment before he looked away. He had finally noticed she was a girl! She had been starting to wonder if he was gay, but maybe not. She smiled. "It's too nice out. I can swim."

"We could get fined."

"Then I'll pay it." Del lay back again. For once she was glad her figure was curvier than Cassandra's, and thankful Serena had made her buy this swimsuit.

Felix called out a warning and the boom swung above Del. The sails sagged, then puffed out again as the boat turned. Now they ran a straight course. "Come help," he called. She scrambled back and squeezed beside Felix on the starboard bench. The sailboat raced before the wind. Del leaned back and laughed.

When they docked, Del asked Felix to teach her how to sail but he claimed he only knew the basics. They separated after agreeing to meet later. He had something planned that involved his friends but wouldn't say what.

Impatient for the evening to come, Del went shopping and bought a camel-coloured jacket on a clearance rack. She loved the big outer pockets, wide belt and inner mickey pocket. Back at the house she modeled it for Luise.

"You might need that coat tonight. It's cooling off and the forecast is saying possible overnight rain," Luise said.

Del showered, changed into jeans and a scoop-necked tank top that she usually wore over a more modest tank. Tonight, she wanted a little cleavage. She took her time with makeup and hair, but still had more than an hour to wait until Felix arrived. The waiting was driving her crazy so she picked up the diary.

16 June 43

I felt so lost today that I had to go back to Tilli's. She looked like she had been crying a lot, but she also had a determined look. She asked me questions that seemed to hint at breaking rules. When she asked outright if I had ever done something not allowed, I confessed that I leave bread for that column of men I have come to think of as "my prisoners," though I do not know how long I can continue because Frau Wechsler is complaining I eat too much bread.

She pulled me over to her small table. Still holding my hands, she sat across from me, looking like an angel with the white kitchen tiles gleaming behind her. She whispered that she wanted to break the law.

I was shocked and said nothing.

"Will you report me?" she asked.

I replied, "Never. You know what I do. We will keep each other's secret."

She confided that she hoped I would join her. Then she told me her plan, and I agreed.

We closed her windows and drew the blinds – she was possibly a widow, after all, and this seemed a natural thing to do. Tilli got out a piece of wire that she had hidden in the springs of the sofa. She explained that Klaus had showed her how to insert the wire through the back panel of the wireless. The normal government-issued radio wouldn't pick up foreign broadcasts, but with the wire its range was boosted. Then we huddled in front of her wireless which sat on a lace doily on top of a low bookshelf. It was smaller than Herr Wechsler's, square with a round speaker that takes up almost all the front. Tilli turned it on and fiddled with the knob until she found the station she was looking for.

I hardly dare write this for it could send Tilli and me to prison, but I promised Papa to always write the truth. We listened to the BBC, Hilde. The British sometimes broadcast in German, trying to break our morale, our government says, so we are forbidden to listen. But what the government does not tell us is sometimes the British report the names of captured soldiers. I do not know where Tilli learned this.

We listened and listened, but heard no names. The announcer did say that names of prisoners would be read this evening, at eight o'clock. I could not stay that long, but promised to return in the morning and find out what Tilli learned.

17 June 43

I went to Tilli's today, as early as I dared. She had not heard the names she hoped to last night, but said that more would be announced this afternoon. We listened to the radio as much as we dared. The BBC today warned that people near factories helping the German war effort should evacuate. We discussed whether that means we are in danger. Hamburg, being a port, is always in some danger, but the shipyards on the other side of the Elbe River are quite far away. I used to be so fearful of the air raids. Now I am a little afraid, but mostly I am tired of having my sleep disrupted.

We walked to the grocer, but the line-ups were too long so we hurried back to the apartment. We only had to listen for a few minutes before the BBC started listing names. And then they said it! They named Klaus's U-Boat as having surrendered because of damage taken. We hugged and cried and tried to listen all at the same time.

They began naming the men taken captive from the U-Boat. My knees buckled when they said Werner Hoenig. I folded down to the floor and hugged my bulging stomach while tears of relief washed my cheeks.

But they never said, "Klaus Gronwald." I could find no way to comfort Tilli. The worst part was, when I was leaving I hugged her and stupidly said, "Thank you for letting me hear that Werner is alive. You and he are my best friends." She tried to smile but her face melted as she closed the door.

I feel terrible for being so happy when she is so devastated.

Chapter Twenty-Seven

Luise clasped her hands on her kitchen table. Evening light filtered through the window behind her, lighting the side of her face. "Would your sister approve of such an outing?"

Del gave an exaggerated shrug. "I don't know what Felix is talking about."

Felix slapped the table. "I'm talking about a Hamburg tradition. How can Del say she stayed in Hamburg for two months but never partied all Saturday night then went to the Fischmarkt first thing Sunday morning?"

"If Cassandra and Mathias were here to say yes –"

"But they're not." Felix leaned forward, his eyes as intense a green as Del had ever seen them. "Tante Luise, you know my friends are decent. Even Dad mostly likes them. This is the night they chose for our annual Fischmarkt party. I was out-voted. Wouldn't it be better for Del to party with a group of ten now than later in the summer with just me? Which would her sister and brother-in-law prefer?"

"That's an unfair question. You know they wouldn't let her party alone with one young man."

"Then it's settled." Felix sat back with a triumphant expression.

Luise turned to Del. "Do you think it's settled?"

A familiar clenching in Del's legs started as she tried to think what words might release her from this corner Luise had backed her into. She marshaled every shred of stay-cool attitude she could. "I think Mathias would let me go. And I think he'd talk Cassandra into agreeing." Under the table Del crossed her fingers.

"Surely you had Fischmarkt parties in your day, Tante Luise."
Felix switched to German.

Luise leaned back; her head bumped the wall by the window.
She stared at the light fixture for several moments. "You bring
her back sober and unharmed, Felix."

"Yes!" Felix punched the air and tapped Del's arm. "Let's go
before she changes her mind."

As they left, Del said, "*Danke*, Luise." Outside, Del belted her
new coat against the growing evening chill. "What did you say
to change her mind?"

Felix vaulted the gate and waited while Del went through the
conventional way. "I reminded her a person is only young once."
He winked. "And promised she could beat me if anything happened."

Del linked her arm with his. "You're the best, Felix."

He flashed her a shy smile. Del's stomach clenched, but in a
delicious way. Best of all, he didn't pull away from her touch.
Tonight, she thought, might be better than sailing.

They met up with the others in Dammtor station and headed
southwest to the Altona district. Max and Monika led the way
into a dance club like royalty leading their entourage. Jan trailed
behind Monika. Erik and Paul, neither of whom ever spoke to
Del and got defensive when pushed to speak English, followed
with two girls Del hadn't met. The bouncer pointed them to a
free table. They danced or watched people dance; the music was
too loud to try talking. Del returned from the dance floor with
Jan to find Max had bought a round of beer for everyone. It was
hot in the club and Del had long since shed her jacket. She drank
down half her beer in one go.

Two hours later they left when guys at a nearby table started
getting rowdy. Max knew of another dance club close by so they

tramped through drizzle, Eric and Paul singing beer hall songs. When Felix asked if she was having fun, Del readily agreed. The next club was just as crowded. They claimed a corner and a few chairs, but couldn't get a table. It didn't matter to Del since she spent most of her time dancing. A lot of the songs were techno-pop, which Del didn't really like, but the beat kept her on her feet and having fun. Jan started asking her to dance more often. She usually said yes. Felix didn't seem to dance much at all.

The heat and the beers – she had lost track of the number – added up to a pleasant buzz. The dance floor was packed. Del was dancing with Jan, who was flushed. When he placed his hands on her hips and made awkward grinding movements she decided he was drunk. Felix, Del saw, watched them with a frown.

Jan slipped his hands around to the small of her back and pulled her close. They bumped noses. The situation made her stomach start to churn – it recalled the time she snuck out of the house to go to a rave. A crowded dance floor. A guy with roaming hands. But she'd been high and had laughed. Bodies pressing. The high soaring higher. It had seemed dream-like when he'd led her outside to a camper van; losing her virginity to a stranger in a parking lot, her high had dived into emptiness. She'd avoided drugs since then, and had kept her distance from guys until Geoff. Now he'd vanished, proving that her dad had probably been right: what had been special for her had just been sex for him.

Jan's hands felt clammy. It was all Del could do to not knock them away. The music changed to a slow ballad and Jan's smile widened. Del put her hands on his chest. "I promised Felix the next dance." She dodged around another couple and grabbed Felix's hand. "Dance with me." She pulled him onto the floor and wrapped her hands around his neck before he could resist. She smiled. "Thank you."

His cheeks were pink. "For what?"

"For saving me from Jan. I'm sure he was going to maul me."

"You seemed to be enjoying it."

"I like dancing. I don't like being mauled." But she did love the way their bodies were swaying together now, even if Felix was keeping a little distance. She liked the weight of his hands, halfway between bra strap and waist. "This is nice."

He looked like he wanted to agree, but couldn't bring himself to. By now she knew he was shy around girls when it came to dating. Maybe Monika's put-downs had done their job. She decided to enjoy the moment, rested her head against his shoulder so she was staring at his ear and his bobbing Adam's apple. He smelled of beer and that spicy cologne he liked.

They left the club at four o'clock. Some guys in front of them starting hooting and shouting something about the Reeperbahn. Del asked no one in particular, "What is that Reeperbahn place? I've seen signs and postcards with, like, Las Vegas showgirls on them."

"Ha!" Max turned and walked backwards, his grin plastered across his face. "You can't go there, little Ananas. Too adult."

"What? Bars and stuff?"

"Ho, ho. No, no. Naked women. And sex shows." He said it, *zzzex*, and punctuated it with a bump of his hips. He started laughing and stumbled as he turned. Monika caught him.

"You mean porn flicks."

Felix replied, "Some, yes. But live shows, too. And prostitutes."

"That I can skip. Easily." Del swung around a lamppost and grabbed Felix's arm. The fresh air had hit her and she thought she might be a little drunk. "Where to?"

Felix replied, "The *Fischmarkt*. There are a few bars we can sneak into until the market opens in an hour."

They took the *S-Bahn* from Altona to the next stop. It was an underground stretch and the car they boarded stank like vomit. Del had to fight the urge to do the same and was gasping for air when they left the underground. Del felt better when they reached a stone bridge overlooking the Fischmarkt. The vendors were setting up in a T-intersection running along the waterfront.

The group descended to the lower street and headed for the intersection where Irish music pumped out of a corner pub in a taller brick building. People had to squeeze sideways to get in or out. The group crossed to a low brick hall with a wrought-iron dome. Two steps in the door Del was hammered by the music and stench of beer and smoke. She dashed outside, around some clothing stalls, and made her way along the side of the hall to the edge of the wharf. She leaned on a wooden piling, fighting wooziness and swallowing bile.

Felix appeared at her side. "Hey, James. You still with us?"

Del mumbled, "Thought I was pretty sober."

"Going to, what is the word? *Erbrechen*." He made a *blarg* sound and motioned something coming from his mouth.

Del groaned and pressed her forehead to the metal cap on the piling. "Don't. Do. That."

"Sorry." Felix helped her sit and lean against the post. He crouched beside her looking more amused than sorry. "You kept pace. I thought you'd give out before three."

Eyes closed to fight the dizziness, Del replied, "Not my first all-nighter."

"Your parents let you party all night?"

"Never."

"Oh." He chuckled uncertainly. "So they'll be angry about this?"

"Cassandra won't tell. She'd never say anything to worry

them." Del opened her eyes and searched Felix's features in the growing light. Soon the streetlights would go off and the night would be over and he'd go back to being nothing more than friendly. Del suddenly knew she had to kiss him, before the night ended and she sobered up. It might be her only chance. She motioned him closer. When he was less than an arm's length away, curiosity curving his eyebrows, Del hooked her hand behind his neck and drew him forward.

Their lips touched. For a few seconds he responded to the movement of Del's mouth and their breaths mingled. Del's tongue darted along his bottom lip. He withdrew, standing before Del could pull him back. He rubbed his nose and frowned at a container ship drifting by. "You're drunk. I should get you back."

Del squeezed her eyes shut and whispered, "Yeah."

"Felix, there you are," Max shouted from the alley beside the brick hall. "Stalls soon will open. Almost time for *wurst!*"

"What's that?" Del asked.

"Sausage."

Del blanched and turned her head away. The pewter light rippled on the water the same way her stomach was quivering. The river seemed to chuckle at her pathetic condition.

"No *wurst* for me," Felix said. "I'm going to take Del home. She's a little green."

Max stopped beside Felix and shook his head. "Monika said you'd do this. Your loss, *Kinderhüter.*" He patted Del's shoulder. "Go sleep it off, little *Ananas.*"

Chapter Twenty-Eight

23 June 43

I am so upset, Hilde. The telephone rang in the evening and Herr Wechsler called me from the kitchen and held out the handset to me. I thought it must be Tilli, but when I took the call, it turned out to be Frau Ott. She said she still wants me to move back and live with her so her grandson can be born in his home.

I hung up on her. And when the telephone rang again, I refused to take the call.

25 June 43

Those poor people in the Ruhr Valley and the Rhineland are being bombed in the daytime now. How awful that must be. On the radio it said that the damage is beyond imagination. I hope the Rhineland does not include Heidelberg, which is so close to the Rhine. Poor Papa would not know how to cope in an air raid. I will write to him on Sunday.

Tilli has received official word from the U-Boat command that Klaus's boat was captured. But they do not know his fate and assume that he was killed. She told me I can write to Werner through the Red Cross. I hope the letter does not take long to reach him. I wish I knew where he was imprisoned, but at least I know he will come home after the war, which is more than Tilli can hope.

29 June 43

It is hard to visit Tilli these days. She is despondent. She has been talking about moving to live with a cousin in Lueneberg southeast of Hamburg. But she has promised she will wait until the baby is born since, she said, she almost feels like an aunt.

She became very melancholy when I told her that the Wechslers are going to adopt the baby. She said, "Then we will both be alone."

Since she said that, the baby has been a lump of unhappiness pushing at my ribs and making it hard to breathe. I wanted to tell her she was wrong, that I have Papa. But do I? He hardly writes and when he does it is to talk about his university classes or the news. His letters read as if I am some distant colleague, not his daughter. Maybe that makes it easier for him, but it makes me feel like I am nothing to him. If only he would ask how I am doing.

Maybe I do have no one. I have been trying to imagine returning to Heidelberg after this baby is born, and I cannot. I would be a constant reminder of my family's shame. And I might never hear from Werner or get the chance to tell him I love him. In my mind, I made him into this wonderful friend but he might not even answer my letters. Will he think I am pathetic, writing every other day? Frau Wechsler certainly thinks so.

Other than writing Werner, my only enjoyment these hot, horrible days have been my morning walks and feeling the baby move. I try to guess if it is the baby's elbow or knee or foot pushing against my ribs; is the big lump the baby's head or bum? There is nothing of Faber in this baby. I can almost pity him now, dead in a Russian grave, except when my thoughts jump back to that night. I wonder if I will ever forget. Will I be doomed to relive it in my dreams when I least expect it?

Though all Del did was nap and read diary entries all Sunday, she was asleep when Mathias and Cassandra returned from Luebeck. The next morning she felt much better. She heard Cassandra in the shower, so she jotted on the message board that she was going to the bakery.

When she got back, Cassandra was sitting on Del's bed with her clothes hamper beside it and the contents of Del's backpack spread across the turquoise duvet. Del stepped back into the hall-way and squeezed her fists. She worked at breathing evenly. Slowly.

Below, a door slammed. Footsteps ascended the stairs two at a time. Mathias called out a greeting and Del spoke through clenched teeth. "She's in there."

Mathias edged past Del into her bedroom. "What's the emergency, Cassandra? Today is my summer class's final exam. I don't like leaving it in the hands of my assistant."

Arms crossed, Del followed Mathias into the room.

Cassandra tossed one of Del's tank tops from the hamper to Mathias. "Smell."

Del's breath hitched. It was the top she'd worn on Saturday night. Mathias wrinkled his nose and dropped the shirt back into the hamper. "It reeks of beer." The look he sent Del was one of disappointment.

"That's not all," Cassandra said. She opened her left hand to show Mathias three condom packages. Her hand shook as she extended it toward him. "Look! This is what she does when we leave her alone!"

Del's control broke. "That is so unfair. So freaking unfair."

She ran down the hall and the stairs, slammed the front door and charged up the sidewalk. She ran into the locked gate and folded over it. She held onto the gate. Every fibre wanted to leap it and run and not come back. She closed her eyes and whispered, "Stay. Stay. Stay."

She released her grip and marched back inside. Cassandra and Mathias were at their kitchen table, the condoms between them, a stark accusation. Del closed the kitchen door and leaned on it. "Thanks for asking before you jumped to conclusions, Cass. I appreciate you making me feel at home. No reason to miss Mom and Dad."

Cassandra's face pinched tighter. Mathias said, "What are we supposed to think, Del?"

"For one, you're supposed to treat me with courtesy. Isn't that the Golden Rule of the Fedder household? How is it courteous to search my bag without asking, when I'm not around?"

"Fair enough. I apologize for discourtesy on our part. Now please explain the condoms."

"Well, they're these nifty little devices –"

"Del." Mathias raised his hand. "No sarcasm. Why are there condoms in your bag?"

Lips pressed together, Del raised her gaze to the chrome light fixture. When Mathias repeated her name, she said, "It was a joke. Serena came over the night before I left and stuffed them in my bag, saying I needed to be prepared in case I met a sexy German guy."

"How many did she put in your bag?" Cassandra asked. "Three? More?"

Del scowled at the three packets on the table. She had to bite down on the word tipping her tongue that described her sister right now. "You know, for someone so pretty, you sure can be ugly sometimes." The expressions that shadowed Cassandra's and Mathias's faces told Del she should have bitten her tongue off. She said, "There were only three. I haven't gotten *too involved* with anyone." She gave Mathias a pointed look.

He poured two cups of coffee, set one in front of Cassandra, scooped up the condoms and threw them in the garbage. Del wanted to ask if he was sure that was such a good idea, given how little they trusted her. When he simply stood behind Cassandra's chair, sipping his coffee, Del asked, "Interrogation over?"

"No," Cassandra snapped. "Explain the shirt. And your jeans actually smelled worse."

Del considered lying but she knew that, if asked, Luise would tell the truth. "I went out with Felix and his friends on Saturday night."

"Out where?" Cassandra's voice had a slightly shrill quality to it. Mathias rested his free hand on her shoulder.

Del's neck ached painfully, as if caught in a vise. She rubbed it. "A couple dance clubs."

The questions came rapid-fire until Del had told everything. She didn't know how many beers she'd had and one had partly spilled on her. She'd been dancing and thirsty and had drunk what was offered. When she said it had been the group's all-night Fischmarkt party, Mathias's mouth twitched, but his tone stayed grave. "You were drunk when you got back."

Del tried to sound casual. "By that time, hungover would be a better word."

Cassandra was vibrating. Mathias looked to be holding her in her seat. He said, "You know what that means."

"Yeah. It means that all day yesterday I felt like, what's the German word? *Scheisse.*"

He set his coffee cup on the table and gripped both Cassandra's shoulders and massaged lightly. "We had this talk, Del. I told you if you ever came home drunk that I'd be the one grounding you. I want you to bring us the bank card, the mobile and your transit pass."

"No freaking way. You can't do that."

"Now, Del."

"I'm not going back to living in a freaking prison. No. Way."

"It isn't your decision. Breaking agreed-upon rules has consequences."

"So says Warden Fedder."

Cassandra pushed her chair back, making Mathias jump to the side. She pointed a stiff finger at Del. "I've had it with this prison talk. We're going for a drive."

Del swatted down the finger. "Good."

"You'll see what prison means."

"What? You're going to drop me off at a jail? Is there one for teens nearby? That'd make your job easier, wouldn't it? You could report to Mom and Dad that, so sorry, I'm tied up at the moment, but I'm doing fine. Following the rules and looking so cute in my grey overalls."

"Shut up!" Cassandra slapped Del across the face.

It surprised Del so much she didn't move. *Okay*, she thought. *Maybe I pushed too far.* Hand on her stinging cheek, Del opened the door. "Let's drive then. Anything is better than being stuck here with you."

Fifteen minutes later Del decided the car was the worst place to be. It was claustrophobic. Between the misery pushing out from deep inside and the tension rolling off Cassandra to pin Del against the back seat, she could barely breathe. She cracked open the window. It didn't help. She was still trapped in a rolling cage. At least no one was talking, lecturing her when she couldn't get away. But the silence screamed so loud it hurt.

One gram of trust. Was that too much to ask for? Sure she had gone out with Felix and his friends but she hadn't gotten into trouble. She hadn't done anything really stupid.

The blur outside became greener as they left the city. Maybe they *were* taking her to a teen jail. Anxiety wrapped around her limbs so tightly it felt like her circulation was being cut off. Del shrank into the corner of the back seat and closed her eyes against a thrumming ache.

Del woke up when the car stopped. She rubbed her neck to massage a knot.

Cassandra said, "You take her, Mathias. Please. I'll wait by the House of Remembrance."

Mathias sighed and got out. Cassandra slid over the gear shift into the driver's seat and stared ahead with a white-knuckled grip on the wheel. Mathias motioned for Del to come.

Del watched the car retreat down the tree-lined road. "Why'd she make such a big deal about coming here, then take off like that? Where is here, anyway?" At least it didn't look like a teen jail. They were in a lush park hemmed with trees and a scattering of buildings, surrounded by farmers' fields and quiet. Almost deserted.

"I think she knows she couldn't handle it today, not when she's already so upset." He swept his arm to the side. "Welcome to Neuengamme Concentration Camp."

"Never heard of it. You're talking World War Two? Was this a... killing camp?"

"People died here. It wasn't a death camp like Auschwitz, if that's what you mean. More a slave labour camp. Not a big one, but still over 100,000 prisoners came through the gates."

The prisoners Garda had mentioned in her journal came to mind. "Were any of them sent to work in Hamburg?"

"Many."

"Did many of them die?"

"Over half." Mathias started walking down a path with long rectangular beds of broken brick and stone on either side. He pointed left. "Those rocks mark where the prisoner barracks were. The one barrack still standing at the far end has museum exhibits in it." He didn't slow down, just pointed to the right. "Those were sick bays. The lone rock pile behind them was the brothel where women were forced into prostitution for the guards. Ahead on the right is where prisoners were deloused. At the end on the right was the bunker – solitary confinement."

Mathias fell silent. He was practically speed walking; Del jogged to keep up. He turned right, passed the bunker's foundation and a line of trees, and halted before a plaque beside another bed of stones. "All that's left of the crematorium."

Del avoided looking at the spot where bodies had been burned. She peered at the complex of low brick buildings behind Mathias. No one was in sight. The lushness of the grass and trees, the palpable peacefulness of the park, contrasted starkly with what this place had been. Del doubted that it had looked beautiful back then. The contradiction of past and present left her with an eerie tingle crawling over her skin. She shivered. "You really know this place."

"Sometimes I bring students. It inspires amazing responsive essays." Mathias pointed to his left, away from any buildings. "You might want to look at the train wagon."

Del obediently trudged across the grass to a reddish-brown train car sitting on a truncated length of rusty track. It looked like there were people standing in the open doorway, but as Del got closer she saw it was a black-and-white painting of gaunt prisoners in striped uniforms. A small window in the upper left was also filled with a painting, this one of faces peering out. In front of the cattle car was a concrete pad inset with all sizes of boot prints. She sat cross-legged on the pad and ran her fingers over the indentations. Garda's words about hearing voices in the night at a train station came to mind. Voices asking for water. Voices ordered to silence. She studied those painted, despairing faces. Tears pressed against her eyes and gathered above her lashes but didn't fall.

Mathias crouched beside her. "Freedom is a funny thing. Now we think a few days' grounding is a punishment so awful that our world is ending. But here, in a time not long ago, freedom did end. For so many. I find it hard, sometimes, fathoming the things that happened in my country under Nazi rule. It scares me to think what I might have done if I had lived then."

Del wiped her eyes with the back of her hand. "But it was so long ago. Who cares?"

"People still live who survived that war. People in Canada and here in Germany. Six or seven decades is not long in a place filled with centuries of human history. Like the dirty fellow in Charlie Brown cartoons. Have you seen him? He carries the dust of centuries. Here in Europe we breathe that dust. We all need to care, Del. That's why I bring my students." He laid his hand inside a large boot print. "That short period of Nazi rule haunts us. We want to put it behind us, but its spectre refuses to be banished. How do we outlive the shame and horror of what our people did? Why do *we*, who weren't even born then, have to live with it at all? But we must remember. It was so horrifically methodical, so carefully planned..."

Del stiffened. Her sister was a master planner. "Is that why it bugs Cass?"

"Perhaps. Though I think it's more the staggering number of people killed altogether."

Del hesitated. "Is the lesson over, Professor?"

Mathias's small smile didn't reach his eyes. "Would you like to see the mound where executions were carried out?"

"No!"

"The factories where prisoners laboured as slaves or the canal so many died to build?"

She shook her head.

"Very well. But I want to take you to the remaining prisoner barrack. The second floor has exhibits of prison life and small histories of some people who were imprisoned here."

"Do I have to?"

"For a few minutes, at least. History becomes more real if you have before you faces and names of people who lived it."

Del knew that. She already had a face and a name. Quiet

Garda, who snuck bread to prisoners and was, in her own way, a prisoner, punished for being the victim of a crime. She stood and brushed off her jeans, then gave Mathias a long hug.

He stepped back and gripped her upper arms. "What was that for?"

"I'm hoping you meant it when you said just 'a few days' grounding."

He laughed, threw his arm across her shoulders and guided her back across the grass.

14 July 43

I had mail yesterday. Papa has sent me a new journal. I was so excited I slept with it under my pillow. I have three pages left in this one but will mail it to him right away anyway. It has too many things written in it that I don't want to Frau Wechsler to see if she finds it.

It is so dry, so hot. The only time I go outside is for my dawn walk, and then I do not go far. I only see my column of prisoners two or three times a week, and it is getting harder to sneak food to them. When pressed, I told Frau Wechsler that I take bread to feed the ducks at the ponds in *Planten Un Blomen*. She thinks it is foolish given the food rationing, but said she will humour me. She makes me lie down in the afternoons. My feet are swollen by then. She props them up and plies me with cool water. I appreciate that.

I want this to be over! My belly is so big I can barely get up without help. My back often hurts. Even the baby moving, which I enjoyed so much, has become painful. It pushes so hard some days that I think my ribs are going to crack or my stomach split open. But when I think about giving birth, about getting this huge baby out of me, it makes me tremble.

Herr Wechsler frowns at me a lot. I did not understand why until last night at the dinner table. The baby kicked suddenly. I gasped and pushed at my stomach to ease the pain of it. He told me to leave the table, which suited me because I had terrible indigestion. As I left the room he said, "You had better be growing me a son."

That is what is bothering him, Hilde. Frau Wechsler's friends and neighbours all cluck over me and say that I am carrying the baby like it is a girl. She reports these predictions to her husband. It has made him unbearably grumpy. He drinks every night now and Frau Wechsler often has to help him up to bed. I hear them going past my door and he is often muttering about wanting a son. What will he do if he doesn't get one?

20 July 43

I found a pamphlet caught in a shrub today. It was in German but claimed to be from the British. It was terrible, Hilde. It said we have a few weeks, then it will be our turn. It said we have peace now, but then it will be eternal peace. I showed it to Frau Wechsler and she tore it up. Someone playing a cruel prank, she said, but I am not so sure. There were other pamphlets scattered around and who in Hamburg has that much ink and paper to spare?

We no longer try to sleep in our own beds but have mattresses in the cellar, our air raid shelter. There are several cellars deep enough on this block so we do not have to share. But cousin Ilsa shows up every evening. She despises the people in her apartment building so prefers to share our shelter. Night after night the air raid sirens go off. We hear airplanes high overhead, but nothing happens. I cannot understand it. Herr Wechsler says it has been discussed all over town and everyone agrees the British will want to capture Hamburg intact so that they can have the harbour. But it is still frightening to listen to the airplanes and wait and wait, wondering, always wondering, if this is the night bombs will fall.

Chapter Twenty-Nine

Grounding was an ugly word. Things are ground underfoot, crushed, flattened. Okay, so Del wasn't being crushed, but it felt like it when her gut twisted and knotted until it squeezed away her appetite. She kept telling herself that it had only been two days. She could handle it. She wasn't actually confined to her room; she had access to the house and yard.

But freedom was on the other side of the fence.

She sat on the deck. The evening was cooling off and she wore her new coat. She didn't want to be inside. At least out here she could breathe that tangy air and she could smell Luise's garden. The last pages of Garda's journal were on her lap but she couldn't focus. She searched the lavender sky, the same sky Garda had feared might fill with airplanes and bombs. Part of her didn't want to find out if those bombs ever fell. "I have a bad feeling about this," she muttered, and wondered what movie that line had come from.

Del heard voices and stuffed the papers into the mickey pocket of her jacket as Mathias spoke in German, unlatched the door to the deck and stepped outside. Felix followed him.

She hadn't seen Felix since Sunday. His shoulders were slumped and he only glanced in her direction. He slouched in a chair and rubbed his thighs. Del watched the long fingers slide over denim and forced her eyes up. Even tired as he looked her breath still hitched at the sight of him. She suspected she was falling in love. It was so different from what she'd felt with Geoff. From the start he'd been so physical, sweeping her away with sensations. With Felix it was about who he was, how nice he was, how considerate and how fun.

Del knew what he was going to say. He studied his hands. "I feel responsible for what happened on the weekend." A quick glance at Mathias, then down.

Cassandra had appeared in the doorway, arms crossed, lips pursed. Del prayed she'd keep quiet. Mathias replied, "Why? Did you force beer down Del's throat?"

Felix frowned at his open palms. "No. But... I didn't keep track of how much anyone was drinking. We all drank too much. I should've paid attention. But it was just beer. Just..." He leaned forward and clasped his hands. "I'm sorry."

"I admit I'm disappointed you didn't watch out for Del. But you are not responsible for how much she drank. She knew our expectations. She was the one who stepped out of line. Thank you for your concern."

Felix didn't respond, didn't move. Del loved that he had tried to take responsibility for her screw up. She never tired of watching him. He was slender, but his shoulders tapered nicely to his hips and leaning forward like this, head down, emphasized the width of his shoulders. She wanted to massage them, to ease the tension there. Any excuse to touch him.

Mathias cleared his throat. "Was there something else, Felix?"

He nodded and Del saw the effort it took to straighten and meet Mathias's gaze. "I know I have no right to ask, but..." He licked his lips. "Some of us are going to *Planten un Blomen* tonight and I was hoping that you'd let Del go." His words tumbled out quickly. "We're going to watch the light show. That's all. No beer. No dancing. Just the light show and back."

Cassandra's face was stamped with disapproval; she exchanged looks with Mathias, then shrugged and looked down. She hadn't vetoed the idea. Del brightened.

Felix said, "Please, let me prove you can trust me. If you even wanted to follow us..." Air leaked out of him and his shoulders sank.

Mathias said, "I thought we should take Del to the light show one night. I'm sure she would rather see it with a friend than an ogre brother-in-law. It might be okay."

Del jumped up. "Really? You mean I'm not grounded any more?"

"You were going shopping with your sister tomorrow, anyway." Del thought but didn't say that shopping with Cassandra was almost a punishment because they shopped so differently, but she'd agreed because it meant getting out of the house. Mathias continued, "You've worked hard at behaving yourself and being helpful since Monday. I think you've earned this reprieve. Would you agree, Cassandra?"

She could squash the plan with a single word. Del bit her lip, expecting spiteful. Cassandra only looked thoughtful. "If you were not Professor Konrad's nephew and I didn't know that – I'm sure you won't repeat your mistake, Felix. I want Delora home by 11:30."

Felix gave them both a relieved smile. "*Sehr gut.* Yes, I'll do as you say."

Mathias returned Del's cellphone before they left. He still had her transit pass and bank card, so all she had in her wallet was twelve euros and change. She hoped the light show didn't cost much. At least she was out of the house.

Planten un Blomen was west of Dammtor station, past the tall Congress Centre's hotel. As the name suggested, it was a botanical garden which, Felix explained, had free water and light shows every night at ten o'clock in the summer. They met Felix's friends on the far side of a small lake where the show would take place. They were an hour early but already people were staking out spots on the lawn.

They settled on a blanket with Max and Monika. Felix passed

Del one of two colas he had purchased in Dammtor station. Monika laughed. "What is this? Our little *Ananas* can have beer no longer? So you aren't having either any, *Kinderhüter*? Such a good watchdog." She ruffled his hair. He jerked his head away.

"Stop calling him that," Del said.

Monika gave her a withering look and tossed her head. "Why? It's what he is."

"He's not childish. He's –"

"Childish? Is that vat he said *Kinderhüter* means? So funny." Monika smirked. "Childish in German is *kindisch*. Very closed to English, *ja?*"

Del waited for Felix to say something. He studied his cola with a blank expression. Del said, "Then what does it mean?"

Monika's smirk grew more smug. "Nanny. Or,… babysitter."

"He doesn't baby –" The meaning hit Del. She stood and rested hands against hips. "I'm no baby. He's not my sitter." She nudged Felix with her toe. "Tell them, Felix." No response.

Monika braced her arms behind her, striking a model's pose as she gazed up at Del. "*Babysitten, ja. Oder Ananas-sitten.*"

The guys on the grass beside Max laughed. One – Paul, Del thought; she could never keep him and Erik straight – said something about *Geld*. That meant money. Felix still hadn't moved. She nudged him again. "Tell them you aren't my babysitter, Felix. Don't sit there like a lump."

Monika laughed again. "Our Felix never for himself speaks up, do you, Felix? But here is nothing to say. Getting money to mind a child is babysitting. This is so in Canada also, yes?"

Money. *Geld*. Del's stomach dropped. She willed Felix to look up and, with his eyes if nothing else, deny what Monika was saying. He didn't move. Del took a step back. Another.

She wheeled around and ran.

Chapter Thirty

Down a wide path, under trees and past a row of square ponds, Del sprinted, not caring where she was going, only wanting to get away from Felix's laughing friends. Felix was somewhere behind, calling her name. Instead of slowing, she dropped her pop bottle and pumped her arms and legs for all she was worth. She burst out of the park. The television tower loomed across the street. She veered right.

She tore across a bridge that spanned the train tracks. Felix was still behind her, still calling. An intersection. People crossed to the left. She bolted across the street as the pedestrian sign counted down. 4. 3. 2. 1. The light changed when she was two steps from the sidewalk.

Winded, she stumbled off the road and turned to see Felix on the other side of swiftly flowing traffic, his hands held high as if in supplication. Hand against her side, she jogged off to the right. She took the first left down a tree-lined street. In places shadows spilled onto the road, creating pools of darkness. Del picked up her pace, but she was wearing down. How far had she come? A few blocks maybe. Not far enough.

Her name rose faintly above the intermittent traffic. She glanced back to see Felix jogging under a streetlight. She tried to speed up, but couldn't manage more than a jog. Then she spotted a blue sign with a white "U" less than a block away. Adrenaline kicked in and she raced that final block, stumbled down the steps of the U-Bahn and onto a tiled platform. A train was pulling into the station and she lunged into it, grabbing the pole near the doors to keep from falling. She clung to it and watched the stairs. Air heaved in and out.

How could Felix do that do her? Who had paid him? Cassandra? The thought made her feel like slime was oozing over her skin.

Felix came running down the stairs. The warning beeps sounded and the doors on the train closed as he reached the edge of the platform. He looked right at her, and cried, "*Scheisse*." She flashed her middle finger as the train pulled away.

Shaking legs would no longer hold her. She swung into the seat by the door and let her head fall against the window, then remembered she had no pass. Did the DB guards do checks at night? She needed to get off. Where was this train going?

A minute later the train pulled into a station called *Feldstrasse*. She thought *Feld* meant field. Germans, being quite literal so often, probably called it that because there was a field. A soccer field? Maybe not the best place to get off. She'd risk one more stop, then get off no matter where she was.

When she got off the train, the sign read *St. Pauli*. Which told Del nothing. Weary from her run, Del trudged up the stairs most of the passengers seemed to be using. She followed the crowd, not looking, not caring where they were going. Crossed a wide street. Walked for a block and suddenly leaned against a building, her energy spent. While she'd been running, escape had been the only thing on her mind. Now emotions tore at her. She felt like her guts were spilling onto the street and no one cared. It took several minutes for a tenuous calm to return.

People strolled by, laughing and pointing. Everyone seemed to be in a party mood. On a Wednesday night?

She started out again, looking around this time. The street stretched ahead of her with flashing marquees and brightly lit signs clogging the space above the sidewalks. It looked like that cheesy street near Niagara Falls she'd seen a few years ago, or a mini Las Vegas. Something twigged. She read some signs. S-S-E-X-X blinked rapidly. In her mind she heard Max laughing and saying, "*zzzex.*" She turned to the brightly lit window beside her. Gaped at the display – a female mannequin wearing a pink-and-black corset, and some sex toys. She stepped back, bumped into someone and apologized. They were already gone.

She'd heard the name of this street on Saturday night, but she couldn't remember what it was. Del hurried away from the window display, looking for a street sign or something to indicate where she was. Because she didn't want to be here, but didn't want to wind up somewhere worse.

She stopped at the next corner, her attention drawn by the four-storey brown building across from her. Massive illuminated letters, glowing white above the second floor said, *Polizei.* If she walked in and asked for directions back to Dammtor or Hauptbahnhof, they'd be able to help. Did she want to walk into a police station on a street specializing in sex shows and prostitution? That smaller building beside the police station, called St. Pauli-Theater – maybe it would have someone manning a box office who could help. The theatre wasn't gaudy and had no flashing signs. Maybe that meant it was a normal theatre, not an X-rated one.

While she waffled, the lights changed twice. *Reeperbahn*, a plain green-and-white sign on the post read. Only the double "ee" sounded like a long "a". Raper-bawn. What a place to be lost. Cassandra would have triple fits.

Forget asking anyone. How hard could it be to retrace her steps? The traffic lights changed again. Del spun away and barreled into a dark blue uniform.

Polizei. The police officer steadied Del and peered down at her. "*Haben sie sich verirrt?* "

Del felt a puzzled frown descend. She hated not understanding. It hadn't been a problem when she was with Felix. But now...

The officer had sounded irritated before. He spoke again, now sounding angry. Mouth dry, Del lifted her shoulders. The officer took her by the arm and turned her around so she faced the police station. He didn't release her, just continued a stream of German as he pointed, tapped her shoulder and pointed again. The traffic light changed. He piloted her across the street.

Del suddenly realized he was arresting her. Her throat locked tight. Fear iced all her thoughts except one: run! She jerked her arm. The officer's hold only tightened as he continued to drag her toward the police station, which now hovered over her like a gothic palace of horrors.

Chapter Thirty-One

Tears started to drip down Del's cheeks. She was being arrested and she didn't even know what she'd done. The police officer pulled her onto the curb. They were only metres from the entrance to the police station. Panic jolted through her limbs in micro-bursts.

"*Nein. Bitte. Nein.* " Del said the only German words that came to mind. Her plea didn't slow the officer. "Please, don't. What did I do wrong? I don't know what I did!"

The officer faced her, hand still manacled to her upper arm. "*Americkanisch?* "

Del repeated the word silently. "Not American. Canadian."

"*Kommen sie aus Kanada?* "

Del nodded frantically. "Yes. Canada. I'm from Canada."

"*Sind sie allein?* "

What did *allein* mean? Del lifted her shoulders helplessly. The officer's expression closed down again. Did he think she could understand him? How did she tell him otherwise? Felix had taught her this. "*Sss... Speck* English?"

The officer blinked. "*Speck?* "

Felix yelled from across the street. The light changed and he raced across the road.

Del exhaled with relief. "Felix! I'm so glad –" The officer's grip tightened even more. "Ouch. Felix, he's arresting me. I don't know what I did and he doesn't seem to speak English."

Slightly out of breath, Felix began talking with the officer. Words bounced back and forth and all around Del. Words that meant nothing to her. But the officer's grip was loosening. Her lower arm began to tingle.

Felix laughed. Del scowled at him. This wasn't funny. But his laugh was like a key that unlocked the officer's hold on her. She rubbed her arm. The officer nodded to her and spoke, though the only word she caught was, *Entshuldigung*. Sorry. Then he said something else and walked away, quickly becoming a dark silhouette outlined by the neon glare of the street. Del watched him go and asked, "Why did you laugh?"

"Apparently you asked him for English bacon."

"What?"

"He said he asked if you were alone. You said, *Speck* English. Literally, bacon English."

"I was trying to ask if he spoke English."

Felix smirked. "That's what I thought. The word you wanted is *sprechen*."

"What else did he say?"

"He wasn't arresting you. He was taking you to the police station to question you. He thought you seemed too young to be here alone at night."

Young. So young she needed a babysitter. The hurt came rushing back, overriding her relief. "Right. So how did my faithful babysitter find me?"

Felix rolled his eyes. "*Scheisse*. Give me a break, Del. You're a fast runner when you want to be, you know that? I thought my lungs would burst and still you escaped. I found you by luck. Pure luck. I jumped on the next train and when I saw the St. Pauli sign, I had a feeling you were headed to Reeperbahn. I guessed right."

Del looked around. "I wasn't headed anywhere. I want to get out of here."

"*Klar!* This way."

They walked past St. Pauli-Theater and quickly left the sizzle and flash of Reeperbahn behind. When they reached a large intersection, Del pointed to a flood-lit statue on a rise. "Can we go there?" Felix led the way. The path up to the statue was bathed in light. They circled the monument and leaned against a stone balustrade to look up at the cloaked figure holding a sword that came to its chest. "Bismark," Felix said.

"A guy from the war?"

"The war? No. Before that. The 1870s. He was a prince who helped unite Germany."

Del had thought Felix was a modern prince, rescuing her from boredom and befriending her. He'd always been so nice; was still being nice. Could she have been so wrong? She faced him. "I thought you were my friend."

"I am."

"Really? How do I know?" The question she wanted to ask got stuck in her throat.

"I like spending time with you. You're fun."

"Did you like dancing with me?"

A smile tugged at one corner of his mouth. "*Klar.*"

"Which means...?"

"Sure."

Felix had sat on the edge of the stone wall. Del swung and planted herself between his knees. Uncertainty shadowed his face. "What are you doing, James?"

"You've been so dense, Altmann. Didn't it mean anything that I only danced slow dances with you on Saturday?" No response. "Did you ever think I'm settling for being your friend because that's all you seem to want?" His face became a white-board wiped clean of marks. "Do you know what I want to do, even when I'm pissed off with you?"

He didn't even twitch, just sat. Like he was a statue. *Fine,* she thought. *I'll get a reaction.* She framed his face with her hands and kissed him. He slid off the wall. Maybe he'd planned to sidestep, but Del flung her arms around his neck, pressed close and deep-ened the kiss. Like the flip of a switch, he was kissing her back. His hands skimmed up her back. Fingers reached her bra strap. Felix stopped kissing though he didn't pull back.

Del opened her eyes to see his, wide and clouded green. He wheeled away so suddenly she almost stumbled. He slapped the stone wall.

Del splayed her fingers over his shoulder blades. "Felix, it's okay. I wanted you to –"

"No! It's not okay. This is all wrong. I can't be doing this."

Del hauled him around to face her. "Why, Felix? Is it wrong because I'm not really a friend? I'm... a job?"

He touched his finger to her bottom lip. "I like you, James."

"Are you being paid to keep me company? Are you my babysitter?"

His lips were pressed together as he studied her upturned face. He looked past her shoulder. Del swore and marched away. Felix grabbed her wrist. "Don't run."

"Let go of me. I'm going home."

"Do you know how to get there?"

Del pulled free. "I'll figure it out."

She had to ask, but she managed. All the way, she ignored her escort tagging along ten or fifteen metres behind her. He melted into the shadows when she walked into Luise's house.

Chapter Thirty-Two

Sleep only came in fits and starts. Since she wasn't sleeping, Del rose early. She threw on clean jeans, sneakers, layered two of her favourite shirts and put on her new belted coat. Her movements were mechanical, her thoughts calm for the first time since leaving *Planten un Blomen*. She'd struggled all night to sort her feelings. The effort had left her numb.

She walked into the kitchen where Mathias and Cassandra were already eating breakfast. Her transit pass and bank card were on the table for her shopping trip with her sister. She stuffed them into her wallet and dropped it in her outer pocket.

"I've transferred money into your account for shopping," Cassandra said. "I'm surprised you're up so soon. How was the light show?"

"Illuminating." Del opened the camouflaged refrigerator and helped herself to a glass of orange juice. She downed it and banged the glass on the counter. "How much are you paying him?" She folded her arms and leaned against the sink.

"Paying who?"

"Felix, for babysitting me."

Unease crowded into the room. Mathias and Cassandra exchanged a look. What was it about married people that they didn't need to talk? Del tamped down her rising hurt and clung to the numbness. Better not to feel.

Mathias said, "We aren't paying Felix anything."

Del straightened. "Really. Your *meaningful look* says otherwise. You know something. Yesterday you mentioned being disappointed Felix hadn't watched out for me. Someone's paying him. Mom and Dad?"

Mathias became interested in his coffee. Cassandra said, "Don't be ridiculous. I haven't told Mom and Dad about you and Felix."

"There is no me and Felix, not when he's only hanging with me because –" Del slapped her forehead. "No way. I *trusted* her."

Del ran from the room, raced down the stairs and burst into Luise's kitchen. She was at her table – with Felix. He looked wiped. Just seeing him made the knife twist deeper. She ignored him. "It was you, wasn't it?"

Luise raised her eyebrows so high they tucked under her salt-and-pepper bangs. "I what?"

"You paid Felix to be my watch dog."

"Del, please. It isn't what you think."

The presence of Mathias and Cassandra filled the doorway behind Del. "And what do I think, Professor Konrad? Do you know? Or care? This whole month has been one big lie. You all knew about it. You all planned it. Laughed behind my back because I was happy. I thought I was being trusted. And all the time your, your spy was reporting back. Freaking, finking rat, making me feel like I had a friend. Like –"

"No," Luise said as she stood. "It's not like that. Felix needed a job and you needed a friend. I only thought –"

"That the only way I could get a friend is if you hired one for me. You said you like fixing things. You fixed this one great." Anguish pressed against her lungs.

Mathias touched her shoulder. "I think you're overreacting, Del."

She jerked away. "Don't touch me. You betrayed me. Every one of you in this room betrayed me. Do you have any idea how shitty that makes me feel? Any idea at all?" Tears slipped down her cheeks and she swiped at them.

Felix took two steps toward her, looking almost upset enough to cry, too. But he didn't. And he didn't speak. His usual reaction to uncomfortable situations. Del was sick of it. She pointed at him. "Won't you and your friends have a big laugh? Little *Ananas* thought she loved her *Kinderhüter*. What a joke." She turned toward the door. "This whole thing is a sick joke. And now you can all have your laughs because I'm out of here. It hurts too much to be near any of you. You're all total jerks."

She pushed past Cassandra and left. She didn't stop until she was at Hauptbahnhof.

Now what? She bought a cola and watched the arrival and departure sign change. A *train just left*, she thought. *I should be on it*. Like she could get anywhere with less than ten euros. She remembered the bank card. How much had Cassandra put in her account? They'd been going to shop for school clothes. At the *ReiseBank* machine, she requested four hundred euros. That didn't work so she tried a smaller amount, working down until she successfully withdrew two hundred and sixty euros. It filled her wallet so she pulled out the photocopy of her passport and slipped it into her mickey pocket with the rest of Garda's journal.

Still at a loss, Del drifted to the railing overlooking the tracks. All those people with places to go. Or homes to return to. She had neither. Had she ever felt so alone? She was used to not having family, but friends had been what got her through the day. Felix's deception was all the more painful because of it. She'd really thought he was a friend. Really thought there might be something more. He had kissed her back. Had wanted to touch her. But no good bodyguard gets involved with his assignment. Oh God, she felt so... cheap.

Her cellphone rang. She hadn't turned it off from last night. She pulled it out and switched it off without answering.

She continued to let the constant movement of the station

distract her. All the while she wondered what to do. Tiny sips of her cola helped it last almost an hour. She was tired of standing. She dropped the empty in a recycle bin and started to walk away.

English voices stopped her. A cluster of black clad, pierced and tattooed people – teens or slightly older – were arguing. She quietly returned to the railing beside them. They weren't just talking English – it was real England English.

"What do you mean, she took off with her bloke?"

"Just what I said, wanker. He's a student here. She left her tickets and scarpered with him. Said she'd rather spend the weekend making music than listening to it."

"Shite. Stupid bi-"

"Shut your mouth. She's my sister."

"We sprung for her ticket, didn't we, mate? You said she was good for it."

"Yeah," a girl interrupted the two guys who'd been talking. "And Sue was the one who knew where to go here. None of us have been to Hamburg. Where do we go now?"

"Don't be daft," the one with the disappeared sister said. "Someone in this place has to speak English." His gaze skimmed past the group, around the station and settled on Del. "What's this? Little German spy? Listening, weren't you?"

Dirty blond hair, a thin goatee, a ring through his nose – his shaggy, scrawny appearance, even if he was all in black, didn't seem threatening. Del smiled. "Yeah. I was listening."

He shoved his hands in a scuffed leather jacket. "Who for? CIA? You don't sound German."

"Canadian. And I don't think the CIA or anyone else gives a rat's ass what you're doing."

The other guy, a heavy-set version of the first, but with a red goatee, laughed. "Got you there, mate."

"Maybe. But you're curious, aren't you?"

Del replied, "Sure."

His lip curled. Del figured he thought he looked tough. He didn't quite pull it off. "Going to Wacken." Del felt her eyebrows curve into a question mark. He continued. "Wacken Open Air. Pissing big metal festival. Seventy bands. Three days."

"Yeah," the heavy-set one said. "And his sister buggered off without paying for her ticket. We're stuck with it."

Three days. Metal wasn't her first choice in music. She preferred a dance beat. But three days away from Hamburg. Del smiled. "I might buy it if you let me tag along."

"You do that and we'll throw in my sister's train ticket for free." The scruffy one smiled; a capped tooth winked at her.

"How much?"

"In euros? We'll give it to you for a hundred. That's a sale."

"You've got a deal." Del extended her hand. "Name's Del."

"I'm Trev. This is Eddy, Chels. Those two wankers are Eddy's cousins." A guy and girl, looking like crows with pale faces, nodded. Trev shook Del's hand. "This'll be a kick-ass weekend. Hope you're ready to party." He returned his hands to his jacket pockets. "So Del, you can save us some hassle if you know how to get to some place called Dammtor Bahnhof."

Del grinned. "This is your lucky day, Trev." She silently added, *And mine.*

Chapter Thirty-Three

Del rested in the tent she shared with Chels and Eddy's cousin, Marcy. She felt like crap. Not hungover but not sober. They had pooled their money to buy cheap drinks from the town and all the guys had brought back was beer, which she was heartily sick of. She suspected her mouth was growing mold. Green, fuzzy mold that smelled like stale beer and *wurst*. She hadn't changed in two days and stank. Every time she braved the portable bathrooms she came out smelling worse.

As awful as she felt, as much as she needed sleep, she had actually had lots of fun. Enough to keep her moving, to keep her from wondering what was happening in Hamburg. Wacken was a little town not far northwest of Hamburg. The town was small, but the festival was huge. Trev had said it usually drew 65,000 fans and Del believed it. The festival site, right beside the town, was packed but amazingly orderly. There were even families and seniors around, an outdoor mall made of rows of tents, and a "beer hall" packed with black-clad heavy metal fans singing German drinking songs. Weird but cool.

Del wasn't sure what she'd expected of so many metal heads in one sardine can, but they were great. They were here to party and head-bang and cheer – the music was like a happy drug for them. She'd hardly even noticed any other drugs floating around.

The English gang had taken her into the fold, shared blankets, teased her about how her camel jacket stuck out in the sea of black, laughed at her attempts to produce an English accent.

But it was Saturday afternoon and Del was partied out, had heard enough metal for years, and wanted to be by herself.

Tomorrow everyone would pack up their hangovers and go home. Where would she go? Cassandra had to be frantic but Del still wasn't ready to face her. Any of them. Especially Felix, because she feared she'd forgive him in a second.

Del dozed, woke gagging from her dry, coated mouth. Dozed again. Woke again and lay staring at the tent roof. It had sprinkled and the nylon was covered with darker blue dots. What if no one cared that she was gone?

She powered up the cell phone. It could only hold three voice mails and the mailbox was full – all the messages were from Cassandra, all some variation of, "Oh God, Delora. Where are you? What am I supposed to tell Mom and Dad? What will they think?"

Is that all that mattered? What Mom and Dad thought? Keep up appearances and to hell with what you were feeling, so long as things looked fine so they could send a good report to Mom and Dad. What had happened to "Are you okay, Del?" Or maybe even, "We miss you. Please come back."

She didn't erase the messages, didn't leave room in the cellphone for more empty words.

11 August 43

Apparently there was a horrible air raid on Nuremberg last night. It is an awful reminder of all that is still unsaid. I have so much to tell you, Hilde, so much to remember. And I do not want to remember any of it. But Papa gave me this journal and he once asked that I always tell the truth in it, so I will tell the horrible truth. Someday no one will believe it, and maybe then I will be glad I did this. Does Papa wonder what has become of me? I should write. But first I will tell you, before I lose my courage.

Remembering 24 July 43

24 July dawned so clear, so beautiful. A perfect Hamburg summer's day. I spent most of the day restless but too hot to do more than rest. In the evening, I took a cool bath to wash off the sweat. Hilde, I looked so funny in the mirror. My belly stuck out like the gigantic base of a snowman topped by two bulging melons, and my belly button had popped out. I laughed at the sight.

In the kitchen, Herr Wechsler sorted the mail. Already his breath smelled of *Schnaps*. I had a letter from Werner! I must have read it ten times that night. He was in a prisoner-of-war camp in England but had heard he and many others were being sent to Canada. I worried about how far away that was and how long it would take the Red Cross to carry letters back and forth. He was happy to hear from me and wanted to keep writing. His reply made me think I could float, though if I had been able to I would have looked like a weather balloon.

Ilsa arrived at nine o'clock and we bedded down in the cellar as usual. Herr Wechsler had been drinking all night and was unsteady on his feet. I lay facing the wall, thinking about the letter, which was tucked under my pillow. Since I was so quiet, the others must have thought I slept. Their words were low, but not low enough. They talked about the baby being due any day. Herr Wechsler was adamant he only wanted a boy. His voice rose a little as he declared that if I had a girl, he would get rid of the thing and find a strapping soldier willing to try again. Frau Wechsler shushed him and accused him of being drunk and foolish.

I could not sleep after that. Did he mean to kill the baby if it was a girl? What did the soldier comment mean? Would he send me to one of those baby farms to be impregnated by an SS soldier? Or invite one here and let him rape me like Faber had? Even if it was simply drunken foolishness as Frau Wechsler had said, did I want this baby being raised by such a man?

I was so upset I hardly noticed when the air raid sirens started sometime after midnight. It was not unusual, after all. But this night the alarms had barely started when the thumping began. Explosion after explosion after explosion. The house shook. With every crash I flinched and covered my head. Herr Wechsler turned on the light but I almost preferred the dark. The bulb flickered and threatened to go out. Worse, I saw stark fear on everyone's faces. The bombing went on for two solid hours. I fell into an exhausted sleep.

I woke after three hours, not because the sirens were still going, but because my body seemed to think I should always get up at six o'clock. The others still slept. I took Werner's letter and snuck upstairs. I had promised myself during that terrible raid that I'd leave the Wechsler home at first opportunity. I could not risk that Herr Wechsler meant what he'd said. Whether he was a harmless drunk or a cruel man, neither this baby nor I deserved such treatment. In my bedroom I threw one change of clothes into a bag along with my last journal, Werner's letter, my picture with Erwin and Papa, and that pencil drawing of Heidelberg, which was pinned over my bed. I would walk to Tilli's. I knew she would help me.

How to describe the world into which I stepped? A pall of smoke hung over the city. As I walked to the lakeside, I noticed a few houses in our neighbourhood had burned. Large flakes of ash floated down like the first snows of winter. On the Aussenalster's shore I took in the extent of the night's attack. I stood in the centre of a ring of fire and smoke. To the west, to the south, farther to the east, the dark smoke of hungry fires billowed. Only the north seemed untouched but it, too, was shrouded with smoke. Across the lake, the Aldstadt spires and buildings burned fiercely. I wept to think the one church that offered me the same peace I'd always found in Heiliggeistkirche – lovely Nikolaikirche – might be caught in that destruction.

I walked north around the lake. My shoes crunched over odd strips of what looked to be aluminum foil. The smoke was awful; I tied my spare blouse over my nose and mouth. I was used to walking but my lower back was so sore that morning of 25 July that I had to stop several times and reach around to rub it as best I could. The sun was an orange disk through the smoke. I wished for rain, to kill the fires and drive the ash to the ground. Its taste lined my mouth. I was so thirsty I stopped to drink from the lake.

Here and there, the rubble of destroyed homes or apartments spilled into the streets. The faces of the people whose homes had been destroyed – had I ever seen such shock and despair? When I reached Tilli's apartment, I collapsed on the front step. Someone came out a few minutes later, asked who I was looking for and brought Tilli to me. She helped me stand and at that instant water gushed from inside me, soaking my skirt and my socks. My knees almost gave way. "What is happening?" I cried.

"We must get you inside," Tilli replied. "The baby is coming."

"Shouldn't we go to the hospital?" I asked weakly.

"Every hospital will be overflowing with injured people. We must see to this ourselves."

Chapter Thirty-Four

Hauptbahnhof was as busy on a Sunday as any other day of the week. Del lingered with the English group, not really wanting to say goodbye. That meant deciding what to do. She felt cut adrift, floating wherever the tide carried her, just as the crowds at Wacken had swept her here and there.

Trev said, "That's bloody great." He kicked the railing with his worn black army boot.

"What's wrong?" Del asked, glad to have something to think about beside her next move.

"My bleeding sister, that's what. Can you believe it? She wants to stay with her wanking German boyfriend 'til school starts."

Chels smirked. "He must be a cracker between the sheets."

"Shut up!" Trev shouted.

Del understood. "Going to be tough to tell your parents?"

"Too bloody right."

Eddy elbowed Trev. "Cheer up, mate. We're not going home for three days. Maybe she'll change her mind."

"Where are you going now?" Del asked.

"Amsterdam," Eddy said with a grin. "The party's only starting!"

"How can you even think of more partying?" Del asked.

"No prob," Chels replied. "Sleep on the train. Wake up ready to roll."

Trev looped his arm around Del's waist and swung her close. His stale breath made her stomach flop. "Come with us. Party's not over, Del." He narrowed his eyes. "Don't have a bloke wondering where you are, do you?"

That was funny. A babysitter was all she had. She searched

Trev's face, looking for some indication that he actually wanted her to come. His grey eyes were clouded and cool, but his hand, hot on the small of her back, made small circles that tingled as he whispered, "You can have my sister's train ticket. It'll be fun."

Going back to Cassandra's would be anything but fun. Del knew she'd be grounded for the summer when she returned. Why not have a few more days of freedom? She gave a jerky nod. Trev covered her mouth in a brief, hard kiss. "Let's go then, luv."

The train hadn't even left Hamburg before Del was having second thoughts. She stood at the door of their car and watched the city roll past. As the train track curved, she caught sight of all the church spires. *Which one is Nikolaikirche? Did it burn in the bombing?* As the train picked up speed, Del realized this city had started to grow on her. Maybe all the people she knew here were jerks, but the city was great. Vibrant. Alive. It felt like leaving a friend.

Before she could change her mind, she turned her cellphone on and dialed one of only two numbers she knew.

"Altmann." Felix's voice stopped her breath. *"Wer ist da? Guten Tag? Hallo?"* A pause. "Hey, James. Is that you? Say it's you. Please. *Scheisse.* Speak to me, James. Everyone thinks you've been raped and murdered. Your sister reported you missing." He swore again. "You're scaring me, James. Talk to me! Please come home. I want to see you. We need to talk." His voice trailed off.

Throat clogged, Del whispered, "I'm okay. Tell Cass I'm okay." She hung up. How she wished Felix actually wanted to see her.

Trev found her leaning against the window beside the door. "There you are, Del. What're you doing? We need to sleep." She twisted so her back was against the window. Trev whistled. "Crying? What for?" He swiped away her tears with his thumb.

Del didn't tell him the truth, that she wanted to go back and talk to Felix, that hearing his voice had made her miss him with a flu-like ache. Or that she'd just realized she actually cared about having hurt her sister. They'd gotten along for the week before things blew up. Instead she said, "I don't want you to get in trouble. My sister reported me missing."

"To the Hamburg police?" Del nodded and Trev swore. Then he grinned. "Even if they spread the word, conductors hardly look at your face. Like Chels says, no problem." His eyes tinted blue; he looked like a kid planning a prank. "This'll be easy. Sis and I carry copies of each other's passports. Mum insists. When the conductor comes round, you pretend to be asleep and I'll show him the copy and ticket. With your eyes closed, head turned, he'll never notice."

Del followed him back to their seats. This car was like a Greyhound bus for space, nothing like the first-class car she'd ridden in from Frankfurt to Hamburg. She took the window seat and rested her forehead against the glass. Trev patted her thigh. "It's okay if you really fall asleep." She could tell he was enjoying pulling one over on the authorities. She didn't feel right about it, not with Felix's words playing through her mind on continuous repeat.

She dozed. Trev woke her with a squeeze to her inner thigh. "All clear. Conductor backed off when I said your real passport was down your knickers." He grinned. "Let's go to the toilet and clean up. Chels gave me some toothpaste and soap. She thinks of everything."

Exhaustion had set in and Del wanted to sleep, but she felt grubby enough that the thought of toothpaste roused her. She stumbled behind Trev. He insisted on crowding into the bathroom together. As soon as he locked the door, his hands clamped on her breasts, shocking her to alertness. "Banging on a train is the best, luv."

"I don't –"

"Yes, you do. You've wanted to all weekend. Dancing and jig-gling these knockers." He cupped his hands over her butt and pressed against her. "You're hot. Panting."

Only because she could feel panic trying to take over. She struggled to stay cool, to keep him talking. "This is a bathroom. No room."

"No problem." He stepped backwards and sat on the toilet, pulling her down to straddle his legs. "See? Lots of room."

Del's stomach began to churn. "I'm going to be sick."

Trev studied her. "You *are* green." He stood them both up. "I'll leave you the toothpaste. You throw up or whatever, clean up, then I'll come back." He opened the door.

Del shoved him across the corridor. "Not on your life, stud. I hardly know you, and I'll never bang you. I'll scream if you touch me."

"Bitch."

"Better that than what you want me to be." She locked the bathroom door and sat on the toilet until her legs stopped shak-ing. When she returned to the seats almost an hour later, Eddy's cousin was sleeping with her shoulder on Trev and she was left to squeeze over the other cousin who was snoring like a buzz saw. She stared at the passing scenery until she fell asleep.

This wasn't freedom. This was the worst trap she'd ever stepped into.

Chapter Thirty-Five

Someone shook Del awake. She started, glanced around, saw the uniformed sleeve of a train conductor and sighed her relief. The fellow gave her a slight smile. He spoke in an accent that wasn't German, but something close. "Hello, miss. This is your stop, I believe. Amsterdam. We are soon departing and another passenger has booked this seat."

She slept all the way to Amsterdam? She had a vague memory of stumbling beside Chels through a station when they changed trains, but other than that, the trip was a blank. Del fell back in her seat. Where was everyone? The conductor backed away so she could get out. She thanked him and squeezed past people loading suitcases and backpacks onto overhead shelves. She jumped off and ran toward the exit. Where was the English group? They couldn't just leave her.

Trev's face when she'd told him to get lost came to mind. Maybe they could.

She took the stairs down off the platform two at a time. She started passing stragglers, brushing past, calling "Excuse me," searching for the flock of metal-heads. She turned one way and stopped when she realized it was almost deserted – except for two guys exchanging something behind a big pillar. She wheeled and ran the other direction. The main doors came into sight, a bottleneck of pedestrian traffic. Del was forced to slow to a walk.

The train station opened to a broad plaza jammed with people and bicycles, busses and trams. Most people were walking across a bridge and down a street that led directly away from the station. There was a lineup to get into a small building across the street labeled "Tourist Information". She took two steps and stopped. She wasn't a tourist. She was a runaway.

Her limbs began to jitter. Some pedestrians circled way around her, as if afraid she was on drugs – which is probably what she looked like, she realized. She spotted a group of black-clad people about a block away walking down that wide main road. It had to be them.

She'd catch up. Apologize to Trev. She still didn't want to sleep with him, but maybe they'd let her hang with them until she figured out what to do. Chels and Eddy seemed nice. They'd help her. But first she had to catch them.

The flow of traffic was so heavy that she could only manage a fast walk. The bicycle paths were almost as crowded as the sidewalks. Trams dinged as they glided past. She lost sight of the group, then spotted them past a rectangular pond, heading to the left. By the time she got onto that side street, she'd lost them again. She charged ahead. Beyond the water the narrow road was stuffed with cars and people.

This had to be a sightseeing area. Del wasn't interested. She only wanted to catch up with the gang. She was bumped by people heading the other way. She had to squeeze around tourists pointing their cameras and fingers. She had the impression of tall skinny houses crammed against one another and leaning over her. Right, down another narrow street. No sign of Trev or his friends.

Hoping for a stroke of luck she continued down a smaller side street. And another. There were still a lot of people, but the shabbiness of the buildings made Del uneasy. Every doorway seemed occupied by a shadowy figure or a gaunt, strung-out looking guy. The press of people forced her near the wall and she heard someone in a doorway whisper, "Heroin. Heroin." Startled, she struggled to the middle of the lane. Someone bumped her. Touched her pocket.

She slapped her hand on it. Her cellphone was gone. She turned but the steady stream of people was oblivious to her.

She checked her jeans pocket, pulled out her wallet, relieved. Opened it to see how much money she had. She was walking, counting, when a hand snatched the leather. Her fingers reflexively pinched. The wallet was gone. She clutched the couple bills she'd saved to her chest, then stuck her hand right inside her coat, fist tight around those few euros.

Where had the hand come from? Had it been white, brown? She didn't know. She only knew dread was slamming through her. The worn buildings leered at her. Pedestrians swept by as if she were invisible, but the eyes in the doorways seemed to track her like vultures preparing to circle. She pushed past people, ran down the alley, needing to get out of this warren. She lurched into a crowded wider street by a canal.

The blue above and the water beside Del gave her space to breathe. A block later she stopped by a footbridge spanning the narrow canal. Turned and turned again. Looking for... what? Her wallet was long gone. Her English so-called friends were long gone. She leaned against the rail and slowed her breathing. She hated this place, her stupidity.

She still felt eyes boring into her. No one seemed to be paying her any attention, unless she counted that church. Its spire rose above four gabled roofs that peaked over four massive arched windows that seemed to look down on her. It had watched centuries of people, she realized. Had watched people loving, living, maybe dying. It seemed to beckon, to offer a haven. She took it, walked in, head down, and veered toward worn wooden benches.

Someone in a red skirt and sandals approached. A softly accented voice said, "Excuse me. There is a fee for entering. To help with upkeep, you understand."

Del raised her head and looked into a kindly face that reminded her of Luise. "My wallet. Someone took it. I don't..." She swiped at the warm wetness on her cheeks.

The woman tsked. "I will give you a few minutes. Yes?"

"Thanks." Del's hand was still tucked into her coat. She unclenched her fist and stuffed her remaining money into the mickey pocket. Her fingers brushed Garda's journal and the photocopy of her passport. At least she still had that. She lowered her head and eyed a carved stone almost the size of a bed. It took her a moment to realize it was a grave marker. She turned her attention to a low row of stained glass windows and organ pipes that were blue and silver with gold trim. Even with her sneakers on someone's grave, the place was... restful. Maybe because it was quiet; maybe because it was almost empty in a city where she'd been caught in crowds from the first moment, a city that had taken her wallet and replaced it with fear. That fear hadn't crossed the threshold. In its place was the cool relief of still air. Silence. Peace. She could understand why Garda had liked to sit in churches.

Remembering 25 July 43

Through the morning and into the afternoon of 25 July, I laboured to bring a baby into the world. Outside, the sirens rang without ceasing. The apartment was stifling but to open a window was to let in smoke. Tilli bathed me with cool cloths. She held my head when I threw up. She paced the floor with me, bracing me when my knees gave way. Her neighbour flitted in and out, giving advice. Her mother had helped birth many babies, she said. She was too busy collecting gossip from the street to stay with us.

She returned with stories of destruction. The Rathaus burning,

Gansemarkt destroyed. The opera house hit. Fires out of control to the west and fire brigades coming from surrounding communities as fast as possible. Mid-afternoon, the sirens changed. The neighbour came in screaming, "Another air raid!" Tilli gathered our bags (everyone always had one packed) and helped me down to the apartment's shelter. Suddenly I had more midwives than I wanted.

I was a distraction. They settled me on a bunk near a corner and surrounded the bed. Even when the all-clear sounded – someone said it was near five o'clock – none of my midwives left. I could not leave. Contractions tore through me by then, hardly giving me time to breathe before another started. I had never been so afraid, even when the bombs had fallen like raindrops. When the women said it was time, raised my legs and exposed my most private parts to the room, I would not have cared if the Führer himself had stood at the end of the bed to watch. I am certain my screams were as loud as any siren.

The baby was born minutes after ten o'clock. A girl. The women washed her and laid her at my breast. All I could think, Hilde, was thank God I had left the Wechslers'. *Gott sei Dank*.

"Excuse me." It was the woman in the red skirt again. Del looked up, anticipating kindness. The woman looked irritated. "This is not a reading room." She nodded at the papers from Garda's journal in Del's hand.

"Sorry. I... needed to clear my head, to decide what to do." Del tucked the papers away.

"Perhaps I can direct you? You said someone stole your wallet?"

Del told her what happened but didn't mention she had rescued a few bills. The woman's face shriveled up like a raisin.

"What a foolish child. This is Amsterdam. No one walks down even a major street with wallet in plain sight. To be in an alley with your wallet out is to ask someone to take it. Have you no brain cells? Have you smoked them away in the cafés?"

What was she talking about? Del recalled walking by the American Embassy in Hamburg and stood. "There must be a Canadian consulate in the city. Someone there could help me."

The woman sniffed. "Canadian? I do not think so."

"But isn't this the biggest city in Holland?"

"Of course, Amsterdam is the biggest city in *The Netherlands*."

"Then... wouldn't there be a consulate? Hamburg isn't the biggest city in Germany and it has a consulate."

The woman's expression grew more wizened. "Is that so? We will check."

She spun and marched away. Del followed with a sigh and waited in the doorway of a tiny office while the woman scanned a directory of some kind. She closed the book firmly and straightened. Smugly, she announced, "No Canadian consulate. It is in The Hague."

"What's a Hague?"

"*The* Hague is a city. It is perhaps twenty minutes by train."

Del deflated. That would use the little money she had saved from the theft of her wallet. Then she asked, "Can you tell me how to get to a police station?"

"Your wallet is gone. But by all means, spend a day in police queues filling out forms. It will give you time to realize how careless you were. How much you deserve your fate."

"Sure. Thanks. The address?"

"The station dealing with tourist issues is on Nieuwezijds Voorburgwal in the 100 block."

Del gave her a blank look. The woman responded with terse

directions. Up the street by the canal, left on Lange Niezel, then five blocks and she'd see it. Del fled before the woman could deliver another sermon, which she looked ready, even eager, to do.

The sun had slipped lower and was on the verge of disappearing behind buildings. Street lights weren't on yet and long shadows gave the streets an air of foreboding. Del shivered despite the warmth. She quickened her pace as she passed two men whose looks and stance screamed 'pimp'. She waited at the corner while an elderly woman in a pillbox hat with a cloth grocery bag and a sturdy cane limped her way up the curb and past Del with an air of dignity. She gave Del a polite nod in passing, as if thanking her.

The directions returned Del to the rectangular pond with ships moored around its edges. Beyond it, the train station's square towers and peaked gables were silhouetted against clouds. Their undersides looked lit by fire. Del reached the main street leading to the station. She wanted so badly to just go there and get on a train and be back in Hamburg by morning. But there was no way she had enough money. The police could at least tell her what she should do.

She trudged on to the police station, paying little attention to her surroundings other than to search for signs. Five blocks, the woman had said. Sure enough, the fifth block had a street sign with an impossibly long name.

It didn't take Del long to find the 100 block. The police station was a brown-grey stone building with bars on the street-level windows and heavy wooden doors that had three small barred windows over top of them. She hesitated, then plunged into the building.

The line-up she joined filed forward quickly. When Del reached the counter, they took her name and told her to wait. She wanted to scream with frustration.

Instead she retreated to a corner and pulled out Garda's journal.

Remembering 26 July 43

Tilli told me the air raid siren went off again that night but no bombs fell. I heard nothing. In the morning four women helped move me and the baby to Tilli's apartment. A good thing because I fainted on the second landing. My legs were like noodles. All that morning I only rested and suckled the baby. Each time I did, the bonds wove more tightly between my newborn daughter and me. I swear she looked into my soul with eyes both innocent and ancient – as if she knew the pain I had endured from the start to bring her into the world and was thankful. By the time the air raid sirens sounded at noon, I would do anything for her.

I named her Hilde.

The sirens stopped before we could get out the door. Later we heard that American airplanes dropped a few bombs south of the river and knocked out a power plant. In my heart, I knew our enemies wouldn't be happy until we were dust. Tilli agreed.

Tilli had gathered donated items from the neighbours for the baby: spare rags for diapers, bits of blanket to wrap her in. We packed essentials – all I had was what I had brought from the Wechslers' – and off we went. Tilli used strips of torn sheets to rig a sling so baby Hilde was tied to my chest. We rigged my journal between two layers of sheets so it was a support against Hilde's back. My pace was so slow an ancient tortoise could have beaten me.

Clouds of smoke still rose from fires to the west and south. We headed north because that was the only direction with no fires, though a low ceiling of smoke hung over everything. We thought if we could get out of the city, we could make our way around to Lueneberg and to Tilli's cousin. We had gone maybe eight blocks when we came to a roadblock. Only bombed out people were being allowed to leave the city. Were we bombed out? No. Then we had to return to our home and continue to follow directions as issued by Gauleiter Kaufmann. What could we do? We turned back.

Chapter Thirty-Six

It's ironic, Del thought, *that while I'm reading about Garda trying desperately to get out of Hamburg, all I want to do is get back there.* She waited as patiently as she could for her name to be called. It wasn't happening.

One area of the station had a sign declaring it to be ATAS – Amsterdam Tourist Assistance Service. Exactly what she needed. They also seemed to be calling people. She decided she'd better get her name in at that desk.

When she approached, a blue-eyed woman looked up from her computer screen and smiled. Before Del could say anything, the woman greeted her and said, "I need to see your police report number so we can help you."

"I don't have it yet."

"Oh. Well, you really need to –"

"Please. I want to phone my sister in Hamburg. My wallet was stolen. I have no money. I just need to call her."

The woman rubbed her eyes. "I'm sorry but you need to register the theft."

Del leaned forward and lowered her voice. "Look. I didn't see who took it so reporting anything is a waste of time. I'm sixteen. I'll get up there and they'll want to know where my guardian is, won't they? Well, she's in Hamburg. I took off without permission, which was stupid. You don't have to tell me that. But I really, really need to call her. Please."

The woman held up one finger. She left and talked to someone at another desk. They both threw furtive glances her way. The person at the desk finally nodded. The woman returned and escorted Del to a telephone in a quiet corner. She didn't know how to dial Germany so the woman had her write down the phone number, which she dialed before passing over the handset.

Del's leg jiggled as the phone rang its elongated beep. Mathias answered and accepted the collect call. Before she could speak, he said, "Del? Where the hell are you?"

"I'm... in Amsterdam."

"You're where?" The last word was almost shouted. Del jerked her head away from the sound. "How did you get there?"

"It doesn't matter. I want to come home. But my wallet was stol –"

"Do you know how bloody worried we've been? What we thought had happened? Then Felix said you called him and – Do you ever think before you do stupid things? Ever?" Fury seemed to vibrate through the phone line.

"I'm sorry, okay?" Del was fighting tears.

"No, it's not okay. Your sister is curled up on the loveseat in her housecoat." Mathias spewed a string of German then paused. "A thread is all I have left to hang onto, Del. Her hysteria. Your selfish –" The line went dead.

Mathias had hung up on her? Del stared at the handset. He had always been the one on her side, and now he wasn't? Panic flooded her thoughts. She dropped the telephone and ran. Out the door, down the street. She ran headlong and blind.

A stitch almost doubled Del over. She clutched her side, slowed to a walk and looked up to see the spire of another church. A slender green spire that didn't look the least bit welcoming, more like a sword. She halted and stared at it, feeling like she was a blade cutting through her family. Destroying it.

She retreated to a side door of the church, sank down and huddled in the doorway. The stone recess still held some heat from the day even though the street was falling into shadow. If only she could curl up here, never move, never have to face any-one, face Cassandra...

Del gulped in breaths, pressed a hand against her tumbling stomach. What had Mathias said? Cassandra was in her house-coat again, gone strange again. He was hanging by a thread. And it was Del's fault. *I'm a sword. I'm destroying them.*

Suddenly she knew: she couldn't run away from this because she couldn't run away from herself.

And she missed them. All of them. Felix and Luise and Mathias. Even Cassandra. They'd only tried to help her, even if she hated the way they'd done it. The fake freedom they'd given her had been better than the freedom she'd grabbed for herself.

She and Cassandra were so different that Del couldn't under-stand her at all. But the thought of her sister in that weird depres-sion again terrified Del. She needed to get back, to find a way to help Cassandra. To find a way to make things work. To make things right.

Her side twinged. One thing Del knew was that she was done running. It wasn't an answer, and the only place she'd find one was back in Hamburg.

She rose and asked a passerby how to get to the train station.

Del needed twenty more euros for a ticket to Hamburg. She sat near the entrance to the train station and wondered how to get it. Even on a Sunday evening, the traffic here was endless. A few times she heard English spoken and was tempted to catch the people and ask for help.

Off to the left, someone started shouting. A bicycle lumbered past Del, the rider standing on his pedals, trying to build up speed. Two men raced after him, shouting, and caught up before he could reach the bridge to the main street. They yanked him off the bicycle, began kicking and hitting him. When uniformed men tore past Del, she pressed herself against the wall, wishing to melt into the bricks. Minutes later, a police car arrived. They handcuffed the man who'd been pulled off the bicycle and shoved him into the vehicle. An attempted bicycle theft, apparently.

Del thought, *I won't be stealing the twenty euros*. Not that she'd considered it.

Near the entrance, a pregnant woman stuffed some papers into a bin and walked toward the trams. Del recalled the pregnant woman in Hamburg sitting on the sidewalk. Begging was better than stealing. What did she have to lose?

Del retrieved three of the papers. Inside the station she borrowed a pen from the woman at the sales counter and made three signs, each reading: Please help me get home. She rescued the lid of a disposable food container, and sat cross-legged on the floor near the entrance, back against a wall so she wouldn't be tripped over. She propped a sign against each leg and held the third in her lap.

Now she knew why that woman in Hamburg had sat with head lowered. The humiliation of what Del was doing weighed hers down and kept it there. Her legs quivered and she felt vaguely nauseated. How could people do this day after day?

A fifty cent piece dropped into the upturned lid. Del blinked to keep tears from falling. This wasn't how it was supposed to go. She'd only been out for some fun. Party a bit, blow off steam then, after the sting of betrayal had faded, return to deal with Cassandra's wrath. But she wasn't angry; she was in one of her weird depressions. Mathias was the one who was angry. Felix had said everyone was worried. She hadn't thought they'd worry. Could Mathias's anger be worry? Could Cassandra getting upset when Del broke one of her rules be worry? She'd sure never translated, "I'm angry" as: "I was worried about you."

After an hour Del couldn't feel her butt, but her legs and neck clenched with pain. She was sick of smelling four days of accumulated stink. The scattering of coins in her cardboard lid looked to be four euros and change. This would take all night.

Someone crouched and raised her chin with ring-clad fingers. Perfume briefly overcame Del's unwashed odour and she looked into a smooth face with dark, unreadable eyes. The man couldn't be called handsome, but he was very... manicured. Creepy. Del stiffened, wanting to escape his artificial perfection. His gaze flicked up and down.

"You need money?" His accent wasn't one Del recognized, especially with him whispering. "You look pretty under that grime. Come with me. I can help."

She knew what he meant. Heart thudding, Del shook her head. He reached into his stylish leather jacket and pulled out a 100-euro note. "How much do you need?"

She stared at the money, wanting it so badly that for a second she thought, *What can it hurt?* She knocked his hand away. "Not interested."

"You'd rather sit in your filth and beg? I could give you food, a bath, clean clothes."

His voice was melodic. Almost hypnotic. And so tempting. All he would want in return was control over her body. Del had seen enough movies to know the deals these type of leeches struck. Del scooped up the coins in the lid and stood, back to the wall. "Get away from me before I start screaming."

"You heard the young woman, Zarc. Move on." A security guard tapped the pimp's shoulder and pointed to the entrance.

The pimp smiled. "I'm trying to be a good Samaritan here. Do you mind?"

The security guard released a stream of Dutch. Whatever he

said, the pimp sneered, waved the 100-euro note under Del's nose, tucked it inside his jacket and sauntered away.

The security guard sighed. "Begging is not permitted here, miss. You will have to leave." He was tall, with sandy hair and firm features. He frowned down at Del, but in a way that was more sad than irritated.

"And go where? The only time I stepped outside this station, my wallet got stolen. I have a bit of money. I was just trying to get enough to buy a ticket home."

"Trains don't run to the United States."

"Canada," Del replied automatically. "I'm from Canada. But I'm staying for the summer with my sister in Hamburg."

His expression seemed to soften. "Does she know you're here?"

"No. Yes. I don't know." Del scrunched her forehead to keep from crying. "I tried to phone from that ATAS place in the police station and Mathias hung up. But I have to get back. My sister's sick and … I need to help her."

The security guard studied her for a moment. "How old are you?"

"Sixteen. Why?"

A smile crinkled out from blue-green eyes. "My grandmother was close to your age when Canadians liberated her village from the Nazis. She loves to tell that story."

Del eyed him curiously, wondering what that had to do with anything. But something in his expression seemed to light a candle of hope inside.

He shook his head and gave a small smile. "She'd be furious if she found out I had failed to help a Canadian. Believe me, you never want to provoke a Dutch grandmother. Her anger would even frighten Zarc." He winked. "It's safer to help you."

Chapter Thirty-Seven

Del's rescuer introduced himself as Gerrit. She had hoped he would give her some money and his address so she could pay him back. Instead, when his shift ended at midnight, he took her to an all-night cafe where he seemed to know everyone. He bought her soup and tea and watched her eat while he talked with a couple in Dutch. By the time she finished eating, her fate was decided.

They offered her a bed of two coats tucked between a shelf and some boxes. Gerrit gave her a stern warning about not taking advantage of hospitality and left. Every time Del drifted off, something woke her. The clatter of pots, laughter, a dream of fingers reaching inside her coat.

In the morning, the woman tucked a hair net over Del's stringy hair, handed her an apron and told her to start earning her keep. She patted Del's shoulder. "I'll explain to the day shift."

Earning her keep meant scrubbing pots. Del kept her jacket on for fear of losing her remaining cash or the copy of her passport. She rolled up her sleeves, donned rubber gloves, and started on a stock pot. As fast as she scoured pots and put them through a sterilizer, the cook grabbed them and piled the counter high with more dirty ones. Twice he yelled at her and threw a pot back in the sink, splashing water everywhere. Del wanted to tell him where to stick it, but knowing she had to find her own way home kept her doggedly in place.

The third time, a waitress said, "Pay no mind to him. He's half French. Very dramatic." Her comment drew a red-faced spew of Dutch from the cook. She blew him a kiss.

During a break at ten o'clock, Del dozed at the staff table by the door to the storage room. The cook woke her by slamming a frying pan on the table. She almost fell off the chair.

The dull ache in her neck, shoulders and feet grew through the day. During her next break, after the lunch rush, she sank onto the floor beside the staff table. The temptation to leave almost made her get up, though her throbbing feet demanded rest. Walking out of this job was another form of running and Del swore she was through doing that. If this was what it took to get money for the train, she'd do it.

Why had Mathias hung up? It just wasn't like him, even if he was angry. Furious. Was he expecting a second call, one more remorseful than the first? Or worse, had something happened to Cassandra and he'd had to hang up? Del ached with the need to get home.

She fell asleep again. A nice waiter with a smile like Felix's woke her up and set a sandwich on the table for her. The cook barked that she had five minutes to eat. At 3:30 her legs trembled with fatigue. Gerrit walked into the kitchen in his security guard uniform. Surprise claimed his expression. "You're still here! Wait one moment." Five minutes later he returned. "Johannes said you worked hard all day. Your shift is over. Come."

The cook snarled, "Who will clean my pots?"

"You should think about that when you're growling and scaring off your kitchen staff. You're a bear. I'm surprised our young friend lasted the day."

Del peeled off the yellow rubber gloves and flexed her fingers. "We have real bears where I come from. They don't scare me, either. I was a girl scout." She didn't mention her scout career only lasted for two weeks in fourth grade.

Gerrit smiled; deep creases appeared on either side of his mouth. He nodded. She dropped the apron over the latest pile of dirty pots and hurried after him. At the till, an older man with a name tag that read "Johannes" slid a 20-euro note across the counter. "It should be more but this is coming out of tips, you understand."

Del pocketed the money. "It's enough. Thank you."

She and Gerrit walked down the street, and for the first time she admired the narrow buildings and their ornate rooflines. Beside them, a long tourist boat glided through a canal. Cobblestones underfoot and blue sky above. It was perfect, except for a slightly nasty odour Del wasn't sure came from the water or from her. No question, Amsterdam was a pretty city when you weren't getting robbed or hustled by a pimp. She touched Gerrit's sleeve. "Will Johannes get in trouble for helping me?"

"Not unless you report him."

"What about his boss?"

"She will understand. She's been putting up with his quirks of generosity for thirty-eight years. I think that's how long they've been married. He is my mother's cousin. Their daughter and her husband were working last night." Gerrit winked. "Where to now, miss?"

"To the train station. I have a train to catch."

"Centraal it is. Very convenient since that is also where I am headed." He tapped his security guard badge. "We all have to earn our keep, yes?"

Del rolled her eyes. "Sure. Tell that to my feet. They're ready to fall off."

He laughed. "Lucky for you, Centraal has wheelchairs for such emergencies."

"Great."

They turned another corner and Centraal, the train station, came into sight. Del said, "Thanks, Gerrit. I mean it. And thank your grandmother for me the next time you see her."

Chapter Thirty-Eight

Remembering 27 July 43

The air raid sirens had gone off during the night, though no bombers came. The British liked to buzz German cities and make everyone scramble for shelter. That morning, though my sleep had been broken, I felt like my strength was returning. Tilli thought my daily walks had helped make me fit. My bottom was still so sore that I didn't feel fit. Whenever I sat, it was on a pillow. I spent the morning resting and watching my perfect little daughter sleep. I had never realized how fascinating a sleeping baby could be.

In the afternoon we tried again to leave. An elderly Volksstrum guard at a roadblock admired baby Hilde, then gave us a lecture about duty and turned us around. We were tired and sweaty when we retuned to the closed-up apartment which had turned into an oven in the dry hot day. There wasn't even much of a breeze to cool things off.

No air raid happened that day. Tilli wondered if we had been wrong. Maybe the British would leave us alone since they'd done so much damage in the raid three nights before. I still wanted to leave. I think part of my fear was that Herr Wechsler would find me and take Hilde away. Tilli was easy to convince since she still wanted to move in with her cousin in Lueneberg.

We would try to leave at night, so spent the evening sleeping as much as possible. At twenty minutes to midnight, the air raid sirens went off and we feared our plans had been spoiled by the British. We had not left soon enough. When nothing happened after twenty minutes, we decided that it was another Mosquito run and we left.

The night was so still, peaceful and clear, and wonderfully cool after the terrible heat. The stars were our only light as we headed out. We planned to go east and south until we reached the Autobahn. We would follow it to Bergedorf, then find a ride to Lueneberg.

At first, we made good progress. There were places where single buildings had been destroyed by a stray bomb or fire. In the day I imagine these looked like gaping holes in otherwise perfect smiles; by night they were ominous ragged caves where terrible things lurked. As much as possible we walked down the middle of deserted streets. I had baby Hilde strapped to my chest again and Tilli carried a bag and one suitcase. We would retrieve our other belongings at a later date.

Farther east, the streets became more difficult to navigate and I realized we had reached the source of all the smoke in the east. Wandsbek, Tilli said, a residential area. Why, I wondered would the British want to destroy homes? Wouldn't it be more important to hit factories? It had happened three nights ago but smoke still rose from collapsed buildings and piles of rubble. In darkness the bombed-out homes and apartments, with little standing except parts of outer walls, looked like moth-eaten lace. We kept skirting to the south to find clear streets.

We were on a street only half destroyed when we heard a drone that quickly got louder. Airplanes. The sound came from the east which made no sense. We began to hurry. Bomb shelters would be long closed, locked from the inside against possible blasts. A short distance to the south, the dark lit up with golden streaks falling from the sky.

In seconds, the night became a writhing monster. Searchlights, flak and bombs that shook the ground. Tilli and I clung to each other in the middle of the street only blocks from this horrendous mayhem. She shouted and I could barely hear though her mouth was near my ear. "Run east. The bombers will fly past us." I felt vibrations in my chest and realized that baby Hilde was crying but I could not hear her.

So we ran. Only blocks away smoke billowed, painted orange by flames below. The ground continued to shake under non-stop explosions. Flashes of light hurt my eyes. My strength drained. Tilli was half a block ahead when the ripple of an explosion threw me to my knees. I braced my hands against the pavement and heaved in air untainted by smoke. We might as well have stayed at the apartment if this horrible death was to be our fate. I was crying when Tilli pulled me up. We stumbled to a ruin. It was shelter from nothing but I had to rest.

The bombs seemed to be dropping closer and closer. We struck out again, arms around each other, heads down. I realized Tilli had dropped the suitcase somewhere. Sparks and red ashes floated down. Everything was lit by an eerie glow. The roar of bombs and battle and fire mixed together to drown out every noise. It all combined to make it seem that it wasn't really happening, that I was walking through a nightmare.

On the block ahead of us, a bomb had blown a crater in the street. We paused in an intersection. An incendiary bomb hit a building to our left, causing it to burst into flame. Instinctively, we ran from it just as that whole intersection was hit by incendiaries. At the next intersection, Tilli grabbed my arm and pointed straight ahead.

I saw, not a string of fires, but one huge fire block to the south. Even from that distance we could feel its heat. Hell had broken through the surface of the earth and its flames consumed everything. Overhead, the bellies of English bombers were bright red. The air itself was red. We ran east, fearing that fire more than the airplanes. Bombs might chance to spare you, but fire devoured all in its path.

Others were in the streets now. Some had come from the south, were frantic and screaming about a sea of fire. Some were terribly burned. It was no longer safe to stay in the middle of the street as people fled in vehicles. Some drove into craters. Still bombs fell. Fires ignited roofs. Timbers fell. Buildings collapsed inwards, sending up clouds of sparks.

Our whole world was burning; we hardly knew which way to turn. Something had struck Tilli's arm in our flight and it was badly burned. Other than tiny burns from sparks, Hilde and I were unscathed. My eyes stung from the smoke. Weariness dragged my feet. I wanted to rest, but to do so was to give up and die. Baby Hilde was tied to me; I could not give up.

A few blocks later, the bombs seemed to have tapered off. But still delayed explosions flashed. To our right, to the south, the sky was glowing an ever-brighter red as the flames grew and spread. The roar of the fire became a howling wind, as if the demons of Hell had been unleashed to torment us. My thirst grew with each step. We reached another intersection and rested against the corner building as we gasped for breath and summoned the strength and courage to keep moving. Suddenly a wind pinned us there, blowing not away from the hellish fire but toward it. As we watched, a tree cater-corner from us was ripped from the ground and its leaves were sucked toward the conflagration. I knew that if a tree could not stand against the storm, we would surely die.

We might have, if not for a strange meeting. Someone joined us against that brick wall: a man in prisoner garb. He wore a patch with a "P" indicating he was from Poland. For one wild second I thought that here was one of my prisoners from the marchers near Dammtor. But it was too far away. He was a large man with a blunt face. I do not think he had been a prisoner very long for he did not have the hollow cheeks and sunken eyes I had seen in so many. He rested a paw on baby Hilde's covered head and spoke in broken German, "*Feuer kommt.*" He pointed across the street. "*Schnell.*" I shook my head. I had no strength for speed.

Before I could protest, he scooped me up and ran. I clung to him, face against his chest, as the wind tried to drag us into the red maw. And just as quickly we were in the next street. He set me in the stairwell of a cellar entrance and ran back toward the intersection. I backed down until I was huddled in the bottom. Then I realized my feet were wet. Had a water line in the building broken? It was a gift. Moments later our rescuer arrived carrying Tilli. We all lapped up the muddy water then left, for the roar of fire was, if possible, louder still. Blocks later we came to edge of a field. A football pitch. The light from the fire showed that people had gathered there. The Polish prisoner capped baby Hilde's head again and said something about keeping my baby safe. He nudged us toward that island of green and ran north along the shadowy edge of the field.

I do not know what became of him. I hope he evaded capture and made it back to his homeland. I think he had his own babies waiting for him there.

The pitch was our refuge for the rest of the night. It was hot but the fire, that horrible cyclone of flames, never got closer to us. I tried to nurse baby Hilde but she was so upset and red-faced from screaming that I could not get her to suckle. Instead I rocked and crooned and watched Hell destroy Hamburg. Where we sat, it looked as if the whole city was engulfed in the destruction. The small band of survivors who gathered there told of far more horrible things than we had seen. They spoke of escaping through the flames over charred and shrivelled bodies, of people screaming in the middle of roads because they were caught in melted asphalt, of others who had become human torches.

Death, so much death. I had to stop listening. Curled against Tilli's back with my baby tucked against my chest and tummy, I slept the sleep of exhaustion.

Chapter Thirty-Nine

This time, Del stayed on the train at Hauptbahnhof. She watched people rush along platforms. Even after midnight the station was a hive of activity. As the train pulled away, she noticed people huddled in the nooks and crannies, under shadowed eaves on the edges of the station, shadows themselves. The homeless.

She felt an unexpected kinship with them, knowing now how easily a person could fall into the cracks, like she almost had in Amsterdam.

The train eased over the bridge separating the two Alster lakes. Del peered across the smaller Binnenalster, alive with dancing reflections, to the illuminated Rathaus and tried to imagine it burning. The whole city burning. She shuddered, glad when the train's speakers came alive and announced their arrival at Dammtor Bahnhof.

On the platform, she hesitated. It was hard to go back. Hard to admit how badly she'd screwed up. Her stomach rumbled and joined with worry about Cassandra to spur her into motion. She had eight cents, not enough to call and ask Mathias to pick her up or to buy food. She struck out, and didn't slow down until the last block.

Somewhere here in Rotherbaum, Garda had waited out most of her pregnancy. Which house? Had it been bombed? Had it burned the night Garda had barely escaped that awful fire?

While Del was lost in thought, her feet carried her to Luise's gate. Her key had been in the change pocket of her wallet so was probably in an Amsterdam canal. She climbed over the gate, then leaned against it. Those last few steps seemed to bridge a canyon of thought and emotion. Would Mathias still be angry at her? Was he even still there? Could she stand and take her punishment or would her body betray her and try to run?

I won't run. I won't. If Garda had survived what she did, Del could face an upset sister and brother-in-law. She could live with a few rules. It was worth it to make sure Cassandra was okay. And Felix's words played continuously in her mind. Everyone was worried, he'd said. They had worried about her. Cared about her. She knew her friends cared, but when had she ever felt like she was important to anyone in her family?

This was the moment to find out. If it was only about the rules she'd broken... she'd find a way to survive August, then she'd leave Cassandra and Mathias to their safe little classrooms and their safe little routines and she'd go back to her friends.

Del reached inside her coat and touched the pages from Garda's journal. *I want to be brave like you.* She pushed away from the gate, more fearful than ever about what awaited her inside but ready to face it.

It was after one o'clock. The house was dark. Del's thumb hovered over the lower of two doorbells, the one that was wired to ring upstairs in the master bedroom. She bit her lip, pushed the button. Her leg muscles tightened and she resisted the urge to run again.

Inside, a light went on in the hallway. Through heavy glass, she could see a figure descending the stairs but couldn't make out who it was. She took one step back. Brightness flooded the step and made Del squint. The door opened.

"Hello, Mathias." Del stepped forward, needing to know he was real. She tentatively embraced him. "You stayed. Thank you. I am so, so sorry."

It took a second before his arms came around her in a hug. He whispered, "I could strangle you for worrying us so much, Del."

He held her at arm's length and his nostrils flared. He was unshaven and wrinkled. Shadows underlined his eyes. "You're really back. Filthy. But back. *Gott sei Dank*. Get upstairs. Cassandra hasn't moved from the loveseat since you called Felix." He frowned. "I cannot believe you called him instead of us. We're your family."

Del noticed Luise at the entrance to her bedroom, one hand holding a bathrobe closed and the other covering her mouth. As she started up the stairs, feet heavier with each step, Luise whispered, "Welcome home. I'm so relieved."

Dim light wavered through the frosted glass on the living room door. Del pressed her hand against the rippled surface, afraid of what she'd find on the other side. Mathias joined her and squeezed her shoulder. "She isn't as bad as last time. Your presence is the medicine she needs."

She gave him a worried look. "You're not angry with me?"

Mathias closed his eyes for a few seconds. "I was very angry with you, Del. And worried *for* you, especially after I called back to that number in Amsterdam and got the police station. They said you had run off. I thought, for the rest of the summer we'd be chasing a runaway."

"Why did you hang up on me? That scared me so much. I thought you hated me."

He shook his head. "I didn't hang up. I had been carrying the handset with me everywhere in the house, hoping you'd call. When you did, the battery died. I had forgotten to recharge it."

Del almost laughed with relief. Mathias reached around her, turned the doorknob and gave the door a gentle push. He nodded for her to go in. Cassandra was asleep, curled up on the black loveseat and looking like pale marble in the faint light from the desk lamp.

"I should shower and sleep," Del whispered. "I could see her in the morning."

"Not a chance." Mathias switched on the main light.

Cassandra jerked upright and looked around with bleary eyes. When she spotted Del, she swung her feet to the floor and started crying.

Del bolted across the room, sat beside her sister and took her hand. "I'm sorry, Cass. I hate what I did to you. Please say you'll forgive me. You have to be okay. You just have to."

Cassandra folded herself against Del's chest and Del held her close, giving Mathias a "help me" look. He didn't move.

It was several minutes before Cassandra whispered, "I've never been so scared in all my life. You disappeared. I had to call the police and report you missing."

"I will never, ever do something that stupid again. I swear. I'm through running."

"You... called Felix instead of me. I can't believe you did that. We're family. Doesn't that count for anything?" Cassandra sat up. Alertness seemed to be reanimating her face. Her eyes seemed sharper, more focused. "But at least we knew you were alive, not drowned in some canal. The police had thought you were just a runaway. Just. Oh God. As if that isn't bad enough."

Del didn't know how many times she could say she was sorry. She sat and waited for the lecture. She knew she deserved that, and more.

Cassandra sniffed. "What is that awful smell?"

Del's attempted smile didn't succeed. "That's Eau de Runaway, the five-day version."

Cassandra blinked rapidly as if processing the information. She shared a look with Mathias who mouthed, "I love you." Cassandra looked back at Del. "Maybe you could tell us where you've been after you shower."

"Could it be over a plate of food?" Cassandra responded with a nod and this time Del did smile. She was sure the punishment would come, but for now, knowing that Cassandra and Mathias were glad she'd returned was enough.

We're family. They had both said that. It had a nice ring to it. Better yet, it finally felt real.

Remembering 28 July 43

The sun always rises. But it could not be seen to rise on this grim Wednesday morning. The heavy smoke made our green island an uncomfortable refuge and Tilli and I soon left. Baby Hilde had finally nursed and now she slept in her sling, in need of a diaper change but we had nothing. We could only hope to find help along the way.

Neither of us considered returning to Tilli's apartment. If it hadn't been destroyed in this attack, it would be in the next. We kept walking toward Bergedorf. When we got there, others were also straggling through the town. Some townsfolk were outside, offering juice and water and what comfort they could. Someone gave me a flannel nightgown to tear up for diapers.

Already there was a word for the horror: *Feuersturm*. It had truly been a storm, the most ferocious one I had ever experienced even though I had been far from its centre. I barely dared to think how many had perished in that firestorm.

We hired a ride to Lueneberg, in the back of a rickety delivery truck. It was a relief after all the walking. Tilli's cousin had no idea she would be asked to shelter three people instead of one, but when she opened the door and saw us, she cried and hugged us. She'd heard about the horrific attack and had worried terribly. She never hesitated to offer me shelter.

It seemed to me that the kindness of strangers was the only thing that kept me from despair, in Hamburg and now in Lueneberg.

13 August 43

I cannot believe it took me two days to write down my account of the Hamburg bombings. We hear such incredible numbers we do not know what to believe. Some are saying as many as 100,000 perished. Even half that many is beyond understanding. The victims were mostly women, children and old men, for every able-bodied man is fighting in this endless war. Will there be anything left of Germany if the British continue like this? Why are men so quick to want to deal out death?

My concern is life, my baby's and my own. I must stay strong so she can grow up strong and healthy. I see nothing of Faber when I look at her. His attack and her arrival in my life hardly seem related, as if the firestorm burned the last thread of terror that bound me to him. This is a relief and a blessing, as is having Tilli and her cousin, Klara, to help. We all find joy in this tiny infant who controls our days and nights, little tyrant that she is. Klara has offered to share her home until the war ends, and I will stay as long as Lueneberg remains a safe haven.

Tilli has heard from the Red Cross. Her husband was injured but is alive. When he was separated from his crew and put in a hospital, his paperwork was misplaced. We are so relieved.

I need to write to Papa today. He does not even know I survived the attacks on Hamburg. Does he wonder? I hope he someday gathers the courage to meet his granddaughter. His is a sad life, I think, controlled by fear. For baby Hilde's sake I will try not to follow his example, though it is hard on nights when the air raid siren sounds. So far, no airplanes have targeted us. Perhaps Lueneberg is too small to bother with. I also hope the bombs stay away from Heidelberg. Though I won't return, it is precious to me.

I hope you don't mind, dear sister, but from now on I will not address my journal entries to you, such an important part of my past though you've only lived in my thoughts. Instead, I will write to my baby Hilde (your namesake), to record our lives so that, someday, she can read about them and understand what a miracle she is to me. She is my family. My future. I pray the war ends soon so it will be a long and happy one.

Chapter Forty

"You never called Mom and Dad, did you?" Del clipped the top of her boiled egg with the *Eierköpfer*, then passed it to Cassandra. Mathias had made their breakfast then left to run errands.

"God, no. I don't know how many times I picked up the phone, even dialed the number but could never finish. Then I fell apart. You wouldn't believe how scared I was."

"To tell them?"

"For you, you little idiot."

Del smiled. That was such a big sister thing to say.

"Why would that make you smile?" Del shrugged and dipped into her egg with the tiny spoon. Cassandra said, "Are you going to talk to Luise?"

"I don't know."

"She'd like to apologize." When Del said nothing Cassandra wrapped her hands around her mug of coffee. "She told us about your reading project. Did you finish the diary?"

"Yeah. It was an amazing story. The girl, Garda, went from being afraid of everything to so brave." Del rubbed her barbell piercing as she thought about the story. She wasn't sure how much to say but decided Garda wouldn't want her to keep silent. "Reading how she felt made me realize that I've been afraid for... a long time."

"You?" Cassandra swept her hair from her face – a loose style that softened her features. "You're the bravest girl I know. I can't leave the house without a list, a plan and a backup plan, but you just... go. It's not always smart, maybe, but it's very brave."

"Not about stuff like that. I mean, Garda's family abandoned her, and I kind of know how she felt because I've never, you know, fit."

"What do you mean?"

"You, Mom, Dad, lists, plans, all blond and thin. You match. I don't."

"Why do you want to be like us? We're neurotic."

"Don't be dense, Cass." Del started pacing the room. Her body wanted to flee, but she resisted. "I'm an outsider. I have my friends but... I've never felt like part of my family."

Cassandra stood and gripped Del by the shoulders. "Oh God, Del. We're so opposite in almost everything, but that doesn't change that I'm your sister. You're stuck with me." She wrapped her arms around Del and held her tight.

I refuse to cry, Del thought. Her hands slowly rose to return the embrace. She whispered, "I wish Mom and Dad felt that way."

"Don't let them drive you crazy, Del. I'm sorry they compare you to me, but they're not really. They're comparing you to some myth that doesn't exist. I'm no more perfect than you are."

No kidding. Del smothered a giggle.

Cassandra asked, "What are you going to do if they get divorced?"

"I don't know. Stay with whoever keeps the house and try to get by. Like Garda did, one day at a time."

"I'm here if you want to call or email. Mathias, too. I know you'd rather talk to him..."

Del stepped back. "He's easy to talk to. Maybe we'll get better at it if we do it more."

"We could try." They stared at each other in silence for a long moment, then both started laughing. Cassandra said, "This was a good start. So what will you do with your second day of grounding?"

"Not sure. Maybe find something else to read."

"You could help Luise in her garden. You both like that."

Del frowned. "Don't push, Cass. I'll talk to her when I'm ready."

"Just remember, you only have three and a half weeks."

Two days later, Del shimmied down the lattice in the early morning and stood on Luise's patio until the older woman looked up from her weeding and spotted her.

Luise strode across the lawn, stripping hat and gloves as she came. She swept her bangs aside with the back of her hand and said, "Please let me apologize." Del tilted her head and waited. An ant crawled over her toes. Luise said, "I'd do anything to reverse my mistakes, Del. Felix likes you. He was reluctant to take money from me, but did so because it satisfied his father that he had a job. I tried to fix a family problem by using you, and it was very wrong."

"It was."

"I deserve your censure."

"What happened to Garda's parents?" Luise looked puzzled. Del explained, "Garda's dad deserved her judgment, too, but at the end she felt sorry for him. What happened to him?"

"Karl stayed at the university and was still teaching when the Americans arrived in early 1945. After the war, Ulla slipped into a depression from which she never recovered. He looked after her and lived out his life in Heidelberg."

"Did he see his granddaughter?"

"Yes. He and Erwin became regular visitors, but Ulla never accompanied them."

"Did Garda ever go back to Heidelberg?"

"As a visitor, after her mother died." Luise put on her gloves.

"I'll answer other questions while I'm working. You can accept my apology or not. You know my preference." She returned to weeding.

Del watched for five minutes then joined Luise, whispered that she did accept the apology, pulled a miniature spade from her tool box and started digging. She didn't ask anything, just revelled in the smell and cool dampness of the earth as she worked beside her friend.

When they finished, Del said, "Is there a memorial for the firestorm victims? Cass said I could ask you to take me since I'm still grounded."

"Did she? You're getting along better?"

"Not bad. But we're sisters." Del loved being able to say and mean it. Sisters. "We'll argue again. It keeps Mathias on his toes."

Luise laughed her loud, relaxed laugh Del liked. "Good. Mathias usually has things far too easy." She leaned back on her heels. "As for a memorial, I know the perfect place. Shall we go this afternoon?"

After lunch, the heat made Del glad she'd changed into a tank top and skirt. They crossed the stone-baked Rathausmarkt and wended through crooked streets behind the Rathaus, over a canal that looked tempting enough to jump into, and arrived at the black ruins of a church, its dark spire stark against a shock of blue sky. They walked along the outside of a plaza that would have been the church's interior and entered through a preserved side door that was black and covered with intricate wrought-iron designs. The portions of walls still standing hinted of beauty and grace. It was still beautiful, but in a sad way – red bricks and beige sandstone charred black in places, unblackened but broken in others.

Del eyed the top of the spire. "Was this destroyed in the firestorm?"

"It burned during the first bombing a few days before the firestorm."

"What church is this? I've seen the tower but I'm not much for old places so I never thought to come here. I didn't know it was a ruin."

"It's Nikolaikirche."

Del looked around. "The church Garda liked."

"Yes. They left it to remind us of the price we pay during war and how precious peace is. It's also a monument to the 50,000 people who died in the Hamburg air raids and firestorm. There is a museum in the crypt if you want to see it." Luise pointed toward the far end of the plaza and a teepee-sized glass pyramid.

"Maybe later. Could I sit for a minute?"

"Certainly. I'm going to stroll the perimeter."

Del sat in the shade of the broken south wall beside an ornate window frame empty of glass. Sunshine cast elongated patches of light across the stone floor. In the shade, the floor was cool. She closed her eyes and breathed in peace. Though traffic hummed on the street beyond, inside a bubble of quiet existed, as if the broken walls still kept the outside world at bay.

This is what Del wanted. Not the history lesson that Luise seemed to think necessary, but a sense of connection – with this place. With Garda.

On the subway ride, Luise had told her more of Garda's story. How she had written to Werner, who'd ended up in a P.O.W. camp in southern Alberta and had laboured for a sugar beet farmer. The farmer had offered to sponsor Werner's move to Canada, but Werner had decided he wanted to help his country rebuild.

Garda and Werner had married (Del knew they would) and had three more children. Hilde hadn't quite had the long life her mother wished for her – Luise had lost her mother (Hilde) in a car crash in 1994 – but until then it had been a happy life.

"Would you like to meet Garda?" Luise had asked. "She lives in a home for the elderly and still has some good days. Though many days she is trapped in the past."

It had taken Del a moment to decide and decline. She didn't want the sixteen-year-old Garda in her mind replaced by an elderly, sometimes senile stranger. That younger Garda felt like a friend who had helped Del through a hard time. Here, in this place where Garda had said she found peace, Del could almost sense her presence. She opened her eyes.

Felix sat cross-legged a metre from Del. Chin propped on clasped hands, he watched her with intensity brightening his green eyes. They were mesmerizing.

Del knew she was smiling. She couldn't help it.

"I didn't surprise you?" He sounded disappointed.

"I knew someone was there." Del gave a one-shouldered shrug. "I thought it might be your great-grandmother."

That earned her a puzzled quirk of eyebrows, followed by understanding. "Is Tante Luise getting you to read that diary she's translating? She suggested I should read it. Family history and that." He gave a small smile. "I get tired of always having the war pushed in my face. I'm not sure I want to read something from the war if I don't have to."

"Your loss. It's a good story."

"You could tell me about it."

She raised her chin. "I don't know if I'm talking to you."

"But I need to thank you."

"For what?"

"You inspired me. When you called and said to tell your sister you were okay, I thought about how much courage it takes to just leave. I decided, if you could be brave enough to do that, then I could explain to my dad how I felt."

Del leaned forward. "How did it go?"

"I still have my head." He shrugged. "I promised when I knew what I wanted to do, I'd go after it with all my strength, but he had to give me space to figure out what that was."

"And...?"

"He agreed. Reluctantly. Gave me one year." Felix broke into a smile, popped to his feet and offered his hand to help her up. He looked so good in his moss-green shirt and jeans. Del sat and simply enjoyed the view. Felix wiggled his fingers and she grabbed them.

He hauled her up. "You know I feel terrible about what happened, don't you? I wish I'd done or said something differently. I should never have taken Tante Luise's money."

"She told me. It's okay. It was a big mess all around. I made the biggest mistakes of all." Before she'd run away, she had thought she might be falling in love with him. From the second she'd heard his voice over the cellphone on the train, she knew she wanted to see him again.

He still held her hand. "I bought tickets to go up the tower. Do you want to come?"

"How did you know we'd be here?" Del glanced around but couldn't see Luise.

Felix gave his shy knee-weakening smile. "Tante Luise isn't just the family's peacemaker. At heart she is a date-maker."

"You mean matchmaker?"

"Yes!" His fingers slid between hers and gently squeezed. "This is almost harder than talking to my dad. I'm not brave about dating. Will you come?" He gave a little tug.

Del planted herself. "What's the point? I'm returning to Edmonton in twenty-four days."

Felix released a slow breath, then stepped close. It was hard not to stare at his slightly-downturned, very kissable mouth. "The point, James, is that I really like you."

"I like you, too, Altmann, but I'm still leav –"

His free fingers covered her lips. "Let me speak before my courage flies. The point, James, is I want to dance with you and hold you close. And the point, James, is I want to be able to kiss you back the way I very much wanted to kiss you back at the statue."

Del swallowed and licked dry lips. "But I'm leaving, Altmann."

"You keep saying that. Maybe, at the end of August you leave and we stay friends. You can tell your friends in Edmonton about your summer fling with that sexy older guy from Hamburg." He gave a self-deprecating eye roll. "But maybe something grows between us that will bring us back together after you leave. Don't you want to find out what will happen?"

Del needed a minute to breathe, to think. "Weren't you taking me up the tower?"

As the lift carried them up, she thought of Garda. With all she'd been through, she had still found the courage to love someone. If Del stopped loving for fear of hurting or being hurt, she'd be no better than a lifeless ruin, a memorial to what might have been.

They started at the southwest window of the viewing platform. Del studied the placard by each window that pictured each view as it had looked right after the Second World War. The pictures of devastation made the rebuilt modern city spreading out form the foot of the tower seem like a miracle. A new city from rubble. Life from death.

A phoenix from the ashes. She touched her tattoo. At the beginning of the summer her life had felt like ashes. Was now her time to rise?

The last window faced northwest and opened to the green roofs of the stately Rathaus, beyond to the squarish Binnenalster and the much larger Aussenalster, both sapphire blue. White dots skimmed across the Aussenalster. The distant sails beckoned to her. She'd never been much for only watching.

Del smiled. "Will you take me sailing again?"

Felix leaned against the dark stone of the tower wall. "Does that mean you'll be my summer girlfriend?"

"I don't know. Actually, I don't even know if you're a good kisser since you've never put any effort into it. I don't think I want a boyfriend who isn't a good –"

Felix pulled her to him and kissed her, she thought, with considerable skill. Enough to leave her slightly breathless. Though she was pleased to note he was, too.

"Well?" he asked. "Does my kissing meet your standards?"

Del smirked. "Maybe with a little practice."

"Where should I get this practice? With you, James, or with someone else?"

"With me, Altmann. Only with me."

✳

ACKNOWLEDGMENTS

Without financial support by the Alberta Foundation for the Arts, this story would never have been written in a timely manner. Many thanks to them, and also to my library board for being supportive of my artistic endeavours by allowing me to take time off to focus on writing.

Though a story is written by one person, so many people contribute in so many ways to the process that I cannot possibly name them all. I can only hope that those I don't mention here still know their help was greatly appreciated.

My family gave me their patience, as always, and allowed me to keep my office door closed for long stretches. My husband, Michael, let my research needs determine the itinerary when we travelled.

In Germany, my niece, Melannie Bass, translated for me when I toured Hamburg and my limited German failed me. She answered countless questions and reviewed German in my text, while her living arrangements provided me with a floor plan for the imaginary house I built in the real district of Rotherbaum in Hamburg.

My friend, Sabine Sattel, showed me around Heidelberg twice – the first time planted the idea that one character's story had to start in that beautiful old city, and the second time unearthed details for the narrative.

Several readers gave valuable feedback, but two who must be mentioned are Dymphny Dronyk for reading and commenting on my work when she was hard-pressed to find the time, and

Gisela Everton for her eagle-eyed line editing and correcting of misspelled German words. If anything is still spelled incorrectly it is entirely my fault.

There isn't a story out there that can't benefit from the input of a good editor. I had a great one in Laura Peetoom and am grateful for her insight, encouragement and friendship.

And of course, thank you to everyone at Coteau Books for working the magical transformation from manuscript to book.

A fourth-generation Albertan, Karen Bass attended the University of Alberta, and received a psychology degree from the University of Victoria. She currently lives with her family in northwestern Alberta, where she continues to work as a librarian. Her first novel, *Run Like Jäger*, has received critical acclaim.

ENVIRONMENTAL BENEFITS STATEMENT

Coteau Books saved the following resources by printing the pages of this book on chlorine free paper made with 100% post-consumer waste.

TREES	WATER	SOLID WASTE	GREENHOUSE GASES
23	**10,757**	**653**	**2,234**
FULLY GROWN	GALLONS	POUNDS	POUNDS

Calculations based on research by Environmental Defense and the Paper Task Force. Manufactured at Friesens Corporation